EARTHRISE

Gus Gresham

This novel is a work of fiction.
Any similarities with names of persons living or not living, or with place names, company names, products or services, etc. is purely coincidental.

ISBN: 978-1-6736-4295-7

.

for Sarah, Alex & Phoebe

Acknowledgements

For their support, kindness and belief during my formative years as a writer, I would like to thank Sue Alphey, Jean Thornton, Kerry Kenihan, Jonathan Evans, Dr Laurie Cusack, Sue Thomas, Mahendra Solanki, Graham Joyce, Catherine Byron, Dr Katherine Frank, Clare Littleford, Angela Readman, Hilary Kirby, Pippa Goodhart, Paul Bailey, Liz Lochhead, Sarah Leigh, Melvin Burgess, Lucy Christopher, Joel Lane, Colin Teevan, Martyn Waites, Saul Reichlin, Martin Jarvis, Ros Ayres, all tutors and fellow writers on the MA writing program at Nottingham Trent University, all tutors and fellow writers on Arvon Foundation and East Midlands Arts courses, and East Midlands Arts for the writer's bursary prize (1999).

A very special thank you to Shelley Routledge for her valuable input and encouragement with EARTHRISE.

1

The Ruins Of Your Heart

Erin would remember this as the night everything started getting messed up beyond all recognition.

"It might be a bit of a shock to see him connected to the machines," said her mother, talking *at* her again.

Seven o'clock, and the sun was making its way down behind the hospital buildings. Just inside the main entrance, Mum added, "There's this horrible respirator pipe in his mouth. And wires, pumps, catheters, and I-don't-know-what-else sticking out everywhere ..."

A couple of days ago, Uncle Dom had had his latest heart-attack. He was on the critical list but stable, and had been transferred from intensive care to a side room. Erin had a recent memory of him behind the counter of the chip shop he owned – wheezing badly; stress and tiredness written across his face; the armpits of his shirt damp. Erin hoped he wasn't suffering, but she'd never been close to him – she even found him a bit creepy.

"How's Dad?" she asked.

"Holding up," said Mum, her heels clicking through the corridor. "I think ... Erin, I think this could be the last time you see Uncle Dominic."

"I ... Okay," she said, trying to look more concerned than she really felt.

"This way now," said Mum.

It was because of Uncle Dom's worsening health that Erin's family had moved to Everdene last autumn. They lived in the southern suburbs, not far from Crow Woods. Being near such an old woodland was a big plus as far as Erin was concerned. She'd already got her name down as a summer volunteer for a wildlife conservation project. Its focus would be on owls and badgers.

"He won't be able to see or hear you, Erin. He's unconscious and – "

"I get the picture, Mum."

"Well, I think the best thing ... We say hello, then go for a cup of tea."

"Tea?"

"Or coffee."

"That's not what I meant," said Erin.

Mum blew her cheeks out and said, "I'm just suggesting that we go and get a drink so that your dad can spend as much time with him as possible."

Erin became aware of an electronic squealing. Up ahead, a grey-haired man in a suit was leading a group of white-coated young men and women.

"... another cardiology case," he was saying. "Surgery pointless. On life support. Not expected to – Hmm, alarms seem to be ..."

"Oh," said Mum. "That's where he is."

Next thing, two nurses rushed by and went straight into the room without knocking. They left the door wide open. The electronic squealing was louder, and beneath it Erin heard her dad and her uncle's voices.

Everybody reached the doorway at the same time.

"Excuse me," said Mum. "I think – "

"I'm Professor Sharman," said the man in the suit. "Sorry. Are you family?"

In the room, Dad was trying to calm Uncle Dom down, but Uncle Dom was marching about opening cupboards and drawers, apparently looking for his clothes. Erin had never seen him move so quickly. The pale-green gown he wore was of the type with a spilt up the back. Only the top tie was fastened and Erin had to close her eyes as he bent over and the gown yawned apart.

"The thing is, Dom..." said Dad.

"This isn't possible," said Professor Sharman. "Must be the wrong ..." He checked his notes. "Supposed to be Dominic Lockwood."

The two nurses who'd entered the room a minute earlier were now standing aside. Erin could feel the medical students jostling behind her for a better view.

"Thought he'd died," said Dad, his gaze drifting from the nurses to the cluster of people in the doorway. He seemed too bewildered to recognise his own family. "Heart-beat monitor went to flat-line ... I pressed the panic button. Waited. And waited. Then he just pulled the respirator out of his mouth."

Dangling by the side of the bed, Erin saw the corrugated plastic tube of the respirator. There were other dangling things that should have been attached to her uncle: an IV drip, a catheter for urine, electrodes.

The alarms were still squealing.

"Perhaps you should lie down again?" suggested Dad.

Uncle Dom ignored him. He spotted some manky old fluffy slippers – not even his – under a chair. He sat down and pulled them on happily.

One of the nurses went to the monitoring equipment and began switching off the alarms.

"Right," said Uncle Dom. "I'm out of here." And he came forward with such determination that everybody backed away except Professor Sharman.

"Mr Lockwood," said Sharman, slight and frail next to the hulking form of Erin's uncle. "I'd advise you to take it easy. Your heart – "

"My heart feels like a gorilla's."

Uncle Dom looked a bit comic in his "found" slippers and hospital gown, but there was something disturbing in the way he moved the professor aside, with no more effort than if he'd been parting a bead curtain.

He set off along the corridor with Professor Sharman, the medical students and the nurses trailing after him.

"... back to bed," called Sharman. "A cardiograph. I just want to help you."

"Can't they sedate him, Toby?" said Mum, hurrying to catch up.

"Well ..." said Dad.

Uncle Dom was setting a speedy pace, but when he was near the main entrance he paused. He went straight up to Dad. With an oily smile, he took the wallet from inside Dad's jacket and slid out some notes.

"You're a diamond, Toby," he said. "I'll square up with you tomorrow."

Registering Erin's presence, her uncle partially turned his head, offering a rosy-veined slab of cheek. The corner of his mouth twitched and his eye sparkled amid the surrounding folds of flesh. In his dilated pupil, Erin glimpsed a fiery flicker that made her legs go weak. She had the impression of looking into the bottom of a well, from which the bucket – or something – was rapidly shooting upwards. She gasped, and stumbled back a step. Uncle Dom smiled and raised his chin. There was recognition in his face, but not of an uncle recognising his niece. It was more like he was sizing her up as somebody might size up a puny opponent. Then he turned away and strode through the exit.

Erin stood there, the nape of her neck sweaty.

The professor and his entourage were already on the move. So were Mum and Dad. By the time Erin arrived outside, a couple of cleaners, a paramedic and someone who looked like security had joined the small crowd.

Uncle Dom was sitting in a taxi. The driver had come around to the passenger side and was standing by the open door.

"... for a Mr and Mrs Singh," he was saying unhappily.

"That's me," said Uncle Dom. "Mrs Singh's been held up. She won't be coming home until later. Ready when you are. Let's go."

"I don't think so, pal. You can ... *Uhhh* ..."

The driver's resolve crumbled. Uncle Dom didn't do or say anything, as far as Erin could tell – although her view was partially blocked. The man's body sagged and he had to grip the edge of the passenger door for support.

Then he straightened up, nodded, and muttered an apology.

Seconds later, the taxi was on its way.

"To the car," said Dad. "Quick!"

It was a brisk walk back through the buildings to the visitors' car-park, and they were delayed by queues at the pay machines. When they arrived at Uncle Dom's house, Erin was surprised to see him only just getting out of the taxi. Then she spotted the pile of colourful Whiz-Go takeaway boxes under his arm.

As he walked up the path, the hospital gown billowed in the warm breeze. Erin had to close her eyes again as his large mottled backside was exposed.

Dad was in a bit of a state. He couldn't even operate the car's door catch. Then he almost throttled himself trying to get out with his seatbelt still fastened.

Erin might have laughed under different circumstances.

Finally, he was out and hurrying along the path, calling to his brother. Mum opened her door, hesitated, and raised her eyebrows at Erin.

"I'll wait here," said Erin from the back seat.

She didn't know what to make of it all. The main thing she was feeling at that point was relief for Dad, although his pleas to his brother seemed increasingly redundant.

Uncle Dominic – now happily devouring a burger – radiated life and vigour.

Mum stood dutifully by, occasionally touching Dad's arm.

The longer it went on, the more uneasy Erin felt. She kept remembering the chilling look Uncle Dom had given her at the hospital.

She reached between the front seats and turned the radio on to distract herself. They were playing the latest Lily Raven song.

"*Dark like night ~ In the ruins of your heart ...*" Erin sang along.

Abruptly, she stopped. Uncle Dom was staring at her. She realised that the car windows were down and that maybe the Lily Raven lyrics weren't exactly in the best taste, all things considered. Although, based on the last half-hour, nobody would ever guess there was anything wrong with her uncle's heart. Now he was smiling and saying something she couldn't hear. At his words her parents turned to gawp at her. He spoke again and they responded with solemn nods. As Lily Raven sang on, Erin's skin prickled.

What was Uncle Dom saying? What were Mum and Dad agreeing to?

The staring continued, then Uncle Dom disappeared inside. Too late, Dad lurched for the front door. It was pretty much shut in his face. He rang the bell, knocked on the frosted glass, called through the letterbox. Mum went to the bay window to peer inside. Eventually, they gave up and came back to the car. Dad took out his mobile and called Uncle Dom. The line was engaged.

"Well, this is all very ..." said Mum. "Are you all right, Erin?"

It was as if the gawping thing hadn't happened now.

"I know what I saw, Wendy," said Dad on the way home. "Nobody can tell me any different. Dom died. Stopped breathing. His heartbeat went to flat-line. I pressed the panic button ..." He sobbed, then struck the steering wheel. "Dom was dead. All I could do was wait. Two minutes. Three. May have been longer. Then he ... he opened his eyes! It was ... He pulled the respirator tube out. Sat up. Winked at me! Threw the covers off ..."

It was about the tenth time he'd retold the story.

At home, he sat in his armchair continually ringing his brother's number, and continually getting the engaged tone. Mum turned the TV on.

Erin said, "Er ... would it be okay if I still went to band practice?"

The rehearsals were always in Kane's garage. Or Kane's dad's garage. Erin was the only girl in the band at that time and she regularly got teased at school over which of the boys was "the one". It wasn't like that, though, she kept telling herself. They were just in a band together.

Kane had a resemblance to Gee-Jay Samson, the rap artist, except that Kane had better cornrows and the band didn't do rap. Logan was quiet and a bit gormless, often to be seen peering vacantly from under his baseball cap. Josh was tall and athletic and ... Okay, Erin had had the odd fantasy about kissing him, but it always ended when she remembered how arrogant he could be.

Some of the songs were almost good. Others were twisted and hateful, with shouted lyrics and screeching guitars, hopelessly out of tune. But Erin's tastes were wide, even if she did prefer softer rock and grungy female vocalists.

"Five weeks," Kane was saying. "That's all we've got."

"Yeah, yeah," drawled Josh, his dark, designer-scruffy hair hanging in his eyes as he rested his bass guitar on its stand.

"So we need more rehearsals," said Kane. He glanced in Erin's direction, but she was trying to stay out of it. He glanced at Logan.

"Uh, well ... like, yeah," said Logan in his slow way.

"Right," said Kane, "because I thought we sounded like crap tonight."

"Speak for yourself," said Josh. "*I* did okay."

Erin knew that there was often a grain of truth to anything Josh said. If they'd really sounded "like crap" –

and, yes, they had – it reflected worst on Kane. He was lead singer and lead guitarist, *and* he wrote the music for Logan's okay-for-a-fourteen-year-old-boy lyrics. Logan was also the drummer.

Erin thought an argument might be about to kick off, but then Kane said, "I know you don't want us to be in the talent contest, Josh."

"It's a school thing," said Josh, standing with his back to everybody.

"So what? We'll be playing in front of *hundreds* of people. What's the most we've ever had at the youth club? Thirty? Erin, what do you think?"

"She's just the keyboard player," said Josh. "And she wasn't a founding member. She's only been with us a few weeks."

"Uh, well," said Logan, "It's more like three months."

"Shut it, Lardy," said Josh.

Erin hated the way he spoke to Logan sometimes, but she wasn't too bothered by the "just the keyboard player" comment. The keyboards was something that she could *do*, not something that she cared about deeply – not like wildlife or the environment. Or singing. She'd never sung publicly and had no plans to try taking over from Kane. She hadn't even let on to the boys that she *could* sing. When they played, she was tucked away at the rear with the keyboards. She was happy enough there. Even if it meant being too close to the flying sweat when Logan's drumming got a bit vigorous.

The double garage was a great rehearsal-space. There was an old sofa against one wall and a fridge that had a stock of cold drinks. On warm nights, like tonight, the doors were open, and further down the long drive they could see the feathery spearheads of the pampas shrubs nodding in the breeze.

"Three months is long enough," said Kane. "So what do you think, Erin?"

8

Josh finally turned to face everybody. As Erin hesitated to respond, a pressure began to build in her chest. The silence of the garage was punctuated by a flicker and crackle from the fluorescent tubes.

She swallowed, then said, "I think it'll be cool to play to a big audience. And it won't do the band's profile any damage."

The expression in Josh's eyes darkened.

"Profile," echoed Kane. "We'll be raising our profile. Then a week later, it'll be the 'Battle of the Bands' at the youth club, yeah?"

That was something Josh *did* care about, but his withering gaze stayed on Erin. He was about to speak when Erin heard the hooting-owl ring-tone of her mobile. It was a call from her mum.

"Erin ... I'm outside ... Sorry if I'm messing up your rehearsal." She sounded distraught. "I need you to come out to the car ... immediately."

2

Don't Look In The Mirror

"What's wrong?" said Erin as she sat in the passenger seat and closed the door.

Mum sniffed and shook her head.

"I had a moment. I think I'm all right now. Your dad went off to Dominic's again and I was feeling ... all alone. Thinking. I just had this overwhelming feeling that something ... apocalyptic was about to happen and – "

"Apocalyptic?"

"Well ... something horrid anyway. Sorry about your rehearsal."

"Don't worry, Mum. Long as you're okay now?"

"This thing with your uncle, Erin. It's too bonkers for words."

"Yeah, I know. Crazy. *Good* kind of crazy for Uncle Dom, I mean. And for Dad. But still really crazy."

Mum smiled and patted Erin's hand. She checked her make-up in the rear-view mirror and started the car. They travelled in silence for a while. Then Erin said, "Are you sure you're feeling okay now?"

"Yes, I think so, Erin. Yes, yes. Really."

"Good. I'm glad. Only ... there was something I wanted to ask."

Mum gave her a sharp look and Erin almost lost her nerve.

"We can't pay the vet's bill for the crow," said Mum. "You know what we agreed. You get a decent amount of pocket money. Only *you* can decide what to spend it on. After that run-over stray cat last December ... Ninety pounds, that was. Just to put it to sleep! We said then, didn't we, we said – "

"It's not about money, Mum. It didn't cost much for the crow at the vet's. I've already paid that. It's... When I was waiting in the back of the car outside Uncle Dom's earlier, the three of you were staring at me."

"Staring? Were we?"

"Uncle Dom said something, and the three of you all looked at me. For a long time. A minute or more. Just staring. Before he went inside."

"No," said Mum. "We didn't. Did we?"

"Well, yeah. You did. It was … a bit weird."

Mum laughed and shook her head.

"I don't remember that, love. No."

"Right … okay."

They were quiet for the rest of the journey.

Back at the house, standing in the hall with the front door closed on the late-evening suburban road, Mum did a quick up-and-down appraisal of what Erin was wearing: combat trousers and a tee-shirt. Probably thinking about skirts and dresses again, thought Erin – which weren't Erin's kind of thing – at least, not very often. With an index finger, Mum drew a line across Erin's forehead to stroke a wisp of chestnut-red hair from her eyes.

"Nobody was staring at you, love. The experience at the hospital … And then perhaps your imagination?" She smiled.

Erin shook her head slightly and lowered her gaze.

"I'll go and check on the crow," she said.

She went out to the garden.

It was dusk now, and cooler, and a gentle wind whispered in the conifer hedge. She opened the shed just enough to scan the shadowy interior. Seeing "Rarke" perched on the workbench, she stepped inside and closed the door. She hadn't told her parents that she'd named him; they wouldn't have understood.

There were smells of oil and sawdust in the shed, and the smell of old grass-cuttings, which usually caked the underside of the lawnmower. There was also the more recent, slightly acrid smell of bird droppings.

Silhouetted against the window, the crow was as big as an adult cat. Erin thought he was probably a raven – members of the crow family.

She'd found him a week ago, lying in a blackberry thicket at the edge of the woods. The local vet hadn't been able to find anything wrong with him, no reason for his apparent distress and inability to fly.

He was on the mend now. Yesterday, he'd flown around the shed again.

The raven wasn't the first lost or damaged creature Erin had brought home. They always had to be kept in the shed, though. Dad wouldn't have animals anywhere near the house because of his allergies.

As Erin approached the bench, Rarke cocked his head to study her with one yellow eye. He looked a proud, fierce, intelligent creature. His plumage was of the richest, most lustrous black, except for his downy head-feathers, which were silver. The vet had remarked that this silver colouring was rare.

All the bread and warm milk from earlier had gone. Erin took the packet of bird seed down from the shelf and sprinkled some out. Rarke ate half of it and then raised his wings experimentally. Erin retreated to the corner. He raised his wings again, let out a loud caw and took to the air.

Erin laughed and covered her head as he clattered about in the confined space. There was a dong like the sound of a bell as his wing struck an old wok hanging from a hook. Before long, he landed on the workbench again and pecked at the seed. Then he cocked his head at Erin. It was obvious that he was ready to go. Erin knew she was probably guilty of keeping him for a few days too many.

She opened the shed door and went to stand on the lawn. Rarke immediately hopped out to the dusky garden and had a good look around. He flew onto the bird table, almost toppling it with his weight. Then he flapped up to the roof of the house and landed on the ridge tiles. Finally, he made a wide circle over the garden before taking off into the velvety sky.

When he'd faded from view, Erin went into the house.

Mum was in her armchair, surfing the TV channels. Dad was back from Uncle Dom's, flopped out on the sofa looking stressed and exhausted.

"Any news?" said Erin.

"Still won't answer his door or the phone," grumbled Dad.

"I'm sorry ..." said Erin. "Er, the raven's better. I let him go."

"Oh," said Mum, not really interested. "That's good."

Dad was dialling Uncle Dom's number again, but he paused to say, "Make sure you wash your hands before you touch anything, Erin."

"What sick or injured creature *will* she adopt next I wonder," said Mum, with a laugh that was somehow supposed to make the comment okay.

Erin said, "I don't go out of my way to find them."

"I was only joking," said Mum. "But you do have a knack for it."

Her parents were good people, thought Erin. They just didn't "get" animals. She couldn't think of anybody else she knew who'd include wildlife documentaries when they searched through a TV guide and moaned that there was nothing to watch.

* * *

Later, while Erin was changing into her pyjamas, she turned her computer on. As usual she found herself trawling through environmental websites and blogs.

13

Sea-levels now predicted to ... Another Pacific island on the verge of disappearing ... Ice sheets melting even faster than scientists ... Polar bears could be facing extinction if they can't learn to migrate ...

If they can't learn? thought Erin. *As if it was* their *fault!*

Don't panic, optimists on other sites said. It's not too late, but immediate action is necessary ... Recycle. Take the train. Plant a tree.

"The best time to plant a tree was twenty years ago," she whispered, "the next best time is now." It was an African or Chinese proverb. On the Internet, the credit for it varied and she kept meaning to do research into its exact origin.

As she stroked her fingers over the keyboard again, her thoughts went fuzzy. She had the oddest feeling that her bedroom was losing its solidity, that she was floating in a vast empty space. Maybe she was more tired than she thought?

She went to the bathroom, surprised that she had to place a steadying hand on the wall. Even after she'd cleaned her teeth and washed her face, the fuzzy-headedness remained. She was gripping the edge of the sink, head bowed. And as the water spiralled away down the plughole, the light in the bathroom spiralled away with it. The air felt charged, potent, as if a storm were about to break over the house. Erin didn't spook easily, but her mouth had gone dry and her heart thumped. She was convinced that something was in here with her.

At first, she imagined it crouching in a corner. Then she imagined it grinning over her left shoulder. She tried to move, but her legs wouldn't work. Tried to call out, but produced only a strangled murmur. A pulse fluttered in her throat: it felt as if little hammers were tapping away at the soft tissue.

14

Then she had a strong sense of standing among trees. She could smell damp earth, toadstools, dripping leaves and mouldering timber – the rich perfumes of a deep wood where the sun never penetrates. In the darkness, there was a faint silvery gleam coming from where the mirror should have been.

The impression of someone or some*thing* at her left shoulder intensified.

No. *Impression* was the wrong word. It was a certainty. But now she was more afraid of *not* looking.

She jerked her head up.

The mirror shone dully, like a sheet of mercury. She could see a figure behind and to her left.

Man or boy – she couldn't decide which – he seemed both young and old, childlike and ancient. His eyes were yellow. He had a lean, strong face and wore a tunic of military appearance.

In the time it took for Erin to blink, the figure had gone, the woodland smells had gone and the darkness had lifted.

She spun around. No figure. Nothing. Just the faint whiff of soap and the tiniest movement of the shower curtain with its fern-leaf design.

3

Orchid

"Any second now!" said Dad. "Keep watching!"

They were waiting for the next article on the regional news. It was Friday, and in the two weeks since Uncle Dom had discharged himself from hospital, he'd been busy overseeing a complete refit of his chip shop. A local journalist had pursued him for his story, without much luck. Now, tonight, he'd agreed to talk about his experience of "cheating death", but only if it were transmitted live on the regional evening news.

Not much else had happened over the past two weeks. No more gawping incidents from Mum and Dad. Even the memory of the man-boy in the bathroom mirror had faded to a point where Erin was half convinced she'd imagined it.

As they waited, she received a text message from Kane: *Hi. We're all going to the canal tomorrow morning. Meet you about 10?*

The canal? Why would she want to go to the canal? Okay, you could see ducks and swans there sometimes, but the stagnant smell always made her feel sick. She was about to answer Kane's text when Dad yelled out.

"This is it, this is it!"

With a studio sofa to himself, Uncle Dom wore a snappy dark-green suit. He looked relaxed and happy. The pink moon of his face had a healthy glow. On another sofa were three people: a woman in a hideous checked outfit; a grey-haired man in a pinstripe suit; and the presenter Amrit Tagore. Amrit introduced the female guest as a cardiologist and writer named Myra Gilchrist, and the man Erin recognised as Professor Sharman from the hospital.

"Myra," said Amrit, following a brief introduction. "You have a question?"

"I'd like to ask Mr Lockwood," the woman said in a cut-glass accent, "why he's stubbornly refused to be examined since his ordeal."

"No reason," said Uncle Dom. He brushed an imaginary speck of dust from the shoulder of his jacket, then winked theatrically at the camera.

Dad jigged about in his armchair, laughing.

"It seems to me," said Myra, still addressing Amrit, "that unless he co-operates, a valuable opportunity for inquiry could be lost."

"How's that?" said Uncle Dom.

"Allow me to intercede," said Professor Sharman. "What you have to appreciate, Mr Lockwood, are the wider medical perspectives ..."

Erin couldn't get over how well her uncle looked.

"... and who knows what these tests could tell us," the professor finished.

"Yadda yadda yadda," said Uncle Dom.

From an inside pocket, he took out a CD-sized device. It was plain white and its round screen instantly began shimmering.

"While we're on air," he said, "I have an important message for viewers. A new burger restaurant will be opening in Everdene on Monday."

"Er, Mr Lockwood?" said Amrit. "That's not really – "

"The name is Black Orchid. We expect to go national very quickly. If you want to be among the first to sample an Orchid burger, come to our superior outlet on Cank Street, Everdene, at midday on Monday."

"Go national?" said Dad. "He's turned his tatty old chip-shop into a burger restaurant. He's worked bloody hard. Probably put his health at even more serious risk. But *go national*? Get a grip, Dom."

Uncle Dom was now holding the device between his fingertips. Erin thought she saw a dark flower appearing on its round screen before the cameras cut to Amrit. Usually a razor-sharp presenter and interviewer, Amrit Tagore was lost for words. The camera cut back to Uncle Dom, who was flashing a huge smile. The image on his CD-sized device had sprung to life.

"Look at that!" said Dad.

"It's... How unusual," said Mum.

The shimmering white background had been filled by a flower, a black orchid, with a fiery orange sun at its heart.

"Black Orchid," said Uncle Dom. "Orchid. Orchid."

The camera shook. There was a cut to Myra Gilchrist and Professor Sharman, but they were as speechless as Amrit. They kept opening and closing their mouths like goldfish. Their gazes were directed at Uncle Dom's device.

There was a confused shifting between cameras, but they were all being aimed at the brand. Then every camera was *zooming in* on the brand.

The orchid's petals began to rotate anticlockwise around the sun.

By some optical illusion, presumably, the brand leapt at Erin from the TV screen. She'd seen digital close-up film of the sun before – its brightness filtered out, its explosive surface stunningly revealed – and this was how the image looked. It was flaming. Violent. Alive.

"Orchid burgers. You've never tried anything like them. They're so tasty, your taste-buds will think they've won the Lottery."

His corny words were a voiceover now. All that could be seen were his fingertips and the image, which seemed to be jumping from the TV screen. Erin saw flares and prominences erupting, all in incredible detail. She had the sensation of falling towards the sun. Its terrible beauty seemed to speak to her, seemed to promise satisfaction and happiness, followed by exquisite incineration in its super-hot depths.

"A trick," said Dad nervously.

"What about the interview?" said Mum.

"He's tricked them. He's not going to talk about what happened at the hospital. He's using this opportunity purely to advertise."

"I like that design," said Mum. "It makes you feel – "

"It's fiendishly clever."

The black petals continued their anticlockwise rotation; the sun grew brighter. It gave Erin vertigo.

With an effort, she looked away. Something was wrong with all of this.

"Don't look!" she said.

"Don't be silly, Erin," said Dad, in a distracted whisper.

"I *do* like that design," said Mum.

"Orchid," came the monotone, "Orchid."

"Mum? Dad?"

Their eyes were growing misty, their jaws slackening.

Careful not to look at the screen again, Erin picked up the remote. She was about to switch channels, but paused at the voice of David Wang.

"Fascinating stuff," he said. "Now. Moving on. Environment minister, Rex Peach ..." He frowned and licked his lips. "Fascinating. That last article featured Dominic Lockwood talking about Black Orchid ... Excuse me. To continue: Environment minister, Rex Peach, was asked today how he justified his attempts to claim, on expenses, the cost of chartering a private jet for a commute between London and Brussels."

He licked his lips again and smiled falteringly.

"Mm. I don't know about you lot, but I could absolutely murder an Orchid burger. What was it he said? Opening in Everdene, midday on Monday? Excuse me. Where were we? Ah. When asked how he could justify the private jet, Mr Peach said, 'Because I'm worth it'. He later claimed it had been a joke, but green groups have ... Mm, those Orchid burgers ..."

Erin stabbed at the remote. On the screen, wildebeests were gathering at a watering hole. David Attenborough was doing the voice-over. Mum and Dad looked cow-eyed about the room, as if waking from a very deep sleep.

"I just fancy an Orchid burger," said Dad.

"Me, too," said Mum absently.

Erin stared at them.

"How can you *just fancy* one if you've never tried them before?"

"You're right," said Dad, grinning. "Anyway, we'll have to wait till it opens after the weekend and ... I know! I'll have an extended lunch-break on Monday and take us all out for burgers. How's that?"

"Count me in," said Mum. "Fancy it, Erin?"

Erin couldn't believe what she was hearing. They hadn't been "out for burgers" or anything like it in years.

"I don't eat meat," she said. "You know I don't."

Mum rolled her eyes. "Oh, Erin. Really. Vegetarianism is so-*ooo* twentieth century."

"Bor-*ring*," said Dad.

Erin blinked.

Maybe they were under more strain than she realised – over the *other thing*. Mum was desperate for a baby. In April, the doctor had put her on sick leave from her job at a mail-order call centre. Stress, apparently. But Erin had checked the tablets online and discovered they were for depression. They seemed to be working. Most days, she was her usual self, though she showed no interest in getting back to her job. A baby might be the only real "cure". Dad had been supportive; he hadn't even said anything about them maybe being too old. They'd tried everything, including IVF, and it hadn't happened.

But what had *Erin* done? She couldn't imagine anything better than having a baby brother or sister in the house. And were they *really* so anti-vegetarian suddenly?

In her room, she walked around touching her things – the desk and computer, the purple duvet, her books, her clothes in the wardrobe. She took out a favourite jumper. It was brown and white, with a butterfly design. Made in Nepal. She pressed it to her face, feeling the coarse texture of the yak wool against her skin. It still had a faint smell of animal. Because she liked the jumper so much, she rarely wore it to go out in for fear of losing it.

There was a muffled burst of laughter from downstairs. Her parents. Were they laughing at some joke? Something on telly? Or at her?

She put the jumper back in the wardrobe.

Then she sat on the edge of the bed, fighting back the tears. Blubbing wasn't something she was in the habit of. She raked a strand of hair from her face, gave her eyes a wipe and blew her nose. With a vicious action, she tossed the used tissue vaguely in the direction of the bin.

They'd know she'd been crying when she went down.

It was too early for bed. She could hardly stay up here for the rest of the evening. So ... well ... maybe when she went down, they'd both apologise and then everything would be all right again. Or not.

She lay back and gazed up at the dark-blue ceiling with the luminous stars she'd stuck there last year. She knew that stars were really suns; that there were billions of stars in the galaxy, billions of galaxies in the universe; that nobody could really say how big it all was, or where any of it had come from.

Her eyelids fluttered and drooped, and the tension began to drain from her muscles. Her head sank deeper into the pillow. Her thoughts became disconnected and dreamy. She was sinking, falling, drifting ...

4

Crow Woods

The furniture seemed wrong somehow. And why were the curtains closed? She looked around, struggling to recognise her own room. Maybe her eyes were playing tricks in the dim light? She pulled the covers aside, though she couldn't remember getting into bed. As she swung her bare feet down to the carpet, her movements felt clumsy. She'd also noticed that she was wearing pyjamas ...

Maybe she was ill, feverish, imagining things?

She drew the curtains and light burst in.

At the end of the street, the sun was between the rooftops, roughly where it should have been this time of evening, so she hadn't slept long. But the street, *her* street ... No, no. It was all wrong. The cars and gardens were different, and nobody was about. It was as if they'd all gone on holiday, or were all asleep.

She turned back to the room. Potted plants crowded every surface. The walls were covered with geometric shapes in vibrant blues, reds and yellows, which reminded her of a favourite Kandinsky painting.

The pyjamas she wore weren't even hers; they were white and silky. And her fingernails and toenails were painted a sparkly silver.

She went to the dressing-table – again, not hers; the mirror was oblong instead of oval. It was a relief to see her own face. Her complexion looked healthy, if paler than usual and more freckly. Her hair was redder and longer, and had more body. She ran her fingers through it, and it made them tingle.

On a chair were some black combat-trousers (at least *they* were the same) and a top that was way too gaudy.

Under the chair were a pair of ankle-boots, similar to hers, but newer and more expensive-looking.

Her mind was in a fog. She felt similar to how she'd felt coming round from the anaesthetic after having her appendix out. She knew that she was awake, but she was cushioned from everything. "Yeah, okay, this is weird," she was thinking, "but I might as well stick with it and see what happens."

She got dressed and went out to the landing. It couldn't be later than seven o'clock but there was snoring coming from her parents' room.

Everything went fuzzy. What ... ? Then black. As if a switch had been thrown in her head. When she came to, she was outside on the street. The summer air was alive with tiny particles in a constant state of flux; they kept disappearing, reappearing, sparkling brighter or fading.

There were no people around. No moving vehicles. The house across the road, where Mr and Mrs Chalmers lived, had a monkey-puzzle tree on the front lawn. That wasn't right; there should be stone chips and a plum tree. On Erin's side of the street, three houses along, she saw Mrs Croxley on the pavement. The old lady was mumbling to herself, which was normal enough. Erin went to her. Walking was like wading in water, and by the time she got there, Mrs Croxley was in the driver's seat of a bright-red Lamborghini.

"Er, Mrs ..."

The engine roared into life and Mrs Croxley cackled. As the car took off down the empty road, the old lady's head snapped back with the acceleration. Amid the dust and the smell of burnt rubber, Erin stood coughing. She wondered hazily if Mrs Croxley knew what all this was about. As she watched the receding sports car, she began to drift in the same direction, like a sheet of newspaper caught on a breeze. She glanced down and saw that her legs weren't even moving; her feet were barely touching the ground. At the T-junction, she came to a stop. The Lamborghini had turned right and the growl of its engine was dying away. The plumes of dust the car had raised were now settling all around Erin. But she wasn't interested in Mrs Croxley any more. She squatted on her haunches. The tarmac felt gritty and real under her fingertips.

Everywhere was deserted, everything still and quiet under the sparkling air. In the distance, the sun hung low over Crow Woods. Erin smiled as she started to sail along again, blown on friendly currents. Faster and faster. Her body arched like a bow. The streets of Everdene blurring.

Into and through Crow Woods she swept, warm sunlight streaming through the patchwork canopy in strobe-effect. She could hear the echoing hammer of a woodpecker somewhere. Gaudy toadstools ringed the bases of trees, sprouted from fallen trunks. The fronds of lime-green ferns dripped moisture. And all about her was the musty, pungent smell of the wood.

Her senses quickened and reeled. She lost awareness of boundaries and contours, of where her body ended and everything else began.

Then, abruptly, the journey was over.

At the edge of a clearing, she stumbled and nearly fell. It was as though she'd reached the end of a moving walkway at an airport, hit solid ground, and now had to do the rest under her own steam. She still felt as if she were sunk in a fog of anaesthesia, but amid this cushioning fog, part of her mind was alert.

In the middle of the clearing, she found a natural pond edged with mossy rocks. A fat frog on a lily pad watched her for a moment, then leaped into the water. A metallic-blue dragonfly flitted past her face with a purring buzz of its wings.

Erin sat on one of the rocks.

Except for the odd birdcall, the dull clatter of wings in the treetops, or the occasional *gloop-gloop* as a frog or fish broke the surface of the pond – except for these gentle noises, the silence was profound. She would have been happy just to sit on her rock forever, soaking up the beauty and the peacefulness.

Tiny insects skated about the pond. Under the mirror-clear water, tendrils of weed wafted like beckoning hands. A pair of green eyes gazed up at Erin, and she realised that they were hers. The reflection of her face rippled and swam. She had an impression of her room – her *real* room. She glimpsed the dressing-table's oval mirror, the magnolia walls, the dark-blue ceiling with its luminous stars. Then the sights and sounds and smells of the clearing snapped back into focus. A long way off, the woodpecker started hammering again.

From near by came a crackle of twigs. She froze as she saw something shifting in the undergrowth – something as big as a person. The creature groaned in pain. Then a hand, an arm, a shoulder and a head rose from the grasses and weeds.

Erin gasped. Her heart was palpitating. With no memory of getting up and moving, she suddenly found herself back at the edge of the clearing. She blindly reached out for branches or trunks. Her earlier, dreamy acceptance was growing thinner; she was becoming more alert, more anchored.

On the other side of the pond, the creature stood to his full height. He looked human. He had a lean face, cropped dark hair and yellow eyes. The grey tunic and trousers he wore hung off his sinewy frame.

It was the man-boy she'd seen in the bathroom mirror.

He went very still as he registered her presence. Then he took a step forward, but his legs gave way. The man-boy cried out and collapsed to his hands and knees. After a moment, he got up and struggled over to the pond, his face muscles clenching, a hand clasped to his torso.

Erin's instinct was to go to him. Try to help. It was obvious that he was sick or hurt. But she'd just noticed a short sword in a scabbard at his side.

The boy glanced at her a couple of times and she wondered if it was pride that stopped him crying out again. He sat close to where Erin had been sitting. She'd decided on "boy" now, because he didn't appear much older than her.

"Sorry if I frightened you," he said, his voice resonant and friendly, even though he must be in pain.

"That's okay," she said, approaching the pond. She was surprised by the calmness settling over her again. Also – and she didn't know how – but she understood that she was safe here with this strange boy.

It was exactly what was supposed to be happening.

"Kree ..." she said. "Your name's Kree."

The name had simply popped into her head. The boy didn't even seem surprised; he just watched her closely as she sat on a nearby rock.

"You have access to the Source?" he said.

"Er ... I don't know what the 'Source' is."

Another wave of pain crossed his face. Around where his hand was clasped to his side, Erin could see a large dark patch on his tunic.

"You're hurt," she said.

"Did you summon me here?" said Kree.

"What? No. I ... I've seen you before, though. Two weeks ago, I saw you in a mirror. You visited me at my house, didn't you?"

"No," he said. "*You* visited *me*. *I* saw *you* in a mirror."

She stared at him. His eyes were amber, the colour of autumn leaves, and the features of his lean face were well-proportioned.

"What are you looking at?" he said.

"Nothing ..." She stopped staring.

The dark patch on his tunic was spreading at an alarming rate. Blood was seeping between his fingers. He took a deep breath and let it out tremulously.

"You're hurt," said Erin. "What happened to you?"

"The skerri. We escaped with our lives. This time."

She wanted to ask about "the skerri", but he was groaning louder – he seemed to be acknowledging how serious the injury might be. With a quick movement, he stripped off the tunic. His torso was muscled, but lean, sinewy, and highly toned. There was so much blood that it was difficult to see the wound at first. Then, as he shifted position again, to take off his sword belt, a terrifying amount of blood welled up out of a long gash. He clapped his hand back in place and looked at Erin urgently.

She didn't know what to say. Kree needed urgent medical attention. The only thing Erin was sure about was that this was real. The "fog" had cleared completely. She was wide awake, sitting by a pond in Crow Woods with a dying boy.

"In here," he said, unhooking a leather pouch from his belt and tossing it to her. "Please. Can you sew me up?"

"What? Sew? How?"

While she protested and questioned with her voice, her hands were opening the pouch. She laid everything out on a rock – vials of coloured fluid, lumpy white pills, a chunk of bluish crystal, a device that looked a bit like a compass with rubber tubes attached, a ball of black thread, a curved needle.

"Will any of these pills or liquids help with the pain?"

"No," he said.

Shakily, Erin picked up the needle and thread.

Not a good situation, she was thinking. Not good, not good. She'd seen how the wound had gaped open. Seen the huge surge of blood ...

"There's a small hole in one end – "

"I know how to thread a needle!" she yelled.

"Good," said Kree. "Should I lie down? You'll need to work fast when I take my hand away. If I ... Any noises I might ... You'll have to ignore my pain."

She got the needle ready and said, "Okay, lie down."

5

The Edge Of Extinction

She knelt beside him. Even with his hand clasped tight to his body, the bleeding was bad. Erin kept thinking about unobtainable things like medical swabs, antiseptic solution, even some clean hot water.

"Okay," she said, and he removed his hand.

Blood welled up immediately. With the needle held between her teeth, she used both hands to squeeze the edges of the wound together. She couldn't see what she was doing because of all the blood. She had to manage by feel alone. At least it was a straight slash, like something done with a sharp blade – a skerri's sword? The tricky bit was keeping everything in place with her left hand while she took the needle from her mouth with her right. Ignoring the renewed blood-flow, she stuck the needle straight into his flesh and pushed it through.

Kree's body stiffened. He grunted as he fought back his cries. Erin pulled the thread taught and made another stitch. His torso was slick with blood, some of it half congealed. It smelt like old copper coins left out in the rain. Her fingers kept sliding as she tried to keep the edges of the gash together.

She'd still only done three stitches when she began to panic. She dropped the needle and covered the wound with her hands. There was just too much blood. It was too difficult. She couldn't do it. He was going to bleed to death.

"All right?" grunted Kree.

"Yes. No. I ..."

Then some other instinct kicked in.

She understood that saving him was vital to a plan or purpose far more important than either of them. She didn't know where she was getting this stuff from, but it was like when she'd known his name; and known that she was safe with him; and known that meeting him was an event that was supposed to be happening. With the same certainty, she now understood that if she failed to save Kree, a cataclysmic chain of events would unfold.

Her mind grew calm and clear.

She squeezed the edges of the wound together. She plucked the needle from the ground and licked it clean. Then she thrust it in and through. Pulled it taught. Over and over. Sewing blindly. Under her touch, Kree's soaked muscles were iron-hard with tension. His stifled grunts of pain echoed around the clearing and up into the evening sky.

When it was done, Erin sat back against a rock, watching the rise and fall of her patient's breathing. Her bloody handprints were all over him.

He hauled himself to a sitting position, then tore off some nearby dock leaves and swabbed at the congealed blood. They both saw the haphazard black stitches; both saw that the bleeding had more or less stopped.

They were sitting on their rocks by the pond again, and Kree was wearing his stained and slashed tunic. Erin still had worries about damage to internal organs, but he seemed fine – upbeat, even. He must have been lucky. And either he was very fast at healing or he was hiding his pain incredibly well. Following a battle wound like that, and a rough-as-rough repair job, anybody else wouldn't have been able to talk and move around normally for days or even weeks.

"Thank you, Erin," he said.

"Oh," she said. "My name."

"Yes. I could probably tell you a few more things about yourself. But not really very much. At one time, we had higher access to the Source, but our powers have diminished as our numbers have diminished."

He gave her a steady look.

31

"It's very unusual, though, for surface dwellers to have access."

"I'm not sure that I ... Surface dwellers?"

"That's our name for you. Until the time your historians call the Dark Ages, we were more common. Living in woods and forests. But too often we became the victims of superstition and persecution. So we moved underground. Where we found new dangers. Or they found us."

Kree touched the hilt of his sword absently, then smiled a sad smile and passed a hand over his face. He considered Erin again, as if surprised now to find her there. His eyes were slightly bigger than any she'd seen before; their amber colour kept fluctuating, going through a series of subtle tones in reaction to the smallest changes of light and shade. Erin had the impression that even though his gaze was directly on her, he was constantly taking in the details of every stone or leaf, the tiny movements of aphids and beetles.

"How do you even know my language?" she said.

"It's an aspect of the Source. We've always known an older version of your language anyway, so it's not much of a leap. Even though our access has become fragmented, memory and language are among the lesser skills."

He said all this simply and without being smug.

"Lesser skills?" she said. "Okay. Well, that's amazing."

"We share the same ancestors as you. We come from the same branch of the evolutionary tree. What we call ourselves is difficult to pronounce in your tongue, but it translates roughly as 'the people'."

Kree used his hands expressively as he spoke. His movements had fluidity and grace, and made Erin think about piano music and waterfalls.

"In human mythology," he said, "we've been given many names, but as you see: no horns; no cloven hooves; not so different from you."

He perked up at a gurgling in the pond. His eyes grew bright. He plunged his hand in the water and brought out a frog, which he raised to his mouth.

Not so different? Erin turned her head away.

Moments later, from the periphery of her vision, she saw him throw into the undergrowth what ever part of the frog he deemed inedible. Then he wiped his mouth with the back of his hand.

She gave him a look.

"What?" he said with a mock-innocent smile.

"That was a frog," she said.

He lifted a shoulder in a partial shrug.

"I was hungry," he said.

"You're feeling better, then?"

"Yes."

"But ... a *live* frog! Can't you eat berries instead?"

"Berries?" he said.

Erin shook herself. What was she doing? Discussing the dietary habits of ... of fauns, or whatever. But he wasn't a faun. He was a boy.

"Definitely, definitely dreaming," she muttered.

"Now that's an academic question," he said.

"Berries?" she said.

"The question of whether or not you're dreaming."

Erin touched the cool damp moss covering her rock, peered into the weeds and saw an ant crawling over a leaf. She breathed the rich air of the wood and watched a squirrel run along the broken branch of a huge hollow oak tree.

Academic ... The question of whether or not she was dreaming ... Her eyes were suddenly heavy and her head was spinning a little.

"This is all real, isn't it?" she said.

"Yes. It's real. And I can't thank you enough, Erin."

"Why did we meet? I mean, I think your injury – you could have died – I think that was part of it. But there's something else. Much bigger."

He looked at her with those amber eyes, studying her face. At another splosh in the pond, his hand shot out. He hesitated, and let the frog swim off.

"I'm not sure I can help you, Erin. I only know that whenever a surface dweller becomes conscious in the Dreamscape, it's for a reason."

"What reason?" she said, surprised by her pushiness. "The Dreamscape? Maybe you could access the answers from ... the Source?"

Kree laughed. "Or maybe *you* could? I told you, my skills are much weaker now. My people ... We're a dying race."

Her thoughts drifted; her alertness was shutting down. She sensed that she couldn't hang on much longer. She was going to lose the "link", or whatever.

"But you must know more than me," she said, stifling a yawn. "It's the first time I've ... Who else am I supposed to ask? Mrs Croxley?"

"Croxley? I don't know this name. I'll help if I can ..."

Drowsiness tugged at her. She couldn't think straight.

"Who are the skerri?" she said, wringing the question from her brain. "Where are the rest of your people? Why are you dying out?"

She let out an involuntary groan. Her head slumped forward.

Kree placed a hand on her shoulder and his touch sent a tiny shockwave through her. She noticed that his knuckles were scarred. His hand was sinewy and strong and had a perfection about it, like something carved from mahogany.

And she understood that he was *reading* her.

"You care about the planet," he said. "Rainforests, biodiversity. Polar bears and whales. I can divine only

34

fragments. I'm sorry. Maybe your purpose has to do with the environment? I don't know."

She swayed on her rock as Kree's words faded in and out of hearing.

On the surface of the pond, her bedroom began to take shape. *Not yet*, she thought. *Not yet.* But a jolt, like an electric shock without the pain, ran the length of her body. She saw the luminous stars on her dark-blue ceiling, the plain magnolia wall, and the dressing-table beyond the foot of her bed.

She sat up, blinking. It was over.

After a moment, she got up and went to the window. The sun had set, but it was still light outside. The usual cars were parked in their usual places. Geoff Sharpe's van was just turning the corner. Mr Buchenwald was trimming his hedge and Mrs Higgins was coming back from walking her Labrador.

The clock on Erin's desk showed 9.12, and she could hear the canned laughter of a sitcom Mum and Dad always watched at this time on Fridays.

Her mobile bleeped with an incoming text. Kane again, reminding her about the meeting at the canal in the morning.

6

Josh, Kane & Logan

Following a night of deep sleep with no dreams, it was already late when she woke from her usual Saturday morning lie-in. She had some breakfast downstairs then went back up for a shower. While she was getting dressed, she heard Uncle Dom arrive; heard his and Dad's muffled voices in the hall.

As she sat drying her hair, she sang the lyrics of "Ditch Me", an old X-Girls song: "*... just like you ~ To ditch me tonight ~ Yeah, ditch me tonight ~ All along the esplanade ~ The music's just right ...*"

She kept thinking about the dream, and Kree. Because, of course, it *must* have been a dream. The most vivid dream ever. But a dream. Mustn't it?

Almost ready. She tied her hair back and put her training shoes on and ...

"Hallo, Erin," said Uncle Dom, his bulky shape filling the open doorway. He glanced about with a leisurely air, smiling at the wall posters. One was of a humpback whale; another was "Earthrise", the classic picture of the Earth rising above the lunar surface, taken during the Apollo missions.

"Er, hello," she said. "I'm ... on my way out."

"You're fourteen now, aren't you, Erin?" he said, clasping his hands across his belly. "Fourteen back in February when I gave you those music credits."

In contrast to his innocuous words, he seemed preoccupied with something else altogether. Neither had Erin forgotten the effect of his TV stunt on her parents last night. And how had he been allowed to wander upstairs like this?

"Did you download some good songs?" he said.

"Er ... back in February ... yes," she said. "Thank you."

"By the way, I'm now on the judging panel for the talent contest. The *head* judge, in fact. It's only three weeks away and I've been sent profiles of all the contestants. There's a group of girls from your school ..."

She frowned and looked past him to the landing.

"Paige and her pals are very pretty," he said. "They could do well."

"Do well because they're pretty? They're just singing. It's supposed to be a talent contest. Anyway, I need to go. I'm meeting friends."

"Friends? Paige, maybe?"

"I'm not really friends with Paige."

"You're not? I see. Well, have a nice time. It's a lovely day out there. The middle of June already! Where are you going? I'll give you a lift."

"No, thanks."

"Why not? It'll be fun."

Fun? She took a step forward. Her uncle stayed where he was, blocking the doorway. He'd always been slightly creepy, but not menacing like this. Maybe the experience of nearly dying had affected his personality?

From nowhere, Lily Raven's lyrics came back to Erin: *Dark like night ~ In the ruins of your heart ...*

Uncle Dom raised his chin and said, "I don't know if it crossed *your* mind to enter the contest? Not your kind of thing, I suppose? And I'm not saying that you *should* enter. Not even saying you'd stand a cat in hell's chance!" He laughed, and it was a horrible, thick chuckle, like stew bubbling in a saucepan. "But I heard you singing on my way upstairs. Not bad."

She didn't bother to tell him about Josh, Kane and Logan's band, and how they still hadn't decided whether or not to enter – although, of course, *she*'d only be playing keyboards.

At that moment, thankfully, Dad called up: "Dom?"

"Coming, Toby," he threw over his shoulder. Then he lowered his voice and said in a conspiratorial way, "Did you see me on telly last night, Erin? I tricked them good, didn't I? Did you see the Orchid brand?"

"No," she said. "I ... didn't watch it."

He took his device from his jacket and held it out, its round screen facing her. She backed away. The screen lit up on the device and the brand appeared. The black petals of the orchid began to rotate anticlockwise around the flaming sun.

"No!" she said.

There were footsteps on the stairs, then Dad's voice: "Dom? Erin?"

Uncle Dom touched a button on the edge of the device and tucked it back inside his jacket. He gave Erin a cold smile, his dark little eyes glittering.

"Go on, then," he said. "Don't be late for your *friends*. And be sure to remind them that Black Orchid opens at lunchtime on Monday."

She squeezed past him, said goodbye to her puzzled dad on the landing, and hurried down the stairs. It was nearly ten o'clock.

The boys didn't see her approach. In tee-shirts, jeans and boots, they sat on one of the huge wooden lock-gates, their feet dangling. Erin was still on the towpath when, from nowhere, the memory of sewing up Kree's wound came back. It was so compelling that – for a crazy moment – she had the sensation that *he* was part of her real life, and *everything else* was a dream. The feeling passed by the time she reached the first set of locks. Josh, Kane and Logan were on the second set, still unaware of her, laughing and whooping and giving each other high-fives over something.

She trod the concrete towards them. All around was the gurgle of sluice-waters and the smell of stagnation. She made sure that her feet didn't stray too close to the bull-nosed edge of the canal wall.

The water could be high or low depending on which way the last barge had passed through. At the moment, it was low. The empty space between the lock-gates was deep, grim and shadowy, like a crypt.

She called "Hi" across the canal. The boys were on the further of the low-slung timber beams. Kane defaulted to his usual mode of easy smiles and raised a hand. Logan called "Hi", adjusted his baseball cap and spread his hands on his thighs. Josh was holding a large toad. For a second, he looked guilty, then he gave Erin a dark glare and crammed the squirming creature into a glass jar.

"Don't hurt it," said Logan.

"Shut it," said Josh. "Wimp."

Logan tried to grab the jar but Josh held it out of reach, laughing.

"What are you going to do with the toad?" said Erin.

"It's a frog, dumbo," said Josh, tucking the jar behind him.

Erin didn't argue, though she knew it was a toad; the warty, slimy skin was a dead giveaway. She glanced into the barge-chamber again, and shuddered at the rank water lapping the green-slimed walls and the blackened timber of the gates. The toad would have to wait a while. She was fairly sure she could talk Josh into letting it go if she bided her time and chose the right moment.

"So," she said. "Did we get together to discuss band business?"

"Josh dived in here last summer," said Kane with a lop-sided grin. "Straight off the locks. I dared him to, and he did it. The nutter."

Josh guffawed, revelling in the idea of himself as a reckless "nutter" who was unafraid of foolish, dangerous feats.

Often enough, Erin had hurled herself from the top board at the swimming baths, where the water was clear and warm and safe. To dive in here would be a frightening plunge into murky depths containing – for all she knew – old shopping trolleys and bicycles, broken bottles and bricks.

It was hot when the sun came out, and she was sorry now that she'd worn a jumper. She pulled it over her head and her tee-shirt rode up. As she straightened the tee-shirt to cover her exposed midriff, she caught the boys staring.

Logan looked quickly away, hiding his face under the peak of his baseball cap. Josh muttered something to Kane, and Kane laughed. They elbowed each other and laughed some more. Then Kane gave Josh a friendly smack across the head, and said, "In your dreams."

It struck Erin how differently Kane acted in different environments. At band practices in the garage, he showed more respect. Here, it was as if he were responding to some kind of masculine territory thing. Still, he was the first to address her discomfort. He even seemed a bit embarrassed and self-conscious as he tried to change the mood: "Er, yeah. Anyway, Erin ... Band dilemma resolved."

"Really?" she said. "What's happening?"

"Josh has agreed to enter the school contest. Right, Josh?"

Josh pulled a face.

"So," said Kane, "we need to talk about organising extra rehearsals. It's only three weeks away. Less than. It was three weeks yesterday."

Erin smiled. Any dates they had in mind could go straight on the organiser on her mobile. She put a hand in her pocket and her fingers touched an unfamiliar wad of paper. It was a stack of vouchers. Printed across each were the words ONE FREE ORCHID BURGER. Uncle Dom must have slipped them in her pocket when she'd squeezed past him. She did a quick count, stopping about halfway at twenty-five.

"What've you got there?" said Josh.

"Vouchers," she said. "Fifty free burgers."

"What?" said Kane. "Fifty? Free?"

"You gonna give us some?" said Josh.

Kane hoisted himself up and came along the lock. He jumped down to stand beside her, the soles of his boots smacking the concrete.

"They *look* real," he said. "Black Orchid?"

"Never heard of 'em," called Josh. "Can't be much cop." But he and Logan were making their way over.

"It's my uncle's old chip-shop," she said, realising that they couldn't have seen yesterday's evening news.

"Everdene Chippy?" said Kane. "We used to go there all the time."

"Yeah," said Josh. "Steak-and-kidney pie and chips ..."

Kane grimaced. "Urrgh, no. His pies were rubbish. All floppy and doughy and full of gristle. Maggot Bags, we used to call them."

Josh laughed. "Yeah. Yummy, though, if you banged 'em in the microwave for three minutes and dobbed loads of tomato sauce on."

"He's reopened now, doing burgers," said Erin.

"How many of these vouchers are you giving us?" said Josh.

"My dad said he was on telly," offered Logan. "Erin told us about her uncle the other week. He's that heart-attack bloke what came back from the dead."

"How many?" said Josh.

"You can have them all, I suppose," she said. "I don't eat burgers."

Josh made a lunge for the vouchers but Kane beat him to it, snatched the lot and thrust them into a pocket of his jeans.

"Hey!" said Josh.

"Don't worry. I'll keep 'em safe for us."

He began walking and the rest of them followed.

Away from the locks, the canal was bordered on either side by thick reeds, narrow towpaths and hawthorn hedges. Clouds had obscured the sun. The pale skin of Erin's arms was goose-bumped, so she pulled her jumper back on. Then she remembered ...

"The toad! Did it get left in the jar?"

"Uh, yeah," said Josh.

"I'll go," said Logan, spinning about-face and almost colliding with Erin.

They hadn't come far, but it took Logan a while.

"It got out by itself," he panted as he reappeared.

"Wimp," said Josh. "Know what he does? I've seen him rescuing flies from spiders' webs! Eh, Kane?"

Kane smiled. Josh laughed and caught Erin's eye. She ignored him.

As they walked on, a dazzle of colour drew Erin's gaze to the canal. A metallic-blue dragonfly was skimming the water. She remembered the dragonfly she'd seen in the clearing in her dream, and she had that strange sensation again.

"Er, do you know Paige Sanderson?" said Kane.

His voice made her jump.

"Er ... only a little bit," she said, almost grateful for the interruption.

Kane and Paige? Erin couldn't quite picture it, but she wasn't a boy, and she supposed that on some base-level a lot of boys would be attracted to Paige.

Then Josh and Logan came too close, play-fighting, and Kane seemed reluctant to say more. Erin brought her lips briefly to his ear and whispered: "As far as I know, she's not got a boyfriend."

Next thing, Josh and Logan's tussle got over-heated and they barged into her. It was an accident, but she went tumbling straight into the canal.

7

Threshold

She sank to halfway up her thighs. The reed-bed near the bank saved her from going deeper. Fury swept through her as Josh's laughter rang out.

"Nice day for a dip!" he said.

Erin scrambled onto solid ground, thankful that her mobile was still dry in her hip pocket. She had wet feet, wet lower legs and one wet arm.

"Sorry about that," said Logan.

"Shut it," said Josh. "Saying sorry! Wanna get off with her or summat?"

As Erin brushed past him, Josh sniffed exaggeratedly.

"She stinks now," he said. "Stinks bad. Like toad's piss."

"Moron," she said.

Kane and Logan laughed.

"Yeah," said Kane. "*Toad's piss*? What a moron."

Josh's face darkened. He glowered at everybody. When they began walking, he pushed ahead by himself.

In the distance, the old corrugated asbestos roofs of the industrial estate were just coming into view. The canal curved through a series of meadows and beneath a humpbacked stone bridge. Beyond the bridge, the waysides were thick with cow parsley and cuckoo flower.

They saw Josh throwing stones into the reeds. He kept calling back, but they couldn't make out his words.

"Water rat," he said, when they were closer.

He fired another missile. With a sharp sucking sound, the stone tore through the water. Three of the long reeds folded over and collapsed. Josh grinned. Erin considered his designer scruffy hair and the profile of his arrogant face.

"You're cruel," she said.

"Yeah," said Logan. "Evil git."

Josh rammed his shoulder into Logan's chest. Logan staggered, but stayed on his feet. Kane stretched his neck to look in the reeds.

"Where's this rat?" he said.

"Dunno," said Josh. "Hiding, I think. Uh – there it is!"

As he teased another stone from the path, Logan slammed into him and sent him sprawling into the canal with a great splash. He went completely under, then his head broke the surface and he spluttered and thrashed and swore his way to the reed bank. The rest of them howled with laughter.

Josh dragged himself out and stood there soaked and fuming. He lunged at Logan, but Kane stepped between them.

"I'll get him for that sometime," promised Josh.

As they walked on this time, he lagged huffily behind. At the next bridge, they left the towpath and followed an uphill trail that was overgrown with thorn bushes. Here, the boys retrieved their bikes from beneath heavy camouflage. Erin regretted not having hers. It was sitting in the shed with two punctures. The trail led up onto the bridge, and a short lane brought them out at the industrial estate. Josh stood a little way off, feigning interest in the forklift trucks operating in a factory yard.

"You've got that family wedding today, then?" Erin said to Kane.

"Yeah. Dad wants to set off for Bristol straight after lunch. We won't be back till late. We'll try and have our next rehearsal tomorrow."

"Right," she said. "I'm heading home for a shower now. What're you up to?"

"Separate ways from here, I suppose," he said. He patted his pocket, where the vouchers were stashed. "Thanks for these."

"Yeah, thanks," said Logan. "Pity we have to wait till Monday."

"We're off, Josh," called Kane.

Josh pretended not to hear, but then wandered over, looking more in need of a shower than Erin. An expression of her dad's came to mind – "drowned rat" – and she smiled to herself at how appropriate it was.

"Rehearsal tomorrow?" Kane asked him.

"No can do," said Josh gruffly. "I told you."

"What? Oh, yeah. You've got that day-trip with your sensei. We'll have to see what we can set up for one evening in the week, then."

Sensei? thought Erin. Wasn't a sensei some kind of a master in Japanese martial arts? Swordsmanship, maybe?

"See you soon, Erin," said Logan as they got on their bikes.

"See you around at school next week," she said.

"You never know your luck," said Josh, apparently himself again.

After a shower and a sandwich, Erin went to Crow Woods. She'd decided that if her experience had any basis in reality, the clearing must exist. Yesterday, she'd floated and sped through the wood as if on winged heels. Her memories of the dream journey were vague, but she was determined to search the woods.

The trails were growing narrower. Brambles snagged at her clothes and overhanging twigs tousled her hair. At one stage, she had the impression of being watched. She paused and listened, but heard nothing except birdcalls and the wind in the treetops. As she continued, sporadic sunlight penetrated the green canopy. She arrived at a fork. While deciding which way to try, a large crow landed on a tree stump at the point where the trail diverged. Erin caught her breath. The silver head-feathers were unmistakable. It was Rarke!

The raven cocked his head to observe her with one yellow eye. Then he cawed. At the sound, any birds in nearby trees abandoned their perches to soar skywards with a clattering of wings. Rarke cawed once more, then took to the air himself, but flew into the wood. Erin

46

watched him manoeuvre expertly between the branches and trunks, until he was out of sight. It was so good to see that he'd established himself back in the wild. She wondered if he remembered her. Members of the crow family were among the most intelligent of birds.

She looked at the fork again. Which way? Left or right? If only because it was the narrowest and least defined, she took the left trail.

In places, it disappeared altogether. The wood grew darker, due not to the time of day – it was barely two o'clock – but to the thickening spread of the canopy. Just as she was about to give up, she saw what looked like a clearing ahead. She approached cautiously. A pair of twisted alder trunks stood either side of a pale green pool of light, which she now entered.

It was the right size, about fifteen metres in diameter. But it couldn't be the place. The undergrowth was too dense, and there were spindly ash and birch saplings everywhere. She waded to the centre, where she found a depression. It contained grasses and ferns rather than water, but, again, it was about the right size. She separated the underbrush with her feet.

A curve of moss-covered rocks ...

From close by, came a caw. She turned to see the silver-headed raven standing on the ruins of a large dead oak tree. All the boughs had gone, and the remainder of the trunk – about the same height as Erin's five foot four – was ragged and open at the top, and it had an oval-shaped hollow at the front.

Although more decayed, the oak was in the same relative position as a dead oak in the clearing in her dream. She walked over, and Rarke watched her from his perch on the crumbling rim. Inside the hollow, a few beetles were scurrying over a damp, mulch floor. Could it be the same tree? The same clearing?

"Kree?" she said. "Are you here?"

She was about to call out again, but hesitated. The atmosphere had changed.

It had grown ten degrees colder.

Rarke cocked his head, as if listening, then he cawed aggressively and lunged at her. She backed away, but he spread his wings and flew at her. She covered her head. He circled the clearing. He swooped her, his eyes fierce and his beak wide as he let loose a sharp screech.

It didn't feel like an attack. It felt like a warning.

Then he flew away, straight up towards the patchy clouds.

A stillness and silence settled over everything. The air felt tainted with malevolence. Erin shuddered. She had the sense of being watched again, and darted her eyes all about. Her instinct was to stay where she was, but a stronger instinct told her that the source of the atmosphere was the clearing itself.

She picked her way through the waist-high undergrowth and between the scrubby trees. Her legs were trembling as she left the clearing.

The growing sense of evil was unbearable. It was gathering at her back, threatening to engulf her. Run, she told herself. Run. But she couldn't see very far ahead. She'd been getting used to the light in the clearing; the rest of the wood now seemed darker than ever.

Struggling to keep a lid on her panic, she walked faster, but kept wandering off the trail and bumping into things.

Then fear took over. Adrenalin kicked in.

Erin ran and didn't look back. She went crashing through and over and under anything in her path. She banged her head. Twisted an ankle. Got the end of a twig in her eye. Lost the trail. Found it again. Tasted her own sweat as it seeped into her mouth. Tore a flap at the knee of her combats. Carried on through the sepia light of the wood. Breathing ragged. Heart thumping and galloping.

Until, finally, between the thinning trees, she saw houses and a road.

She jumped a shallow ditch and scrabbled up the bank to the pavement.

Feeling gradually calmer, she was near the park when her mobile bleeped with an incoming text: *Come to my house now. Urgent. Paige.* Erin thought it had to be a mistake. But then another text came through giving the address.

When Erin came to Everdene last autumn, she'd attempted being friends with Paige. It had fizzled out, though. They just weren't very compatible with one another. But how strange that she should be in touch now, after Kane asking about her this morning.

Erin texted back: *What's wrong?*

Paige replied: *Just come. Please.*

Please as well as *Urgent*? It had to be serious if Paige was saying "please". But why contact Erin? Either way, she felt compelled to go along and offer any help she could offer. And, of course, she was curious.

So she set off for the Claymore Estate.

8

The Hunger

"Paige?" said Mrs Sanderson, who had thin yellow hair, sunken cheeks, and a harried look. "Course she's okay. You better come in if she wants to see you."

A snarling black dog was tearing chunks of foam from the arm of the sofa. Two boys lay in front of the telly. They had a control unit each and were grunting as they jerked levers and prodded buttons. On the screen, soldiers' heads exploded and rained blood over some bombed-out urban battleground.

Mrs Sanderson lit a cigarette.

"She's in her room," she said, pointing to the stairs. "Past the bathroom, first on your left. I'll bring some drinks up."

Erin noticed a pram wedged under the stairs.

"Oh, a baby," she said.

"Yeah, the great lump," said Mrs Sanderson, joining her at the pram. "Eleven months and she's not far off two stone."

As they stood there, Erin tried to suppress her horror at the woman smoking anywhere near a baby, or even in the same room. The sleeping baby had wisps of downy blonde hair and bee-stung lips. A pink cover was tucked up to her chin.

"She's gorgeous. What's her name?"

Mrs Sanderson blew a stream of smoke from her nose and smiled.

"Moonflower," she said.

Erin stroked the baby's head and thought about Mum's desperation.

"You'd better go up if Paige is expecting you."

"Oh," said Erin. "Okay."

Upstairs, she was knocking on the door for the second time when Paige shouted above the noise of a telly, "It's open!"

The bedroom was immaculate and, well, very pink and fluffy. Cuddly toys crowded every surface. The walls and ceiling were pink, the bed linen was pink, even the deep pile of the carpet was pink. Still wearing a nightie at three in the afternoon, Paige was ensconced in a leather recliner, her blonde hair tousled. She didn't even glance at Erin, just kept her eyes fixed on the telly.

"Re-runs of *Ski Academy Nights*," she drawled.

Erin frowned and sat on the bed.

On the opposite wall were posters of Donna Wowcat the pop sensation, Luke Summerton the footballer, and the new boy-band, Yes Can Do.

"Er, nice room," said Erin.

It was too warm, if anything, but she felt as if she were shivering inside. The experience in Crow Woods still lingered like a kind of psychic pollution.

"I just met your baby sister downstairs."

"The baby's not my sister, you idiot. She's my niece. My sister's, like, twenty-two. Mum's too much of a fossil to get pregnant again."

"Well, Moonflower's gorgeous," said Erin. She nearly added that Mrs Sanderson didn't look much older than Erin's mum, who was still hopeful.

"She *can* be cute. Not when she's crying all night. Or vomming everywhere. Mum'd have a job getting knocked up, anyway, with Dad off the scene."

"Oh?" said Erin. "Where is he?"

Paige looked at her in disbelief.

"Prison. Don't pretend you didn't know."

"No, I didn't! Honestly, Paige."

"Don't lie." She narrowed her heavily made-up eyes. "And it was ABH, before you pretend you didn't know that either."

Erin was relieved to hear a knock at the door.

"It's open," Paige called irritably.

Her mother came in with a tray. Before setting it on the pink dressing-table, she cautiously moved aside some of the cuddly toys.

"Coffee all right?" she smiled.

"Yes," said Erin. "Thank you, Mrs Sanderson."

"*Coffee*?" shrieked Paige.

"Sorry," said her mother, embarrassed. "Did you want something different? Tea? Coke? Hot chocolate?"

Paige glowered.

"I. Wanted. A. Strawberry. Smoothie."

Mrs Sanderson laughed and rolled her eyes, as if this were all in playful good humour, but Erin didn't think there was any mistaking Paige's over-pampered, spoilt behaviour. In the middle of this, Erin gained brief, sudden "access" to secrets about the Sandersons that she couldn't possibly know. *Paige had recently had cosmetic surgery – breast implants. And liposuction on her thighs. To pay for it, her mother had taken out a dodgy loan with stupidly high interest ...*

There was something else, but Erin lost the "link".

"A strawberry smoothie," said Mrs Sanderson. "I'll see what I can do."

She gave Erin another smile and left.

"Is that biscuits on the tray?" said Paige. "The silly cow knows I'm on a diet. She's brought them up deliberately, to wind me up. You wouldn't believe how vicious she can be. Nobody would."

Erin reached for a coffee. *Got to get out of here*, she thought. *Fast.* But an unhealthy curiosity was delaying her. It was all she could do to keep her eyes away from Paige's breasts. There must be a scar underneath each one, where the implants had been inserted. A boob job at *fourteen years old*!

"Er, Paige – there was something *urgent*?"

"Is that an Ever So Chocolatey?" she said, trying to get a better view of the tray without actually moving. "I thought we were out of Ever So Chocolateys."

"I think it is. Do you want it?"

"Course not, idiot. I just told you I'm on a diet."

The coffee was too hot. Erin took the biscuit herself.

"I saw Kane earlier today," she said. "Kane Whitman."

"Yeah? What's he got to do with anything?"

No connection there, then.

"Er, you said *urgent*, Paige."

Paige aimed the remote and the TV screen went blank. Her hand strayed to a fluffy rabbit, which she scrutinised then threw across the room.

"Your uncle," she said. "Heard about his new burger place. He was in the *Advertiser* the other day as well. He's one of the talent contest judges."

So *that* was it.

"I don't have a lot to do with Uncle Dom."

Paige frowned. "Where's Mum got to with that smoothie? Do me a favour and see what's happening, will you?"

Erin caught her bottom lip between her teeth.

"It's okay," said Paige, laughing. "All you've got to do is stand on the landing, lean over and shout down."

"I don't know about that."

"What?" she said, incredulous. She waited to see if Erin would comply. A whole minute of uncomfortable silence passed. Then Paige got up and flounced across to the door. "I'll just have to do it myself! I need a wazzle anyway."

She shouted down the stairs, then went into the bathroom.

Erin took another biscuit, but it slipped from her fingers and skittered under the bed. She got down on her knees. When she lifted the edge of the duvet, she saw the biscuit lodged next to a small suitcase. Her heart was pounding. *Access*, she kept thinking. Access to the Source? It was what Kree had talked about in the dream. So ... could she tell what was in the case just by using her mind? The answer was no. The feelings she'd had earlier were absent.

It wasn't in her nature to pry, but she thumbed the sliding catches of the case and they sprang open. She drew the case out from under the bed and raised the lid. Inside, were ranks upon ranks of chocolate bars.

The toilet flushed.

When Paige came in, Erin was sitting on the bed, nibbling the biscuit.

Paige flopped back in the recliner with an expression of pure innocence as she said, "Right. Your uncle. The contest. Can you pull a few strings?"

"Like I said, Paige, I don't have a lot to do with him."

"Come on," she said. "It's not like Josh and Kane's band's got a chance. Get real. What are they called? Big Red Baboon's Bum?"

"Er, that was before I joined them. And it was more of a joke than anything. They were doing a gig at the youth club last year and just came up with that for the night. The band hasn't got a name at the moment."

"Oh, I really think you should keep the old name," she grinned. "It's kind of appropriate. From what I've heard, Kane's voice sounds like something you'd expect to hear coming from a baboon's bum anyway."

Erin let Paige laugh at her own joke, then said, "I need to go."

"You'll talk to your uncle, though?" she said.

Unbelievable. Erin shook her head.

"I'm not going to help you cheat."

"*Cheat*?" shrieked Paige. "Cheat? What do you take me for? To think that when you came to Everdene, me, Madison, Beth and Nisha – we gave you a chance. Offered you *friendship*. But you thought you were better than us. Right, Lockwood? Then you start hanging out with Josh and Kane and Fatty. It's probably true what everyone's saying at school – you've got all three of them on the go. Bitch. Well, if you can't even do me one little favour, you might as well get out now. Go on. Get out. *Out! out!*"

On the stairs, Erin passed Paige's mum carrying the strawberry smoothie in a tall fluted glass and said a polite goodbye.

For the rest of the afternoon, she alternated between doing homework and trying to replicate the vivid dream state. She wasn't sure what to believe, but she knew that *something* was going on. Too many coincidences were stacking up.

So she kept lying on her bed and looking at the stars on the ceiling; or concentrating on the dressing-table mirror; or closing her eyes and trying to visualise the clearing as it had been in the dream. Nothing happened.

It was a frustrating weekend, what with her parents banging on about Uncle Dom's burger restaurant. They both only picked at their Sunday lunches. Then Dad produced a wad of glossy vouchers, and with a distracted smile began setting them out in patterns on the table.

"I know you're veggie, Erin," he said, "but we're going to Orchid tomorrow at midday on the dot. Why don't you meet us there and just – " (he laughed, as if even *he* couldn't believe what he was about to say) " – just try one."

"Daaaaad."

"Yes!" said Mum. "Try one! I bet they'll be – "

"Muuuum."

" – so tasty that nobody's ever tasted anything like them before."

"That's right, Wendy," said Dad, smacking his lips. "And *I* bet they'll be so tasty our taste-buds will think they've won the Lottery! How about that?"

"Brilliant!" said Mum.

"But they're exactly the lines he used on telly," said Erin.

Dad looked at her suspiciously.

"Really?" he said. "I thought I'd just made it up."

At school, too, the excitement was palpable. In the corridors and stairwells, and all through history and English, students talked excitedly about *lunchtime*. Miss Parlinka was annoyed by the chatter, but Mr Thewlis was more relaxed than usual; he admitted he'd been thinking about the "grand opening" all weekend.

It was a hot day. During the mid-morning break, Erin was wandering about the playing fields when she strayed too close to Paige's little clique. Sitting on their blazers, Madison and Nisha were doing their mascara, and Beth was brushing Paige's hair as if attending a princess.

On the grass, lay a copy of *Snog!* magazine, its cover featuring Donna Wowcat. Erin remembered that Paige had a poster of the pop singer on her bedroom wall, and that the girls were planning to do one of her songs in the talent contest. She'd heard them rehearsing behind the chemistry labs. They'd sounded more "cat" than "wow".

"I dread to think what this sun could do to my skin," said Paige.

"Your skin's perfect," said Beth. "It's like marble. Only better."

Paige made an approving murmur, which was about the closest she ever got to thanking anybody. She *was* pretty, thought Erin, but Nisha was prettier. Nisha's looks were natural and unaffected, while Paige was all push-up bra, short skirts, dark eye-make-up and smouldering glances.

"We'll have to go back any minute," said Madison.

"Don't remind us, then," said Paige. "I've got enough trouble with mouth ulcers, after that putrid kiwi fruit you made me eat."

"I was only saying."

"Well, don't," joined Beth, smiling sweetly.

"Mouth ulcers?" said Nisha. "Nobody *made* anybody eat anything."

"*You're* even worse," said Beth. "All that five-a-day rubbish you whine on about. You're much better off with a big fat Orchid burger and fries. Yu*mee*!"

"*Dee*lish!" said Madison.

Erin watched in morbid fascination. It was insane. It was just like when her parents had been talking about Orchid as if it were already established.

"Where did *you* spring from, Lockwood?" said Beth. "And what do you think you're gawping at? Get lost."

"Don't ever ask her any favours," said Paige. "She's too selfish."

Erin stood there, trying to think of a clever response.

"What's going *on* with you, Lockwood?" said Beth. "I *said* get lost!"

"A seriously weird cookie," said Madison.

They all laughed. Nisha, the least bitchy, only went along half-heartedly. Then the bell rang. With huffs and sighs, beauty aids were put away, blazers and bags were picked up, and the girls sashayed off.

"She's not even on Facebook or Twitter!" said Paige.

At lunchtime, Erin didn't think she'd seen a bigger stampede. Not even at the end of term. Could they really all be going to Orchid? She checked the dinner hall, the quadrangle, the playing fields. Nowhere was deserted exactly, but everywhere was far emptier than usual. By the time she reached the school gates, crowds of students and some of the tutors were marching along the road in the middle distance. She wondered if Josh, Kane and Logan were among them.

And that was the only reason she followed.

9

Herd Effect

On High Street, the big-chain Whiz-Go burger place stood empty. Around the corner on Cank Street, it was difficult to get near Black Orchid.

Traffic was being diverted. Police cars straddled the roads and pavements. Officers strutted about. Although a voice through a PA system urged patience, people were shuffling forward peacefully, with dozy, ruminating expressions, like cattle traversing a field. There wasn't a disorder problem. It was just a problem with the volume of people choking the area.

The powerful pong of burgers made Erin feel ill. It didn't help that it was a hot day and she was lugging her blazer on her shoulder.

Over the sea of heads, she saw a sign on the roof of the old chip-shop. The legend BLACK ORCHID was curved around the top half of the orange-and-black brand. It was an inanimate, crude representation of its digital parent, and looked like a sign adorning the entrance to a fairground ride. It was as if her uncle were having a joke, but there was no denying the masses gathering for his product.

A helicopter appeared and began circling, and for a moment Erin thought it was him; then she recognised it as a traffic-spotter from the city. Its blades made a grumbling, chopping sound, but the Orchid PA could still be heard: "Those with vouchers, please come forward. Everybody else, please queue patiently. The wait is worth it! We promise you've never tasted ..."

In a joint effort by the police and the council, a temporary gangway had been forged from Orchid's entrance to the edge of the crowd. Bunting was strung between posts that were attached to dumpy bases. And through this gangway, customers who'd been served started to filter. They still moved like cattle, but their eyes were fiery and glazed.

"Look at them," Erin said to herself. "Scoffing their filthy burgers, the slaughterhouse death-juice dripping down their fingers."

Then she spotted her parents. They came straight over.

"You don't know what you're missing!" said Dad.

"Absolutely ... mmm ... Yes!" said Mum.

An elderly couple shuffled up behind them – Mr and Mrs Chalmers, neighbours from across the street. Normally gentle people with impeccable manners, they were both gobbling the last few bites of their quarter-pounders.

"Another," said Mrs Chalmers. "I want another."

She had a feral look in her eyes and grease on her chin. Her husband was picking stray morsels from his shirt.

"Great minds think alike, dearest," he said.

"Come on, Erin," said Dad. "Plenty of vouchers left."

"I don't think so, Dad."

He laughed and led the group back to the gangway.

Erin watched in horror. Mr and Mrs Chalmers were vegans. Or had been. They'd even been her inspiration for becoming vegetarian.

Then she saw Josh, Kane and Logan. Each boy had a burger on the go, and each was also balancing a takeaway bag in the crook of an arm. They appeared happy enough, but not manic or wolfish like the majority.

"Hi," said Kane.

"Uh ... hi," said Erin. "Good burgers?"

"They're okay."

"Yeah, about the same as any others," said Josh.

He tore off another bite and looked Erin up and down. She raised her eyebrows at him. In her experience, most people would be embarrassed if they'd been caught staring. Josh just grinned and carried on as he worked the burger round in his mouth. There was more than a hint of amusement in his dark eyes.

"Thanks," said Kane. "Got served quick. It was cool."

"Oh, the vouchers," she said. "You're welcome."

"Yeah," said Logan. "Cool as."

Then Paige and the girls came through, except that Nisha wasn't with them. Paige ate with what Erin supposed was "normal" enjoyment. But Madison and Beth were rolling their eyes and cramming their mouths. Before they'd even finished, Madison was saying, "*Deee-lish*. I'm getting another."

"Me, too," said Beth.

"What's *wrong* with you?" said Paige. "You'll have to queue forever now, anyway." Then she added, with a look at Kane, "Unless ..."

He smiled, took out his vouchers and peeled a few off. Madison and Beth snatched them from his fingers, and paused only to say to Paige, "Coming?"

"I've had enough. See you at Ultra."

Ultra was an Internet café a couple of streets away.

"At least *some*body's generous with the freebies," added Paige, giving Erin a withering glance, and then Kane a little pout.

"Er, can I ask you something, Paige?" said Erin.

"What?" she said, affecting a look of extreme boredom.

"Did you see my uncle on the news on Friday night?"

She knew that Josh and the other two hadn't.

"No-*ooo*," said Paige. "Like I'd even care. Madison and Beth did. And the way they're acting, anybody'd think they'd been hypnotised."

She spun away on her four-inch heels.

* * *

The evening news programmes were full of reports about the "Orchid burger rush", the disruptions to traffic, the people who'd carried on queuing and failed to go back to their work or education.

At school the next day, there was no let-up in the excitement. Mrs Osugbu couldn't have missed all the secret eating, but she said nothing. Behind the cover of maths text-books, students happily ate takeaways, which must have been cold and stale. At one point, while writing on the whiteboard with her back to the room, Mrs Osugbu sneaked something into her own mouth. Just visible in her open briefcase on the front desk was a paper bag bearing the Orchid logo.

Lunchtime saw another pilgrimage to Cank Street.

That evening, Erin concocted one of her special salads: sun-dried tomatoes, onion, watercress, avocado, pine nuts, seaweed and quinoa, with a spicy garlicky dressing. Her parents usually enjoyed it, but now they left it untouched in favour of their takeaway burgers. They didn't even apologise.

The rest of the week passed in a similar vein.

Apart from a so-so band practice on Wednesday night, Erin didn't see much of Josh, Kane or Logan. Neither did she dream about Kree, or have any more experiences of accessing the Source.

On Friday, she was about to leave for school when Mum came into the hall and said, "Not saying goodbye this morning, love?"

"I was going to call out."

"I know you would have." Mum smiled. "And I wanted to ask you, Erin. Are you all right? You've seemed preoccupied lately. A bit distant."

Me distant? she thought. But she was grateful for the concern.

"I'm doing okay, Mum. Really. Thanks."

"Good. I can't help thinking ... You could do with more interests."

"How about a dog from the rescue centre?" said Erin.

Mum put her hands on her hips and rolled her eyes in a comic way.

"You know your dad's allergic to animals," she said.

"It doesn't stop him eating them."

Mum sighed and said, "You could come back to the operatic society. A good voice, you've got. It's wasted singing to that modern stuff in your room."

"Lily Raven's kind of retro," said Erin.

"Hang on a sec," said Dad, appearing from the kitchen. He had his suit and tie on, ready for the office. "You've forgotten something."

He came forward, smiling, his empty hands carrying an imaginary load.

"It's your head, Erin."

"Ha ha, Dad."

It was the old joke about forgetting her head if it were loose.

"And what's this?" he said. He raised the pretend head to his ear and mimed shaking it. "Something's rattling around inside. Yes. It's full of daydreams!"

Erin laughed. It was genuine laughter, but it had more to do with relief at seeing Mum and Dad acting a bit more like their usual selves.

At school, she bumped into Josh and Kane in the quadrangle.

"All right, Erin?" said Kane. "What's going on?"

"Nothing very amazing," she said, trying to sound cool. "Mind-destroying physics to look forward to after the break."

"Yeah? I really like physics." He laughed. "It's okay if you don't."

"No, what I meant ... Some of it's just a bit ..."

Josh sighed and folded his arms across his chest. Erin noticed, not for the first time, how broad his shoulders were, and she estimated that he had to be about six or seven inches taller than her.

"Anyway," said Kane, "It's probably 'cause me and my dad, you know, we're really into astronomy. Got this new telescope in the attic."

"A telescope?" said Erin. "That's great."

"It's a good one. A reflector. You can see planets in detail and galaxies and – "

"We going, Kane, or what?" said Josh.

"Yeah," said Kane. He gave Erin a lop-sided grin. "Meeting Logan. To talk about designs for the band poster. You know, the contest."

Right, she thought, thanks for including me!

"Are we rehearsing again tonight?" she said.

"No can do," said Kane. "Let's fit one in tomorrow or Sunday."

"Good job Logan ain't here," said Josh. "He'd be getting jealous."

He swept his gaze over Erin, as if assessing – with doubt – the likelihood of anybody getting into a state of jealousy over her.

Such a rude pig! But she couldn't help admiring the intensity of his dark eyes. He had no idea how wasted on him those eyes were!

"Er, I'll see you two around, then," she said.

"Don't build your hopes up," said Josh.

10

Perfect Alignment

Wearing a swimsuit, she stood on the lock-gate, her toes curled over the edge. The air was as hot as a blast-furnace. Sweat ran down her body in tickly rivulets. On the opposite locks, Josh, Kane and Logan sat watching. Behind them, blotting out half the sky, was a monstrous flaming sun surrounded by the petals of a black orchid. Everything shimmered and blurred in the heat-haze.

"She's too chicken," said Josh. "She won't do it."

Mum and Dad were among the watchers gathered on the concrete either side. Old friends and relatives Erin hadn't seen for years were there. Her maths tutor Mrs Osugbu was there, and her physics tutor Mr Tomlinson.

Below her, the walls of the empty barge-chamber went down and down. Green slime and moss coated the ancient brickwork, upon which frogs and lizards crawled or clung with their suckered feet.

"Oh, she'll do it, all right," said a woman holding a baby swaddled in sackcloth. "I taught her well enough."

It was Paige's mum, Mrs Sanderson. The baby ratcheted its head slowly towards Erin, revealing a rosy-veined cheek, a small dark eye. She expected to see Paige's niece, Moonflower, but the baby gave her a surreal knowing wink, and she realised with a lurch of horror that it had Uncle Dom's face.

"Don't even try," he said. "You'll fail."

A big rat appeared on Mrs Sanderson's shoulder. It scurried down her dress and over the bull-nosed edge of the slimy wall. Fifty, eighty, a hundred feet down, until it disappeared. Erin couldn't see the water. She could only hear it sloshing about somewhere in the deep darkness. Curling her toes tighter into the wooden beam, she tried to fight off the spiralling vertigo.

"Get on with it," said Paige, her goodie-case open before her. "I haven't got all day. Consider me for a change, instead of yourself."

Behind Paige, Mr Tomlinson was scribbling formulae on a flipchart.

From the thrown-back hood of the black orchid, the massive sun threw out its heat. It was twenty times normal size, but Erin could look at it directly, could see prominences and flares erupting from its violent surface. She felt as if her brain were melting. It might at least be cooler in the canal.

Kree appeared among the crowd. He looked unhappy and was pacing back and forth, turning Uncle Dom's CD-sized device in his hands.

"This could be a problem," he told Erin. "Be careful who you trust. Don't give in to weakness. Or, next thing, you'll start believing *that thing*'s lies."

With a mahogany finger, he pointed across to Mrs Sanderson's sackcloth bundle. The baby with Uncle Dom's face gave Erin another wink.

She said to Kree, "I thought we had a deal?"

"A deal?" he said. He waved a hand to encompass the whole scene. "Not until you wake up from this madness."

The heat was slamming into her, almost knocking her off her feet. She looked desperately around. Paige had been scooping chocolate bars out of the case and making short work of them. Now she was holding open a plastic shopping bag, and retching out a stream of fluorescent pink vomit.

"You bitch, Lockwood," she said between heaving spasms. Then her hair caught fire. It burnt away, until all that remained were black and smoking ashes.

Then everybody's hair was on fire, and their clothes were smouldering. If Erin stayed here, she was going to be incinerated.

She looked into the yawning void.

Despite another jolt of vertigo, she steepled her hands, flexed her knees, swallowed hard, then sprang up and out ... into a stomach-churning descent.

The canal walls flew past.

Curious amphibian faces peered at her from the slime.

Daylight dissolved. Then she was falling through darkness. She knitted her hands tighter. Stretched her arms as far as they'd reach.

The wind rushed by. Faster and faster. She was freefalling through the abyss. How much further?

Finally, a cold, violent impact, and the canal closed over her. Her taut body powered down, down, down ...

What unseen dangers awaited her?

She might hit something, knock herself unconscious. Lie in the sludge at the bottom. Blood streaming from a head wound. Her last air bubbling away. Would her eyes protrude horribly when she was dead? Be eaten out by passing perch and chub?

But the resistance of the water slowed her to a stop. She opened her eyes, expecting to see nothing, but saw dim light at the entrance to a cave. Something shifted within. She had the impression of a lizard-like creature, the size of a human, with a flat, pug-ugly face and a neckless lumpen head sunk between muscle-bound shoulders. A beady red eye found Erin.

She screamed, and produced a trail of bubbles.

Wings of panic beat in her chest. She kicked her legs. Powered upwards. Saw light filtering weakly from above, and thrashed harder. Her chances of survival seemed non-existent. Her lungs were bursting.

If, against the odds, she made it, her immediate priority was air. Then she had the problem of finding handholds and footholds on those slime-encrusted walls. But the air and light were too far away; and she was growing weaker by the second; and the creature ... There was a moment of creeping horror, filled with the certainty that she'd die. That she'd be captured and devoured.

Then light flooded down through the water.

She broke the surface; felt and heard the air rasping in and out of her heaving chest. Water streamed from her hair and over her face.

Instinctively, she reached for the walls, even though she already sensed that she hadn't emerged in the barge-chamber.

So where was she? Silvery light was dazzling her, filling her vision. It was too bright to open her eyes beyond a squint.

She bobbed in the water, breathing hard. Her fingers touched a rock. She clutched it with both hands, pulled herself up, and clambered onto its flat cool mossy surface. The air was cold. Her teeth were chattering. She sat there, exhausted, panting, shivering, still fearful of the creature she'd seen in the cave deep under the canal. But that fear was fading, and her eyes were becoming accustomed. She could see ... Was it ... ? Of course.

The clearing in Crow Woods. And she'd arrived here by coming up out of the pond!

Everything was bathed in silver-white light. The water shone like polished zinc. The clearing and the shapes of the trees around its edge looked like an overexposed photograph, but were gradually gaining focus.

Erin could feel her swimsuit clinging to her wetly. Could smell the pungent earthy tones of the woodland. Hear an owl hooting somewhere.

An owl? In the day?

She looked up, but the sky was too bright.

Dreaming ... She was dreaming.

The moment she formed that thought, she woke up.

Wide, wide awake. Yet she was sitting on a rock by the pond. The swimsuit was dark blue with a jagged red streak – nothing like her own, which was plain black. Memories from the canal pulled at her: the evil sun with its thrown-back hood of orchid petals; the baby with

Uncle Dom's face; the terrifying plunge into darkness; the creature in the underwater cave ...

She heard a rushing sound. At the same time, she glimpsed something over by the hollow tree. It all happened too quickly, but it was as if the ground and the woods came to life. As if a great mass of particles and fibres, leaves and earth went spilling through the air, clustering together to form ...

"Erin," came a resonant voice.

"Kree," she said, standing up.

He'd begun walking towards her. Now he caught his breath and froze. She wondered what was wrong, then realised that he'd been stopped in his tracks by the sight of her in the swimsuit. Her heart speeded up and she felt a flush rising to her cheeks. Kree lowered his gaze. The moment passed.

In a fluid movement, he was beside her.

"It's good to see you, Erin."

As they sat down, his amber eyes sparkled. He was struggling to control the smiles springing to his face.

"It's, er, good to see *you*," said Erin. "I ... I'm awake. It's like last time, only I ..."

There was another owl hoot.

"An owl in the day?" she said.

"It's night," said Kree.

And now she saw that the dazzling light wasn't from the sun or the daytime sky, but from a full moon. It hung there magnificently – close enough to touch, it seemed – filling the hole in the canopy, bleaching the clearing.

"Beautiful, isn't it?" he said with pleasure. "It's the only night of the year that a full moon achieves this perfect alignment."

"Yes, beautiful."

"Wait," he said. "You're shivering."

And before she could say anything, he vanished in a reversal of the same process by which he'd arrived – an

69

explosion of particles that dispersed into the surrounding woods and undergrowth. The particles had barely settled when they came together again. Kree was back, with a garment draped over his arm.

"This belonged to my grandmother," he said, wrapping her in a cloak. "It'll warm you up and dry you out."

"Oh ... thank you." She felt instantly warmer. "Kree, I was having a bad dream. I don't understand. If it was *bad*, why were *you* there?"

He looked a bit startled. Then he said, "I was having a bad dream myself, Erin. You shouldn't have dived off the locks. If anything had happened to you ... It only took you deeper into the nightmare."

"I *had* to dive in, didn't I? To get away from the sun."

"No. You only had to wake up to the Dreamscape."

"And that's where we are now? So the canal and the giant sun and the creature – that was just a nightmare? None of it was real?"

He looked away.

Erin shuddered and rearranged the cloak about her shoulders; its fabric was coarse on the outside, soft on the inside. Amazingly, she felt nearly dry underneath. She glanced up and saw that the moon was edging out of alignment.

"If I'm awake," she said, "how did I get here?"

"Physically, you're in bed," said Kree. "You're having a waking dream."

"So it *is* a dream? I'm still dreaming?"

"We both are," he said.

"We? *We?* You're dreaming, too? How can *you* be dreaming? I thought you lived here. In Crow Woods. I thought – "

"No."

"But – "

"As I said before, the few of us who are left live under the Earth. We don't travel to the surface, except in waking dreams. Hundreds of years ago, during what you know as the Dark Ages – then, yes, my distant ancestors lived here."

"Why aren't there many of you left?" she said. "Maybe that's what I'm supposed to help with. Maybe that's why I'm here?"

"No," said Kree. "We can't be saved."

"From what?"

"Extinction," he said. "We only number seventeen."

"It's not many," she admitted. "But – "

"All male."

"Oh ... oh, I'm sorry. What happened to your people?"

"The skerri are what happened. The Thousand Year War with the skerri. Don't worry. The last of us are safe. We should live the rest of our days in peace. Then in fifty, sixty years ... It comes to every species eventually."

"The skerri?" she said. She felt groggy; her vision was blurring. "I saw something under the canal ... a lizard creature, as big as a person. Was that a skerri?"

"Skerra. Skerri is the plural." His eyes grew wider and brighter. "Yes, what you saw under the canal was one of their amphibious cousins."

Shapes and lights and shadows swam at Erin. Spiral galaxies turned in the blackness, and a great sweeping arm of the Milky Way. In the next moment, she was looking at a flat dark rectangle studded with lifeless stars. She rolled her head on the pillow and saw the "Earthrise" poster on her bedroom wall. Then she was asleep, slipping into "normal" dreams. Josh appeared with a sparkle in his dark eyes, which were partly hidden by his long fringe. Somehow, she knew that the sparkle was for her. Yeah, ri-*iiight*. Like I'd ever ...

"Erin?"

Kree was gripping her by the shoulders. She was back in the moon-washed clearing, her senses sharp. His lean, kind face showed concern and maybe a hint of

71

tenderness. She liked the feel of his hands on her, but all too soon he took them away. Behind him, stood two figures in grey trousers and tunics, short swords at their belts. A second later, they were gone.

"Your friends were here," she said.

He smiled and said, "You were dreaming about one of *your* friends."

"Er ... yes."

"Josh," he said. "Josh reminds me of myself when I was younger."

"How did you ... ? When you were younger? I thought we were similar ages."

"We are. Or, at least, we've both lived on or under the surface of the Earth for fourteen orbits of the sun."

"Kree," she said. "I want to know what's going on."

He laughed. "I'm not sure I have the answers, but you saved my life. I would have died but for you. If I can help you, I will."

"Good!" she said. "I want to know about the Dreamscape and the Source. About the orchid sun in our nightmare. And about that trick you did – how you went off to get this cloak. Most of all, I want to know what's going on."

11

The Source

"Sorry, Kree," she said. "I don't mean to pressure you, but you *know stuff*. I've had sort of glimpses myself. Just glimpses. But *you* can see everything."

"No," he said. "I can't. Believe me."

"But you *can*. All you have to do is put your hands on my shoulders and you can read me like a book. My uncle's up to something dodgy. Maybe that's what it's all about. Try it now. Tell me about him."

Kree frowned. "My access to the Source is a pale shadow of what it used to be."

"Just try it. Please."

"The hands-on thing is more of an anchoring technique. It's not strictly necessary for reading somebody's ..." He shrugged and put his hands on her shoulders, then closed his eyes. He opened them immediately.

"Your uncle is dead?"

"No. He *nearly* died while he was in hospital. He survived a massive heart-attack. But he's okay now. What else can you tell me about him?"

Kree concentrated for a short time before shaking his head. "Nothing. I'm sorry ... He's a blank. Just his brand, the orchid sun. That's very important to him."

"It's the brand for his new company. Before, he only had a chip shop. Now it's burgers, and everybody's mad about them. I think he sees himself as some kind of genius fat-cat businessman. It's embarrassing."

"I know about the power of advertising in your world," he said, though he seemed distracted by something in the pond. There was a burbling sound, and Erin looked just in time to see a large frog hop onto a lily pad.

"That reminds me," said Kree. "Are you hungry?"

She glanced from him to the frog and back.

"No, no," he said. "I don't mean *that*."

He stood and offered his hand. It felt cool and strong and fit perfectly with her own. Her skin tingled. She sprang to her feet and let him lead her away from the pond. Then he stopped and turned to face her. They were exactly the same height. As he looked at her, the amber of his eyes darkened to copper and his pupils dilated. Erin smiled falteringly.

Kree raised her hand in his and examined it, turning it this way and that, studying every finger and knuckle and nail. His eyes met hers again and she wondered if he was going to reach out and touch her hair or face. Then he seemed surprised at what he was doing – shocked, even.

"It's ... just over here," he said, letting go of her.

Upon a carpet of overlapping dock leaves, near the big hollow oak tree, lay a feast of berries. Strawberries, blackberries, raspberries, gooseberries, blueberries – every kind of berry she could imagine.

"Kree! This is ... Wow!"

When they were sitting, she chose a fat strawberry and bit into it. Zest sprayed up in front of her face, deep scarlet against the bright moonlight. Juice ran from her lips, down her fingers and along her bare arm under the cloak. She was startled by the rich flavour that exploded in her mouth.

"Mm, fantastic. I didn't think all of these kinds of berries were in season yet."

"The Dreamscape has longer, more abundant seasons," he said.

"Does the Dreamscape just happen in Crow Woods?"

"No. Its geography corresponds with everything in the physical universe."

She remembered how overgrown and neglected the clearing had been on Saturday, how much more decayed the hollow oak tree had been.

"Are we in the past here?" she said. "An earlier time in history?"

"No. Just a different place, where nature is more vibrant. It has strong parallels with the physical world, but the Dreamscape is separate and autonomous."

"Okay – corresponding geography. In the nightmare, I dived into the canal but then I came up out of the pond. Here in the clearing."

"You transferred yourself here without realising it," he said.

"And how did *you* get here?"

"I ... followed you. I was concerned."

"So how do *I* do that? How do I 'transfer' from one place to another?"

"By concentrated focus on the location or person. It takes practice."

She scooped up some raspberries and lost herself in their succulence. Her hands were smudged with juice. She knew that her face probably was as well, but she didn't care. When her mouth was empty enough to speak, she said, "So the natural world is heightened here. Almost like it's having a waking dream itself?"

Kree paused, a rowanberry halfway to his lips. Erin could tell that it wasn't an idea he'd thought about, even though – to her – it just seemed obvious.

"Maybe," she continued, "maybe that's why I don't know what my purpose is? Because I didn't really choose to come here. It chose me."

His eyes had been distantly focussed. Now he finally popped the rowanberry into his mouth, chewed and swallowed, before saying, "Erin, that's really profound. Whether or not it's true, I ..."

Erin smiled. "I've always thought of the Earth as a living thing. Not in the sense that it has a brain or a personality. But just how, when you consider all the life in the sea and in the air and on the land. All the ... interdependent and overlapping ecosystems. I mean, it's easy to think of it as being alive as a whole."

Kree wandered off in his thoughts.

The moon had shifted out of alignment now, but its strong beams penetrated the edge of the canopy. Lattices of deep shadow lay across the silver. A faint breeze whispered through the boughs. Night birds called.

"Is this where everybody comes when they die?" she said.

"No," he said. "At least, I've never met dead comrades or family here. Only the projected dream-bodies of the living."

"The Dreamscape," she said. "Where we project our dream bodies. It sounds a bit like cyberspace. Like when people sit at their computers in different places, but meet up in chat rooms or virtual worlds."

Kree picked up a strawberry and rolled it in his palm.

"I understand," he said with a smile, "and it's a good metaphor. My people have never needed information storage systems."

"But you have books, libraries?"

"No."

"*What?*"

"We don't keep written records of any kind," he said. "All our knowledge and history are preserved in our memories."

"Don't things get lost, or forgotten?"

"No," he said with a frown.

"*Some memory!*"

She looked at his fingers and the scars on his hands, and tried to picture him holding a book. It didn't fit. She could only picture him snatching frogs from ponds, clambering through subterranean passages, or wielding a sword.

"Your entire history in your memory? Including all the battles in the Thousand Year War with the skerri?"

"Especially those," he said, passing a hand over his face. "The circumstances of the loss of every comrade. The cries of every wife or child who ..."

His eyes glistened in the moonlight. He toyed with the strawberry and it looked too delicate in his tough, sinewy hands.

No, she thought, not a pen or a book. But she could picture him holding a wife or a small child. Then she *did* picture that. She saw him with his arm around a girl who was breast-feeding a baby. Erin was accessing the Source. It lasted only a moment. Kree and his spouse looked so happy together, but Erin understood that the girl and the baby were dead, gone, killed by the skerri ...

"Are you all right?" said Kree.

"Yes," she said, choking off a sob. "Er, tell me about the Source. What is it?"

"It's a vast ocean containing the collective knowledge and experiences of all that lives. Our philosophers believed that if any subtle part of us survives death, that's where it goes. But our identities are lost. Going back to the Source is like a drop of water being absorbed, or re-absorbed, into a boundless ocean."

"Ri-*iiight*. That's *deep*."

She took another berry and savoured its juice.

"Our dream bodies," she said, touching her face. "If we're here, now, separate from our sleeping bodies, isn't *this* what lives on after we die? Maybe we don't lose our identities in the Source; we survive like this."

"As I said, I've never met any dead comrades here."

"But there could be other places?"

He smiled sadly. "Who can say? But for my people, it seems that our two bodies are interdependent. If we die physically, we die in the Dreamscape. The reverse is also true. We've battled the phantoms of skerri in the Nightmare Realm, and when a comrade has fallen, his physical body has also died."

"You fight the skerri in nightmares as well?"

"We used to. Hardly ever in nightmares or underground now. We try to stay hidden. The skerri have a particular hatred for my kind. I couldn't have lingered in the canal nightmare. They would have quickly sniffed me out."

A sudden wave of tiredness washed over Erin.

"Your – our nightmare," said Kree. "Some things were real, and others false. When we're not fully awake, the boundaries blur. Our perceptions play tricks."

She peered into the moon-shadows at the edges of the clearing.

"Don't worry, Erin," he said. "I've never seen skerri in the Dreamscape; only in Chthonia, the Nightmare Realm. And all too often in the bowels of the Earth. Anyway, it's different for your people. If you were hurt in a waking dream or waking nightmare, your physical body wouldn't be harmed. And if ... if ..."

He gripped her arm gently and gave her a tender look. Her blood tingled in her veins. She felt a warm glow in the centre of her chest. For a second, she thought he was going to kiss her, but then a complicated, regretful expression entered his face.

"Erin, I should return to my people soon," he said.

Her heart banged a little faster.

"Not yet," she said. "Er, sorry, I didn't mean ... But I've been asking you too many questions. And I still don't know why I'm here."

He stroked his hand down the length of her arm.

"The environment," he said. "I believe your purpose here has to do with the environment. It's the only thing that make sense. The way you care about it."

"And?" she said. "What can you see?"

"It may not be relevant."

Another wave of tiredness crashed through her. She forced herself to sit up straighter, gulped in some deep noisy breaths and hung on to the image of Kree's face.

"Tell me," she said.

"Your uncle is still a blank," he said, "but there's a man connected to him. A figure in your local government. And there's a connection to endangered species. Polar bears. Giant pandas. I don't know if any of this – "

"Is that what it's all about, do you think? Something to do with a councillor that my uncle knows? And to do with endangered species?"

"Possibly. Erin, I really don't know."

"What else can you see?"

"He's ... This man is not a good person. He has an office at the town hall. You shouldn't ... His mind is close to unravelling ... He has more than one face. A gentle push and he'll go straight over the edge. But you need to be careful ..."

Erin could feel the softness of the pillow against her cheek, the coldness of a foot sticking out from the duvet. Her tongue felt thick in her mouth as she tried to speak again. Her last impression was of his big amber eyes, with pupils that contracted and dilated in response to the subtle play of shadows and light.

She tried to stay awake, to stay with him, but it was impossible.

Deep, irresistible sleep dragged her under.

12

Garage Band

On Saturday morning, she kept thinking about the waking dream. She no longer doubted that everything was real. After breakfast, she sat at her computer doing research into local government. She knew already that Tansy Warrilow was a champion of the environment, but Tansy was a woman. None of the male councillors seemed to be involved in green issues.

Then it occurred to Erin that it was more likely to be somebody who took a stance *against* green issues – whether or not that part of their lives was public knowledge. She went through the profiles of every councillor, male and female, looking for clues. Then she concentrated on their photographs, while trying to recapture the feeling she'd had when she'd "intuited" the stuff about Paige and Kree.

Nothing. Twenty minutes and she came up with nothing. All she had was the strong feeling that she shouldn't ignore Kree's insights. *He has an office at the town hall.* She couldn't think what to do, except by maybe staging a small demo in the square to see if anybody took any notice.

And she'd need some help, she decided.

She texted Josh, Kane and Logan to ask what they were up to. The ford, apparently. They were going out to the ford. What was it with boys and water?

During lunch – omelette for her, Orchid takeaway for her parents – Dad said, "I don't see you riding your bike much these days, Erin?"

"Uh, no," she said. "Punctures in both tyres."

"I think you'll find they've been mended," he smiled.

"What? Hey, thanks, Dad!"

Before she left, she gave him an extra kiss and a hug.

It felt good to be cycling again. She arrived at the ford under blue skies. Most of the year, the water was shallow and only about six feet wide, and vehicles were able to cross easily. Other times, with the river in spate, the road was impassable for the average vehicle. Today, the conditions were somewhere in between and a warm breeze was furrowing the surface.

Josh was crossing back from the other side using the footbridge. He carried his bike on his shoulder. Its rear wheel was buckled.

"Did it count?" he said as he stepped down from the footbridge.

"It counted," said Kane.

"Good 'un, Josh," said Logan.

On either side of the ford, a crude ramp had been set up. The ramps had been improvised from bricks, wooden planks, and corrugated iron, and the distance between them was about fifteen feet.

"Hi," said Erin, pulling up at the side of the gravel road. The boys were all sitting on the grass verge now. Kane waved a hand towards the ford.

"You can go next, if you like, Erin."

She laughed and shook her head.

"*I* flew across," said Kane. "The back wheel just clipped the top of the other ramp, then I landed perfectly. I've always been good at bike stunts."

"It was a fluke," said Josh. "I'm going again."

"You can't," said Kane. "Your bike's knackered."

"I'll use yours."

"No way."

"Or Erin's," said Josh, smirking at her.

"No way," she said.

"Use mine, if you like," said Logan.

"*That* pile of elephant dung?" said Josh.

Erin thought about the demo, but knew she couldn't come straight out of leftfield with it. They'd laugh at her. They'd probably laugh anyway, no matter how and when she introduced the subject. Or Josh would. She began to doubt herself. Maybe Kree was right about his insights being random and irrelevant?

"You still okay for a rehearsal at four?" said Kane. "I've rustled up an audience. Just to keep us on our toes. My parents, sister, some cousins."

"Audience?" she said. "Er, great. Do you think ... ?"

But Kane's attention had wandered to his mobile.

"Okay, Logan," said Josh. "Get on that scrap-heap and show us how it's done."

Logan's bike was odd. It had small wheels and a slanted crossbar. Erin hated being unkind about his weight, but she thought that fifteen or sixteen stones of boy, on *that* bike, would have to be going fast to clear the distance.

"Maybe ..." she began, then changed her mind.

Logan walked up the slow gradient of the approach road, his bike like a toy beside him. He was about twenty metres away when a car nosed into view.

"We'll have to shift the ramps now," groaned Josh.

But the driver did a many-point turn and went back up the lane. Logan got on his bike, gave a thumbs-up sign then started pedalling.

"You know what's going to happen?" said Erin.

Josh trained his dark gaze on her. He rubbed his hand over his chin and worked his jaw, as if chewing a hunk of raw meat. Erin blinked, but stopped herself from looking away. With a faint smile, Josh scrutinised her hair and face, her denim jacket and her combats.

"Logan *wants* to do it," he said with a chuckle.

When Logan hit the plank-and-brick construction, it collapsed – but, for a second, boy and bike became airborne.

Splashdown was about halfway across.

"Priceless," said Kane.

He and Josh clutched their stomachs, so debilitating was their laughter. Erin fought hard to hold back her own, but couldn't help herself as Logan came wading out of the water, completely drenched, all smiles, his baseball cap still in place, dragging his toy bike by the handlebars. Even though it was a warm day, by the time he reached the grass verge, he was shivering.

"You should go home and get dry," said Erin.

"Who are *you*," said Josh, "his mum?"

The boys laughed again. Then Josh said, "I've had enough of this. Are we going to Orchid with the last of them vouchers, Kane?"

Erin was surprised that any vouchers were left – although, of course, none of the boys had seen the animated brand on TV. And since that initial rush, the crowds on Cank Street had been lessening.

Kane and Logan got on their bikes. Josh shouldered his own bike and sat sideways on the parcel rack of Kane's. Kane made an annoyed grunt, then laughed as if he were fine with the arrangement.

"I suppose," said Josh, grinning at Erin, "we could treat you to a burger with one of your own vouchers."

"I'm veggie," she said.

"Yeah, me too," said Logan.

"No you're not!" said Josh. "Since when?"

"I just mean I *want* to be," said Logan.

Josh shook his head in exasperation. Then he turned his attention to Erin again, regarding her as if she were an alien life-form.

"That's why you're so undernourished," he said.

"What? No, I ..."

Somehow, in three months, they hadn't noticed she was veggie and she hadn't mentioned it either. Now she felt herself bristling. She wanted to tell Josh he was wrong; wanted to say she was probably better nourished than he was. Wanted to, but didn't. She was always doing this – stating her principles or opinions on something, then letting people rubbish her without making a stand.

The boys began to move off on their bikes.

"See you at band practice," called Logan.

"Er, I was just thinking," she called out.

Kane and Logan stopped and turned. On Kane's parcel rack, Josh swayed off-balance and looked irritated as he adjusted his broken bike on his shoulder.

"I've already had lunch," said Erin, "but I could come with you and have a coffee. Er, and Ultra's good. Why not go there instead? We could chat about what songs to do later, and which one to do for the contest."

"Ultra?" said Kane. "Yeah. They do yummy toasties."

"We can use the Orchid vouchers later," said Logan.

Josh scowled. He opened his mouth to speak, but then had to struggle for balance again on the parcel rack as Kane set off.

Erin jumped on her bike. It was good being part of the band – even if they didn't have a name; even if Kane couldn't sing; even if Josh was a tosser.

She laughed to herself.

Thoughts about the waking dream and the demo were evaporating.

As they locked their bikes up at the Internet café, Erin saw something through the window that made her skin prickle. On a leather sofa, away from the computer terminals, Uncle Dom sat laughing over coffee with two men in suits. Erin thought she may have seen at least one of their faces in her online search.

"You okay, Erin?" said Kane.

"What's up?" said Logan.

She'd backed away from the door, a strong sense of wrongness making her heart race. In that moment, she knew only one thing – she couldn't face Uncle Dom.

"Sorry," she said. "I just remembered something I was supposed to be helping Mum with. I'll have to go. I'll see you later at rehearsal."

"What?" said Kane.

"This is stupid!" said Josh. "Plan A, then. Orchid."

"Yeah," said Erin. "I think you should."
Kane and Logan looked at her, totally baffled.

Erin started out from home again later in the afternoon. She could have cycled all the way to Parkfields by road, but couldn't resist a short cut through the western elbow of the woods. It was far enough from the clearing, and it cut a mile off the journey to Kane's house. She kept an eye out for Rarke. She might have felt happier if he were there to warn of any danger.

The trees were thinner in this part of the wood and the landscape was hillier. Erin rode into the dazzling warmth of the sun, through the coolness of the shade, and over mounds that reminded her of ancient earthworks or long barrows.

At one point, she stopped to sit by a little stream. Less than a metre wide, it was so shallow and clear that the stones on the bottom were visible. Wispy threads of weed waved in the current.

Erin rolled up her sleeve and dipped her hand in. It was cold for the first few moments, then her skin felt refreshed, invigorated. She smiled as she watched her fingers warp from the lens effect of the water.

Turning her face towards the sun, she closed her eyes.

If anything ever troubled her, she always felt strengthened by being close to nature. In a world of technology, concrete, society's pressures and rules, it was so easy to forget the mysteries of life.

How had that physicist on *Horizon* put it recently? *The mystery of a particularly clever species of ape living on a blue planet orbiting an average star in the blackness of infinite space.*

"Yeah, something like that," she said aloud.

Kane's house had a pale-blue stucco front topped with mock-Tudor gables. On the wide driveway, pampas shrubs swayed in the breeze. Erin leaned her bike against the fence and entered the double garage. The amps and microphone were set up at the rear, along with the drum kit and guitars. The walls were hung with the familiar faded posters of Jimi Hendrix, Bob Marley, Tom Waits, Courtney Pine, Nina Simone, and incongruously one of the comedian Bill Hicks.

"Most of the posters belong in a museum," Kane had joked on Erin's first visit earlier in the year. "They were my brother's. He's emigrated to Canada."

There'd been mention of a small audience for this afternoon, but except for Josh and Logan drinking from cans on the sofa, nobody else was here yet.

"Hi, you two," she said.

"Hi, Erin," said Logan.

Josh glanced at her from beneath hooded eyelids. He took a leisurely swig of his drink, sniffed, then gave her a barely perceptible nod.

She tried to pretend she didn't care, but the muscles in her stomach tensed and her throat felt constricted. Even though she was warm, she did up a couple of buttons on her denim jacket and looked around for Kane. Some days it was easier to cope with Josh than others, and this wasn't one of them. She'd tried hard to be friends with him. Maybe she had to accept that he didn't like her and never would. Maybe it was *her* problem that she found it hard to deal with people not liking her. Paige was more extreme than Josh, of course, but Erin had a lot less to do with Paige.

Then Kane was placing a cold drink in her hands.

"Thanks," she said.

A quarter of an hour later, a dozen people had arrived and the playing kicked off. Erin went through the numbers automatically, trying not to think too much about Josh, or Uncle Dom, or the demo idea.

After six songs, they took a bow to politely energetic applause.

Some people drifted away. Others stuck around to chat, mainly with Kane, since they were his relatives. Josh and Logan talked among themselves and Erin ended up feeling a bit left out. She knew Kane's mum and dad to speak to, but they'd disappeared soon after the playing. Eventually, the rest of the audience went and Kane broke out cold cans from the battered fridge.

"... gelled well today, musically," Logan was saying.

"It all sounded okay," said Josh. "Apart from Kane's ropey singing."

Kane laughed, unfazed. He'd never claimed to be a good singer.

"Yeah, yeah," he said, "and you know what I've been thinking? We should do 'Darker' in the contest."

Erin thought it was a great choice. Where most of the other numbers were so-so, "Darker" had a haunting, indefinable quality.

"What about the *new* song?" said Logan. "What about 'Rich Bitch'?"

"Nah," said Josh. "We should just scrap that one."

Kane said nothing; Logan hung his head.

Erin steeled herself and said, "I agree about 'Darker' for the contest. But 'Rich Bitch' is good. I wonder if it might work better a bit more up-tempo? I don't know, sort of ..." The idea of singing in front of them was terrifying, but it was the best way to demonstrate what she meant. So, avoiding eye-contact with Josh, she went for it. *"I don't care, baby, I don't care ~ I just wanna ..."*

She stopped, aware that Kane was staring.

"Carry on," he said.

"Yeah, carry on," said Logan.

Josh was looking ever-so-slightly shocked.

"Better still," said Kane. "Give it a go with the music."

Before she had a chance to protest or even think about it, Kane was looping the strap of his guitar over his head and Logan was manning his drums. Josh wouldn't look at Erin, but he, too, was reaching for his instrument. With a flushed face, she was left tripping over her own feet as she approached the mike.

"I ... I'm not even that familiar with the words."

"I'll sing as well," said Kane, "till you've picked it up."

Four messy run-throughs later, she knew the lines well enough to sing alone, and the boys had been cranking up the beat to allow for her faster delivery. As she sang for the final time, there were moments when she knew it was going okay, but she kept stumbling and wandering off-key. When it was over, she was convinced that she'd bombed. Her hands shook as she slotted the mike back on its stand.

"It was only an idea," she said, her mouth dry. "It's your song. If you don't like what I was suggesting, just keep it how it was."

The boys stood in absolute silence.

Was it respect? Or something else? Maybe she *had* bombed and they couldn't find a single thing to say. Logan pulled his baseball cap down low and wrung his hands together. A smile flickered over Kane's lips. Josh stood perfectly still, his eyes gleaming oddly under the fluorescent lights. Erin raised a hand to drag some hair from her face and his dark gaze followed her movements.

She began to turn awkwardly towards the door.

"Thanks for letting me have a go. It was fun."

"Hold on a sec," said Kane. "It was more than fun! You can *really* sing."

Oh ... they liked her.

"Er, thanks."

"A tiny bit nervous and shaky," Kane continued, "but that's just a lack of familiarity and a confidence thing. *You're good!*"

"You sounded fantastic," said Logan.

"Josh?" said Kane.

Josh sniffed and folded his arms.

"Yeah," he muttered. "She can really sing."

"Next rehearsal's on Monday night," said Kane. "Erin, why not take a copy of the lyrics to our other songs, so you can go through 'em at home."

"What? I ... don't know about that," she said.

Kane looked at Josh and Logan, then back at her.

"Why not?" he said. "It's just casual. Not as if we're asking you to be lead singer for the talent contest."

"*What*?"

"I said, it's *not* as if we're asking that," he said, smiling playfully. "We're only asking you to sing the rest of the songs on Monday. For now."

"Yeah," said Logan. "Come on, Erin."

Josh seemed to have recovered from what ever pause Erin had given him over her voice. He was tuning his guitar now, his back to everybody.

Kane presented Erin with sheet-music, complete with lyrics. She remembered that all their material was original and that Kane composed the music. It was impossible not to be impressed by that, or be tempted by the offer.

"I'll ping you over the recorded sound files as well," he said. "If you don't mind singing along to my voice."

She still felt self-conscious, but was flattered at being asked, and a bit excited. But there was just no way. Was there? To *really* sing with a band and end up performing in the talent contest? There was just no way.

"Okay to Monday," she said. "Er, there's something I wanted to ask you three to help me with on Monday as well? But earlier; before the rehearsal."

13

Lizards Under Rocks

The clock above the town hall showed just before five o'clock. She'd wanted to come straight from school, but hadn't been organised enough.

They'd stationed themselves midway between the fountain and the wide steps that led up to the main entrance. Erin wore a tee-shirt with a motif of a polar bear in sunglasses. Logan was handing out information flyers about leatherback turtles. More were spread over the fold-up table Erin had lugged here on the bus. A steady trickle of people passed in and out of the town hall, and she stayed alert for anybody taking an interest, but so far everyone was woefully indifferent.

"Not much of a demo," said Kane. "Sorry about Josh. I'll text him again in a minute. You still coming to rehearsal later, if he doesn't turn up for this?"

"Of course," she said.

In the middle of the square, the winged bronze lions at the fountain spouted water that fell turbulently into the large basin. Occasionally, the fine spray got caught on the wind and reached their faces.

"You're not even doing a petition?" asked Kane. "Is there a particular councillor you want to target with the issues?"

"No!" she said. "I'm not *targeting* anybody."

"Okay," he laughed. "Don't look so worried."

"No ... no," she said, forcing a calmer voice. "It's just to raise awareness."

Across the square, a woman from the tourist office was taking in an advertising board. On the side adjacent to the town hall, a stationary queue of buses and cars clogged Luxor Street.

Erin wished she'd made more of an effort for the demo. She'd run out of time; had spent most of yesterday singing along to the band's numbers.

"Do you think the other two are okay about me singing later?" she said.

91

"You mean, is Josh?" said Kane, smiling. "He likes you more than you think. What ever impressions you might have about him, he already sees you as a potential lead singer. Same as me and Lo. It's, like, we're a complete package now." He laughed. "Apart from needing a name. And a keyboard player."

A man in a dark suit was coming down the town hall steps in a medium hurry. When he saw the demo, he paused, then approached. He was tall and thin, had white hair and a tanned, lined face. Erin was sure she'd seen his photo on the website, and that he was one of the men she'd seen with Uncle Dom in Ultra.

"Sea turtles?" he said, his upper lip curling. "You want to save sea turtles?"

"Polar bears, too," said Erin. "And giant pandas. Er, especially them."

A vulnerability entered his reptilian eyes, but it was fleeting. He glanced at the polar bear motif on her tee-shirt.

"I hope you kids have got a licence to be here?"

"Er, I don't think we need one," said Kane.

"You sure about that, son?" The man's voice was velvety. "I could have you removed in an instant. Now get going, and don't come back."

He walked away towards the gridlock on Luxor Street, pausing to say something to Logan. Logan came straight over to the table.

"He said we've got to clear off!"

Erin watched the man leave the square and join the pedestrians, not even bothering to glance back. Could he be her "target"? It had seemed too easy. Even if it *was* him, he'd been irritated by their presence, but not ... *A gentle push*? She didn't understand. No, no. Something didn't add up.

Automatically, she began gathering the flyers together.

"We're finished?" said Logan. "We've only been here fifteen minutes."

"We don't have to go because of *him*," said Kane.

"Er, could we do it again tomorrow?" said Erin. "And come earlier?"

"Maybe," said Kane with a grin. "You gonna tell us what it's really all about, though?"

Erin said nothing. She hated being ambiguous, but didn't see how she could tell them about Kree and the Dreamscape.

Later on, at band practice, Kane and Logan exaggerated the story for Josh's benefit, and Josh regretted that he hadn't been there. They did all of the songs twice over. The boys were impressed by Erin, even though she'd been distracted and thought it had gone badly. Josh had that gleam in his eyes again. He did his best to appear neutral, then gave her a casual nod.

Logan said, "Your voice makes my lyrics sound great."

"Erin's voice could make a shopping list sound great," said Kane, passing cans around. "The contest is less than two weeks away. Not much chance of getting a keyboard player now, but with *you* singing ..."

It was a bit overwhelming.

"Hey, thanks," she said. A sensation of vertigo rushed through her but she knew what she was going to say. "Er – okay. I'm prepared to give it a go."

"Yes!" said Kane. "We'll do extra rehearsals; build your confidence up."

"And we do the demo again tomorrow?" said Erin.

Josh snorted. Logan frowned and scratched his neck.

"*I'll* do it," said Kane. "That posh geezer can't just tell us to get lost for doing a little demo."

"Yeah," said Logan. "Me, too. I'm in."

"Thanks," she said. "All you have to do is turn up. I'll take care of the rest. And I need to include something about giant pandas."

Josh's laughter echoed in the garage. He quietened down as Kane gave him a sharp look, but then he couldn't help himself.

"Tell you what! My mum manages a costume hire place. They've got a giant panda outfit that never gets used. I'll see if I can borrow that if you want!"

"What?" she said. "Yes! If you can get it, we'll use it."

"You're serious?" said Josh. "I was being sarcastic."

"*I'll* wear it," said Logan.

"If it'll fit you, Lardy."

"Don't call him that!" said Erin.

Josh scowled. Then he licked his lips and said, "If Logan's wearing a panda costume in the town hall square, I'm coming on the demo!"

They all laughed, and Josh added, "And if Erin's gonna be lead singer, it's only on the condition that we don't all have to turn veggie."

"Oh, I think it should be compulsory," she quipped back.

Vern Hawkes, Member of Parliament for Everdene West. As soon as his tanned, smug face came up on her computer screen, he was recognisable as the man from the town hall square. She knew him by name as the local MP of course, but had never before put a face to the name. As far as she could discover from online searches, he had a squeaky-clean record and had done a lot of work for community centres and for people with disabilities. She thought about some of the things Kree had said ... *Not a good person ... More than one face ...* For ten minutes, she alternated her concentration between Hawkes's on-screen photo and any impressions she remembered from earlier that evening. No intuitive thoughts or feelings surfaced.

She cleaned her teeth and put her pyjamas on, then sat in front of the computer and tried again for a few minutes before giving up.

On Tuesday afternoon, Erin was passing the gym in A-Block when a movement caught her eye. The door was closed, but through its window she saw a lone figure pacing the empty floor. It was a boy in black jogging bottoms and a black vest, and he was going through some kind of choreographed routine. His arms and shoulders had well-developed muscles; his skin shone with a fine layer of sweat. The boy stopped striding and settled into a stance, knees bent, one leg planted forward, the other behind. He swiped at the air with a short wooden pole. He ducked low to the left, low to the right. He thrust out again, then mimed sheathing the pole, which Erin supposed represented a samurai sword.

He took three long strides, stopped for a beat, turned through 180°...

Erin darted away from the door.

She wasn't sure if he'd seen her or not. Her breathing was a little fast and shallow. Voices rose and fell and echoed somewhere near by. She glanced both ways along the corridor. It was empty. She listened for sounds from the gym. Nothing. She stroked a lock of hair from her eyes and approached again.

The boy hadn't seen her, she decided. He was too focussed on what he was doing. His steps were light but certain: not a single squeak was produced by the passage of his trainers over the wooden floor.

He unsheathed the "sword" and marched forward, slowly at first, then faster. He carved at the air, this way and that. Stepped backwards, forwards, to the side. Turned again. Sheathed and unsheathed. Struck out.

Twisted his lean muscular body in precise, graceful, perfectly timed movements.

The boy's face was rigid with concentration.

His eyes were dark and intense.

The boy was Josh.

Erin tried to detect arrogance in the display, but there wasn't a trace.

Josh was alone and didn't know he was being watched. Yet here was an entirely different boy from the one she thought she knew.

She stepped away from the door.

Of course, he *was* still rude and mean and unfriendly.

Erin started along the corridor. Then she stopped, ran a hand through her hair and leaned against the wall. For the first time in about six months, she had to consult her timetable to find out what subject she was doing next.

Josh failed to show up for the demo, which meant they didn't have the costume either. Erin had managed to get some A2 posters printed off in the media room at school, one of a polar bear, one of a giant panda. These she taped to the front edge of the table. The sight of Josh doing his swordsmanship routine in the gym kept intruding into her thoughts.

"We're better off without him," she said aloud.

"Who?" said Kane. "Oh, you mean Josh."

"Yeah. He'd probably just be rude to people."

By "people", she meant Vern Hawkes. Things could be tricky enough without some macho face-off. But in the end, neither Josh nor Hawkes showed.

"I can tell how disappointed you are," said Kane. "I suppose you want to come back tomorrow as well? I'll have another word with Josh."

At home, Dad told her Uncle Dom would be appearing on the national news. The *national* news? Erin was curious, but planned to leave the room if he produced his brand device. Thankfully, the Cank Street crowds had continued to get thinner, and she was glad to see that her parents had left their burgers unfinished tonight.

When the main news was over, there was a recap of the Orchid story so far, then a cut to Rupert Frith, the programme's camp and floppy-haired icon. At his interview desk sat Uncle Dom and a stick-thin lady with a permanent pout. Also – beamed in by video-link – was a po-faced bald man of about seventy.

"... heady times," Rupert Frith was saying. "What a story, Mr Lockwood! You stuck two fingers up to a killer heart-attack, re-branded your business, and here you are beside Letitia Brown, CEO of Whiz-Go Burgers UK."

Uncle Dom mimed straightening his pink cravat and the collar of his dark-green jacket, then jiggled his head.

"I'm doing pretty good for myself, aren't I?"

"You certainly are!" said Frith. "I hear they've been flocking to Everdene from all over the region? How do you explain it?"

"Oh, you know. Word of mouth."

Frith blew out his cheeks.

"So your burgers must be exceptional?"

"The recipe's a trade secret, of course."

"Of course. But your digital brand had quite an effect when it was shown on *Everdene Tonight*. There's been speculation about hypnotic content."

"Rubbish," said Uncle Dom. "All experts agree that mass hypnosis through a TV screen is an urban myth." He winked at the camera.

Frith laughed like a hyena.

"We've seen clips of what it's been looking like outside the Black Orchid restaurant. And although there's now been a tailing-off, demand for your product is still generating concerns about public order."

"It's just a question of supply," said Uncle Dom, giving Letitia Brown a smile. "Once supply is addressed – "

"Yes," said Frith. "Ms Brown. CEO of Whiz-Go UK. I believe you have a bombshell announcement to make?"

"You bet we do," said Letitia, who'd retained her Los Angeles accent after twenty years in London. "By the weekend, all UK outlets of Whiz-Go will be trading under the Orchid brand."

"*Trading as Orchid*? All outlets?" It was obvious Frith had been briefed, but he always played to the viewers. "Is that even logistically possible, Letitia?"

"It's been a roller-coaster of co-ordination. Our own food and packaging plants are working round the clock to meet the dead-line. But it's a done deal."

"Surely this is unprecedented? A tin-pot start-up company like Mr Lockwood's calling the shots with the UK arm of a multinational?"

"I know a good thing when I see it. And I have the full backing of our American mother corporation."

Letitia glanced at the bald, elderly man on the video screen.

"Some analysts might call your enthusiasm naive," said Frith. He tossed his leonine head to get his floppy fringe out of his eyes. "Isn't the initial rush for Mr Lockwood's product now losing steam?"

"Yes, that's true," she said, "but we're confident there'll be an exponential rise in demand at the weekend."

"Not by showing the notorious animated brand on the national news, I hope?" said Frith, turning to Uncle Dom.

Uncle Dom smiled cryptically, and a security technician could be seen hovering briefly at the edge of the picture.

"If he shows it, don't look," said Erin.

"Don't be silly," said Mum.

"Let's bring Clark Jefferson in," said Frith, his gaze moving to the video-link. "Clark, thanks for talking to us on behalf of Larry Bratwurst, Whiz-Go America's CEO. I understand Larry's enjoying a final stay on his Pacific island of Lulawaikiki, before abandoning it to the vicissitudes of climate change?"

"Now, hold your horses," said Clark. "I was told ..."

There was a cut to a colonial-style mansion in the middle of a flooded park-like landscape. Beyond the grounds of the house, lost beaches could be made out below the turquoise water. As a news helicopter got closer and its camera zoomed in, a swimming pool on the flat roof of the palatial building came into view. By the pool, a flabby man wearing a thong was being attended by three bronzed women in bikinis – until he saw the helicopter and waved his fist.

"Larry Bratwurst bidding a sad farewell to his Pacific island of Lulawaikiki," said Frith, back in the newsroom.

"That was cheap," said Clark Jefferson. "One more crack about namby-pamby green issues and I'm off-air."

Frith threw up his hands and released a blast of his trademark hyena laughter.

"Absolutely certifiable," said Dad.

"Clark Jefferson?" said Erin.

"No, you moo. Rupert Frith."

"... an offer we couldn't refuse," Clark was saying from the video screen. "Five per cent of any increased profits. That's all Mr Lockwood's asked for, and that's what we've signed up to. He'll still own the brand, of course, but we – "

"I'm struggling to understand," said Frith. "Did any of you even *know* Mr Lockwood when he recently opened Black Orchid?"

"Let me answer that," said Letitia. "Alongside the Everdene launch, Mr Lockwood had the foresight to email a business plan to Whiz-Go directors across the UK, and a short digi-film of his idea for a TV advert."

"Ha!" said Frith. "Did it include the animated brand? Have you since joined the fray laying siege to his restaurant?"

"I didn't need to. I met with Mr Lockwood at his home. He cooked and served me one of his burgers personally. And to use an old Whiz-Go tag-word, the experience was *fabulotissimo.*"

"I see. Clark? Have you sampled an Orchid burger yourself?"

"Sure thing. Letitia mailed me one over by airfreight."

"It must have been cold?"

"You don't say," said Clark. "And it was still so good that my taste-buds thought they'd won the Lottery."

For the camera, Frith assumed his dumbfounded face.

"I suppose you'd also seen the animation?" he said. "Embedded in Mr Lockwood's proposed TV advert?"

"Yep. It's ingenious stuff. I gave Letitia the go-ahead to have the ad remade using two of Britain's top actors."

"Who – ?"

"All part of the surprise."

"Well. You *have* been busy beavers," said Frith. "We're running short on time now, but I believe viewers can see the advert this Friday night?"

"It'll be aired on all major UK channels," said Letitia. "Ahead of Saturday's nationwide roll-out of re-branded Whiz-Go restaurants."

"Is the advert even *legal*? In view of the hypnosis allegations?"

"It's entirely legal. Our corporate lawyers in the UK and across the Atlantic have checked under every stone."

"And they didn't find any lizards, Letitia?"

"No lizards."

"Let's be clear," said Clark Jefferson, "all effective, good-quality advertising is a form of legal hypnosis."

Uncle Dom aimed another wink at the camera.

14

The Target

It was a humid evening. Erin thought Logan would be too hot inside the costume and felt sorry for him, although he seemed to be enjoying the attention of the small children who kept dragging their mothers over. The novelty soon wore off for Josh and he was looking for ways to relieve his boredom.

"Are you all vegetarians?" said a little girl.

"We're vegan warriors," said Josh, making his eyes go dopey. "We live on carrot juice and lentils, and talk to dolphins telepathically."

At that moment, two community officers approached.

"Everything all right?" said the woman.

"Er, yes, thanks," said Erin.

But the woman was looking at Josh and Kane.

"We've had a complaint," she said. "To the effect that you've been hassling members of the public for money."

"Not true," said Kane. "We're just handing out flyers and trying to raise awareness about endangered species."

Erin saw the "target" watching from the doorway of the town hall. His steely gaze met hers and she held it defiantly for moment.

"We haven't asked anybody for money," she told the officers.

The male officer said something to his colleague that was drowned by children screaming with laughter at Logan's antics. Despite the humidity and the heavy costume, he was doing star-jumps to entertain them. Both officers laughed at the spectacle, then turned their attention back to Kane and Josh.

"Where've you had the costume from, kids?" said the man.

Josh told them about his mother's job. They asked for and wrote down a contact address and phone number.

"Okay," said the woman. "Watch how you go."

The officers walked off.

"Nobody can touch us," said Josh.

"Yeah," said Kane. "One guess who made up the lies."

A few minutes later, the officers had left the square altogether and Vern Hawkes was coming down the town hall steps.

"Make way there, please!" he said.

At his authoritative tone, mothers scooped up or led their children aside. Hawkes planted both his hands palms-down on the display table and looked back and forth between Erin, Josh and Kane.

"Didn't those officers just tell you to move on?" he said.

"No," said Josh. "We were told it was okay."

"Yeah," said Kane. "It's a peaceful demo."

Hawkes cast a glance at Logan fooling about in the costume.

"Well!" he said with a sneer. "I should think you'll have the giant-panda hunters trembling in their boots if they see this little set-up!"

"We're not causing any trouble," said Erin.

He ignored her, pointed a finger at Josh and lowered his voice to say, "Who put you up to this?"

"Nobody," said Josh. "And we know our rights."

"It was all my idea," said Erin.

He brought his face close to hers. She could smell something unsavoury on his breath. The lines on his forehead deepened, some riding up beneath his feathery white fringe. His reptilian gaze had a penetrating, frenetic quality. There was a tic in his left eye and a pulsing vein at his temple.

His mind is close to unravelling, she remembered with a shudder.

"Leave her alone," said Josh, standing straighter. "It was my idea."

Hawkes turned on Josh and seemed to consider something that he quickly changed his mind about. Then he addressed them as a group.

"Who's *behind* it? That's what I want to know." He darted a look at the town hall. "Is it Lee Redmond?"

"Who?" said Josh. "No. Nobody. Just us. Mainly me."

"You've got five minutes to get out of here," said Hawkes before sauntering off. He went back up the steps, stationed himself in the doorway and made a show of checking his wristwatch.

"Ponce," said Kane.

Logan let out a muffled sigh. With both paws, he pulled off the fluffy black-and-white oversized head. His face was like a big red lantern.

"Sweltering," he rasped.

"You should take the whole thing off, Logan," said Erin.

"Why?" said Josh. "We're not going, are we?"

"I just mean that he needs a break."

"I'll be all right in a sec," said Logan.

"Who is that jumped-up idiot anyway?" said Josh.

"Vern Hawkes," said Erin. "MP for Everdene West."

"He thinks we're packing up," said Kane. "Just look at him standing there with that stupid smarmy smile on his stupid smarmy face."

"Yeah," said Josh. "Put the head back on, Logan."

Logan put the head back on and began entertaining children again. Hawkes was furious. He kept pointing at his watch or up at the town hall clock.

"Tosser," said Josh.

When the five minutes was up, Hawkes put his hands on his hips and glared at them from the top of the three wide steps.

"Don't even look at him," said Josh. "Just carry on like he's not there."

A minute later, Hawkes went back inside the building. Erin imagined that he'd reappear accompanied by security personnel, but he didn't.

Another half hour passed and he didn't reappear at all.

At six o'clock, they packed up.

"Same again tomorrow?" said Josh.

"What?" said Erin. "Er, maybe that's enough now."

"So it *was* him you were targeting?" said Kane.

"Hold on a minute," said Josh. "If we don't come back tomorrow, he'll think he's won. We've *got* to come back."

"The timing's a coincidence," said Erin. "It doesn't matter if he sees it as some kind of victory. If the demo was over anyway ..."

Josh looked at Kane, and Kane said, "It's Erin's thing, I suppose. We're just helping out, remember? Let's go and do this extra rehearsal."

"You're saying it's over, then?" said Josh, looking at Erin intently.

But she didn't know. She wasn't sure what to do.

The next day at school, she noticed how the contest talent entrants had been upping their marketing campaigns. The most striking efforts were those of the girl group, Pink Ocean. Their colour posters adorned the walls in every classroom and corridor; some were even stapled to trees on the playing fields.

It was a head-and-shoulders composition of the girls, with Paige at the centre. Madison and Beth flanked her, but their images were smaller and fuzzier. Nisha was absent from the poster, which confirmed Erin's recent suspicions of a fall-out. Paige's blonde hair flowed about the shoulders of a pink top, and her eyes were so blue it seemed likely they'd been digitally enhanced. What really captured the attention was her angelic smile.

Between morning lessons, Erin saw the girls flouncing through the quadrangle, Paige in the middle of Madison and Beth. But this wasn't the angelic Paige of the poster. This was a pouting, smouldering, super-confident Paige, in the shortest skirt she could get away with, believing herself the role-model of all girls and the desire of all boys. Believing herself a goddess among lesser creatures. Believing that Pink Ocean were the all-but-named winners of the Schools of Everdene Talent Contest.

As the trio bore down on Erin with their contemptuous sneers, she stood aside rather than be barged aside.

On the playing fields at lunchtime, she came across Nisha, crying and alone, her face turned towards the trunk of a sycamore tree. Erin offered her a pack of tissues and she accepted them with a slender, ringed, manicured hand.

"What's wrong?" asked Erin.

"Nothing," she said through her snivels.

Erin touched her lightly on the arm.

"Is it Paige? Something to do with the contest?"

Nisha blinked her large, dark, almond-shaped eyes.

"She kicked me out of the group."

"Oh," said Erin. "No chance of – "

"We had arguments about the music. I can play the keyboards, see, and it's a talent contest, so that's another talent we'd have. Even if the rest of the music was a backing track ... Do you see? But Paige wanted the four of us standing together in a line. The worst thing is, she must have planned it. She texted me last night, right? And this morning the posters are everywhere. But the four of us posed for promo-pics weeks ago. They couldn't have had time since last night to do a new picture and get posters made up."

"I suppose not ..."

"I don't *care*," said Nisha, another sob wracking her body. "Better off without friends like that. Don't care."

"Er, I don't know if this is the right moment," said Erin, "but Josh, Kane, Logan and ... We need a keyboard player for *our* band."

Nisha looked at Erin with interest but said nothing.

"I used to play keyboards," said Erin. "I'm sort of lead singer now."

"Yeah? Wow. You kept that quiet."

"It's pretty recent."

Nisha smiled and dabbed at her tears.

"I don't know," she said. "Would they even want me?"

"They definitely want a keyboard player. I think they're desperate." The moment the words left Erin's mouth she regretted them.

"Desperate?" Nisha said in a cracked voice. "They should be prepared to take on a reject like me, then?"

"I didn't mean ... I'm really sorry."

"Don't worry, Erin. I know you didn't mean it like that. It'd be good to still be in the contest. And I love playing. I get the odd wedding gig with my brother's band, but they're a lot older and their music's stuck somewhere in early Corner Shop. Every song sounds like a variation on 'Brimful of Asha'."

They both laughed. Impulsively, Erin reached out and hugged Nisha.

It was humid again. Storms had been forecast but none had materialised yet. Although Erin had offered to wear the panda costume to give Logan a break, he was insistent that it was a job he wanted to do.

"I just don't get it," said Kane. "I've looked into Vern Hawkes, and he's not involved in environmental issues, not even on a local level."

Erin shrugged and said nothing.

The clock was just striking five when the target burst aggressively into view from the town hall. Erin and the others fell silent. Logan lifted off his panda head and moved nearer to the display table. Around the square, people stopped and stared.

Vern Hawkes had another man by the jacket collar and was forcing him down the steps towards the demo. Shorter, skinnier and younger, the other man had crew-cut hair and a rodent's face. At the bottom of the steps, he managed to escape Hawkes's grasp. Hawkes lunged for him, but the man ducked.

Then they were skipping about – Hawkes making continual attempts to grab, and the other man on the defensive, backing further from the town hall and closer to the fountain. His protestations were lost in the tumbling of the water, the roar of the traffic and the comments from onlookers.

The paved area around the fountain was on a lower level, so Erin and the boys had a clear view over the heads of the swelling crowd. A security guard was keeping his distance, but talking into a two-way radio.

Hawkes's voice was too frenzied for any of his words to be made out, but he kept pointing in the direction of the demo.

"Hope we get some blood," said Josh.

Erin's heart banged against her ribs.

In the next moment, Josh got his wish.

Hawkes grabbed a handful of his victim's jacket and thrust his head forward. Erin winced. She thought she heard the smack of the impact but knew it was impossible above the general noise. The man staggered against the fountain's safety rail and held his hands to his face. Even from a distance, Erin definitely saw blood trickling between his fingers. The security guard had been joined by another, and they were now pushing their way through the crowd.

"Nutted him," said Josh. "Brill."

"Looks like he's bust his nose," said Kane.

Erin put a hand over her mouth. As she watched, the security guards restrained and questioned both Hawkes and the presumably innocent man.

"It ain't your fault, Erin," said Logan.

"Now it's getting *interesting*," said Josh. "Wonder if he'll be done for assault? Wonder what'll happen at tomorrow's demo?"

"Tomorrow?" said Erin.

"It's your gig," said Logan. "Up to you. It's over now if you say so."

"Oh, I don't know," said Kane, smoothing a hand over his cornrows. "Like Josh says, it's getting interesting."

15

Impasse

For the rest of the evening, Erin fretted. She couldn't eat. She sat in her room reading a book on birds of the

British Isles. The colour plates of owls usually cheered her up, especially the one of the tawny owl in flight. But not this time. She put the book down, set up some music on her computer and sang along. It was Funnelweb's new album, "The Other Side of Forever".

It didn't help. Nothing helped.

Her mobile rang. The caller was Logan.

"Hi, Erin. You seen the news tonight?"

"Hi, Logan. No, I haven't."

"Vern Hawkes is in trouble," he said. "They released him, but they've not finished. The assault only got mentioned once, and there weren't nothing about the demo. Apparently they want to interview him again, about fraud. It weren't clear. Dodgy stuff with tax and business. Now Customs and Excise are investigating him. Yeah, so ... is the demo on tomorrow?"

He was talking too quickly, making her head spin.

"I'm sorry, Logan. I need to go. I'm not feeling well."

Erin lay back on the bed. She didn't know whether the news about Hawkes was good or bad. Neither did she want to think about it. The assault was still playing on her mind. She felt exhausted. Swamped by tiredness. She closed her eyes and saw spiralling red shapes against blackness. Then a fizzing ran the length of her body, like an electric shock without the pain. She opened her eyes and the room distorted and swam. Then it resolved itself into ... Oh ...

Twilight at the gap between the drawn curtains. Kandinsky designs on the walls. Lush green plants on every surface. And her, all tucked up in bed in silky white pyjamas. She threw off the covers and got to her feet.

Her movements felt strange, poorly co-ordinated.

Hanging on the back of the door was the cloak that had belonged to Kree's grandmother. She wrapped it about her and did up the tarnished star-shaped clasp at her throat. The cloak was of a rough black fabric and had woodland creatures embroidered on it in gold: an owl, a squirrel, a fox, a badger.

There were clothes folded on the chair, which she ignored. She put on the boots and walked out to the landing and down through the dusky silent house.

A cool breeze blew in the twilit street, and countless tiny particles were spangling the air. She saw the red Lamborghini parked at Mrs Croxley's house, but no sign of the old lady. Some boys of pre-school age were playing with a football. Otherwise the street was empty and there were no moving vehicles.

She thought about the clearing in Crow Woods, and began to drift along, quickly gaining speed, her feet barely touching the ground.

Houses and familiar landmarks flashed by. Erin smiled. Her mind and body felt sluggish, but in contradiction to this, she was sailing along at a rapid pace, her thick red hair flying out behind her like the tail of a comet.

I'm back, she thought. *Back in the Dreamscape.*

From around the corner came a pack of dogs, twenty or so, snuffling and bounding. They raced beside her, nuzzling and sniffing. Then the forerunner, more wolf than dog, led the rest off on a different journey. Erin wanted to follow, but a stronger instinct took her to the southern edge of Crow Woods.

The trees rushed at her and by her. But her easy passage ended abruptly before she reached the clearing.

She stumbled and fell to her hands and knees.

The canopy bore down, thick and low.

In a moment of clarity, she watched a green beetle moving across the hard ground. She saw the details of its eyes and antennae, the creases of its folded wings on the glossy carapace. Then her alertness was dampened.

111

She felt clumsy and oafish as she got up from her knees. The clearing was just ahead. What light it offered looked bleak and unwelcoming.

Erin struggled forward.

Half-asleep. Dull-witted. Anaesthetised.

It was a place of shadows. Ferns squatted in hollows, dark and spidery. She could smell stagnant water and decomposing timber. An alarm was triggered somewhere deep in her thoughts. She should leave. Get out now. But she wasn't sure if she knew *how* to leave. One way might be to wake fully to the Dreamscape; another might be to let go of this flimsy hold on consciousness, give herself up to conventional sleep and dreams …

No. She had to hold on. She felt it instinctively. If she let go now, she wouldn't find sleep or dreams; she'd tumble down into some horrible nightmare.

Wake, then. Wake, wake.

It wouldn't happen, and her dream body still felt as if it were an unresponsive avatar in a computer game.

"Kree?" she called.

Although dull and grey, the clearing was a living, breathing place. Erin had an impression of hidden faces and laughter in dark corners, cruel eyes watching her. She remembered Kree talking about focus, the levels of wakefulness, and the boundaries of perception getting confused.

A dragonfly rose up from the pond. With a purr of wings, it flew right up and hovered near her shoulder. Its body was metallic blue. Its robotic-looking face swivelled one way then another, as if trying to understand what kind of creature Erin was. Then in a dazzle of movement, the dragonfly was gone.

"Kree? Kree?"

She went to the big hollow oak and put her ear to the opening. Nothing. Reached her hand inside as far as it would go. Nothing. Ducked her head in and peered around in the semi-dark.

Currents of warm air caressed her face. There was a smell of rotting wood, strong but not unpleasant. At the bottom of the hollow, she made out a deep earthen chamber. Criss-crossing this chamber, in the empty dead air, were the exposed roots of the tree, and all along the roots hung sleeping, upside-down bats, strung out like lines of washing. An eye blinked open and closed again; an ear twitched.

Erin's careless fingers brushed one of the furry bodies and she leapt back from the hollow, banging her head on the rim of the opening.

The twilight had grown deeper.

There was a burbling *gloop-gloop* from the pond, and an enormous bullfrog broke the surface. It blew out its cheeks, then croaked harshly. An owl hooted. Some other creature rustled near by. The bullfrog let out a bellow, and went under the water.

Then the air exploded with bats. They issued from the hollow in a continuous black stream, their leathery wings beating close to Erin's face. They shot into the evening sky where the first stars were out.

"Kree. I don't know what to do. It's all going wrong."

There was a pulling at her ankle. Her foot was tangled in the undergrowth. She yanked it free, but then her other foot was caught. It kept happening. Each time she lowered a foot, the brambles wrapped about her ankles. They wound tighter, rose higher up her shins. She wrenched herself free. The thinner tendrils snapped and tore, but the thicker ones were like rope and their spikes penetrated her pyjama bottoms and her skin.

Even though she couldn't wake beyond this drowsy limbo-state, she could still experience fear. And now she realised that what ever intelligence was at work in the wood, it wasn't trying to imprison her. She was being coerced in a certain direction, being expelled from the clearing. As brambles encircled her ankles from behind, so the previous ones would release their hold.

Before she knew it, she was at the edge of the clearing.

Suddenly, she was seized by the arms and flung to the ground. Who ... ? She looked in time to see the branches of the nearest tree swing back into place.

Her focus slid further; her muscles relaxed. The ground felt soft, more like a duvet, and the stars she saw were dotting the sky at her bedroom window.

She sat up, feeling thick-headed, blinking and gazing around at the plain magnolia walls. Consciousness was coming in a flood. The summer air entering the open window brought with it a smell of freshly mown grass.

Her mobile bleeped with an incoming text.

It was from Kane: *Everything's cool for tomorrow. Josh has got his dad to print off loads of colour flyers about humpback whales.*

Erin still felt rocked by the vivid dream. It had nearly become a waking dream. But not quite. She hadn't seen Kree and she didn't have any answers.

The boys obviously thought the demo was a winner because it had precipitated violence. Josh and humpback whales! Josh was the least ecologically aware person she'd ever met. How could they think it was all right to go ahead tomorrow? How could *she* allow it to go ahead?

16

In Your Face

The whole of Friday, Erin was troubled. She avoided the places she'd be most likely to cross paths with the boys.

After Kane sent two more enthusiastic texts, she felt guilty and sent a short reply: *See you there 5.15.*

She understood there'd be no putting them off. The fact that the demo had progressed to a dangerous new level was something they relished. Any attempt to talk them out of it would fail. If she didn't go this evening, they'd probably turn up anyway, and might even do something stupid.

Her final class was netball. Afterwards, she had her shower and got dressed quickly. The combined scent of shampoo and other toiletries was strong, though not strong enough to mask the smells of old trainers and sweaty kit.

The communal aspect of the showers and changing rooms affected her more than usual. There was too much raucous laughter, too much squealing and gossip. She was almost ready to go when Beth came over.

"Good ball that was, Erin," she drawled, running her fingers through her short wet hair. "Yeah, you can really turn it on when you want to."

"Thanks," said Erin, suspicious. "You did pretty good yourself."

Beth nodded and popped a stick of chewing gum in her mouth. From the shower area, voices sounded metallic amid the splash and surge of water. A scream of laughter rang out and a bar of soap came rocketing across the floor.

"Thing is," said Beth. "Paige, right? She was telling me how you two had a chat in her bedroom the other week, about the talent contest, yeah?"

Erin blinked at the abrupt change of subject.

"Yeah, so," said Beth, cocking her head. "What we want to know – me and Paige and Madison – is, like, have you thought any more about it?"

Frowning, Erin finished tying back her hair.

"Er, I'm not sure what you mean."

"Talking to your uncle! Uncle? Judge? Contest?"

"Sorry, Beth. There's some kind of mistake. I didn't say anything about talking to my uncle. I don't even – "

"You *could* though," said Beth. "You *could*. He's your uncle, yeah? Your stinking rich fat uncle with the burger business. Ate so many last week I was puking my guts up. He's *your* uncle. Just flutter your eyelashes at him. Flash your boobs. Put a word in for Pink Ocean, yeah?"

"I don't think so."

Beth started breathing rapidly through her nose and darting her eyes about the changing room. She chewed her gum viciously.

"Just have a word with him, yeah?"

"Sorry," said Erin. "No."

Beth slapped her hard across the face and strutted off.

Erin's cheek burned. She wanted to go after Beth and slap her back twice as hard. But she left that option as a fantasy. She wasn't interested in fighting anybody; she just wanted to be left in peace.

Faces were peering at her now – the smirking, slightly awed faces of spiteful girls who were glad it hadn't been them, but glad they'd been around for the entertainment.

Erin zipped up her sports bag. She could feel her cheeks reddening, from embarrassment as well as the slap.

Later, as she climbed on the bus with the fold-up table under her arm, she worried that her day might only get worse. But the final demo passed quietly. Neither the target nor his victim put in an appearance. Logan did star-jumps in the panda costume for the children, and rode around on the micro-scooter he'd brought with him. Josh and Kane handed out flyers about humpback whales. Erin reminded the boys about Nisha, and a big rehearsal was planned for Saturday afternoon.

When she got home, she heard a familiar TV signature-tune from the hall, and guessed that it must be the end of

Open Heart, a poor-quality Friday-evening soap set in a hospital. Her parents never missed an episode.

"Erin?" called Mum from the living-room.

"She's just in time ..." said Dad.

"Hi," said Erin, putting her head around the door. "In time for what?"

"Everything all right?" said Mum.

"Yeah, good. I was doing that awareness-raising thing with some friends again." They hadn't questioned her, so she'd been keeping the details vague.

"It's good you're making more friends," said Mum. "Who are they?"

"It's the boys from the band, okay? They're ... interested in the environment now as well. One of them, Kane, he's into astronomy, and – "

"We're glad," said Mum. "It's all right, isn't it, Toby?"

"Course it is. Bring 'em round sometime. 'Bout time we met 'em. Oh! Hey! Here we go. We should see Dom's advert now. Come and sit down, Erin. The first adverts after *Open Heart*. That's what he reckons."

Erin stayed in the doorway.

"If they show that weird animation again ..." she said.

"Shush," said Dad. "This is it."

"I'm worried about you," she said, and realised how parental she sounded. But they hadn't heard anyway. They looked like children waiting for sweets.

A camera was zooming in on a suavely dressed couple, who held hands across a bright-orange plastic table and smiled lovingly at one another.

Mum said, "That looks like – "

"Shush," said Dad.

"It *is*. It's – "

"Shush, Wendy. Please. You'll ruin it."

Erin recognised both actors. One was the very beautiful Persephone Stark, who'd been in several supporting roles in recent British films. Her acting was average, but she had a good line in sultry glances. The other was Will Forecastle, of the hangdog looks, who usually landed the lead in period dramas.

Two clown-outfitted waiters had arrived at the restaurant table, a man for the man, a woman for the woman.

"In Your Face Burger, sir?"

"In Your Face Burger, madam?"

"Oh, yes!" said Persephone. "It's our orders, darling."

"So it is," said Will. "Oh, darling!"

Erin blinked. The acting was atrocious.

"Assume the position," said the waiters.

Persephone and Will leaned back, smiling faces tilted upwards. Each waiter took the top from a sesame-seed bun and the camera zoomed in on the halves containing the filling – a juicy, steaming burger daubed with relish.

"Looks like well-presented poo," said Erin.

"Shush," said Dad.

The camera zoomed out and, unbelievably, the waiters pushed the open burgers into the faces of their respective charges. The only reactions from Persephone and Will were muffled groans of pleasure.

"Eat, you pigs!" cried the waiters, as they massaged the burgers into the customers' faces. "Eat, eat!"

Dad flopped about in his armchair with laughter.

"I'm surprised at Will Forecastle," said Mum.

"They won't really do that tomorrow," said Dad, though he seemed a bit unsure. "Not with real customers. It's just a gimmick."

The clown-outfitted waiters cocked their legs up on the table to get better leverage, and chanted, "Eat, eat. You know you want it!"

"Mmmm," said Persephone, managing briefly to angle her soiled face to the camera. "This is heaven ..."

The waiters stood back, and looked at the customers with disgust and contempt before walking away.

Persephone and Will sat up straight. They exchanged adoring glances as they raked smeared burger into their mouths.

"How's yours, darling?" said Will.

"It's so yummy, my taste-buds feel as if they've gone to the moon!"

She leaned right across the table and started licking Will's face. He licked back. Then they were licking away at each other like a pair of affectionate cats.

"Oh, darling."

"Mm, darling."

The scene went into soft focus and a voiceover began:

"At a Black Orchid restaurant near you, tomorrow. Only at Orchid, the In Your Face Burger. Let us send *your* taste-buds to the moon. All Whiz-Go outlets around the country will be opening under the Orchid brand tomorrow ..."

It seemed as if the advert was about to end. Then the flaming sun with its orchid petals appeared, filling the screen. Flares erupted from the incandescence. The black petals began their anticlockwise rotation ...

Erin's body sagged against the doorframe.

She shook herself and looked for the remote. She couldn't see it, so she rushed over and hit the TV's manual off-button. Her parents already had sleepy, cow-eyed expressions, and there was a delay before their brains caught up.

"Erin," said Mum. "That was very rude."

"Sorry. Remember last time, though? All the burgers you kept eating? You'd been hypnotised. It was wearing off, but now this new advert – "

"Don't you ever do that again, young lady," said Dad, in the most menacing tone she'd ever heard him use.

"I ... I'm sorry, Dad. I just – "

"Go to your room," he said.

She lowered her head and walked out.

"Bloody nerve," she heard him say. "So much for these *friends*. Influence, Wendy. A bad influence."

"Oh, Toby," said Mum, and she sounded tearful.

Erin paused in the hall, glad of the support.

"Oh, Toby. We didn't see it to the end."

The advert! She was upset about not seeing the whole of the advert!

"Don't worry, Wendy," said Dad. "It's being aired quite a lot tonight, Dom said – on most commercial channels."

"I just fancy a burger," said Mum. "We could nip to Orchid now. I know there won't be In Your Face Burgers until tomorrow, but – "

"Yes, we'll go now!" he said. "We can have a Mr Scrummy each. Or a couple each. Don't you fret, darling."

Darling? Erin couldn't remember the last time he'd called her darling.

In her room, Erin told herself she wouldn't cry.

It wasn't their fault. They'd been hypnotised once, so they probably didn't need much exposure to be affected again. They were blind to the freakish power of the brand. Erin didn't doubt that it could tear apart families and communities. A few weeks ago, half of Everdene had fallen under its influence following a single showing on the regional news. Tonight, it was being shown on national channels.

She heard the clunk of the front door.

So they'd gone. Without even calling goodbye.

Erin wanted to run after them, but what good would that do? They were totally focussed on getting burgers. They'd probably forgotten they'd been mean.

Probably forgotten they had a daughter.

17

Slaughterhouse

Erin knew it wasn't true, the idea about forgetting they had a daughter. She swiped at a tear on her cheek, then scrolled down the contact list on her mobile. Of the boys' names, she came to Josh's first. Obviously. Josh, Kane, Logan. J, K, L.

She paused. Into her head came the memory of Josh in the gym – his precise, graceful movements; his quiet strength and skill; his serenity and focus. Competing with this was an image of him slouching on the sofa in Kane's garage, giving her a bored, heavy-eyed, superior look.

Erin called him anyway. There was no answer, so she tried and got Kane.

"Have you seen the advert?" she said. "My uncle's Orchid burger advert? It's just been on telly. About five minutes ago."

"No," said Kane. "I'm in the attic with Dad. We're doing some astronomy. Waiting for Venus to come out from behind a cloud."

"Listen. This is important. Please believe me. Don't watch the advert. It starts with Persephone Stark and Will Forecastle sitting in a burger restaurant."

"*What*?"

"Seriously. That's who's in it. As soon as you see those two, turn over, or walk out of the room, or – "

"Erin. Hold on. What – what're you talking about?"

"Trust me. Something really bad is going on with my uncle's company. I can't explain it. But you've seen what it's been doing to people. I know it's been wearing off lately, but it's starting again – tonight – and it's going to be much, much worse."

Kane was quiet, then he said, "My mum and an aunt and a couple of cousins went a bit loopy over those burgers the first week. Didn't rate 'em too much myself. Nor did Josh or Logan. They were just okay. Like any others."

"You hadn't seen the animation. Neither had they. Or Paige. But remember how Madison and Beth were?"

"Yeah ..." said Kane. "Josh and Logan! They both just texted me, a minute before you rang. Wanted me to meet them at Orchid."

"They've seen the advert. The burgers are the same as any other crap on the market. It's about the brand; it's hypnotism on an industrial scale!"

"That has to be illegal."

"My uncle's got influence. In business and in TV networks. Maybe even in politics and law. That must be how he pulled off the Whiz-Go coup."

"It all just sounds totally crazy."

"Yes. Please don't watch the advert."

"Okay," he said. "You've convinced me. I'll ring Josh and Logan. Try to talk some sense into them. I don't want anything interfering with tomorrow's rehearsal. 'Bye."

Erin sat on the edge of the bed, thinking; then she made another call.

"Hi, Nisha. This might sound a bit ... I don't know if you've been watching the news about Orchid? My uncle ... Embarrassing, really."

"I heard about it," said Nisha with laughter in her voice. "All those people must be mental. Your uncle's got his business head screwed on, though."

"Did you see his advert tonight on TV?"

"I hardly ever bother with TV," said Nisha.

"You might come across it online. It hypnotises people."

"Yeah, well, all TV does that."

"Okay," said Erin. "But if the animated brand or the advert come on anywhere, turn away. I'm talking about computers, screens in public, anything."

"Yeah, got you. Thanks for the advice ..."

Erin could tell that she was being humoured.

"I'm looking forward to getting it on with the band tomorrow," said Nisha, "but I gotta go now. Family here from London for the evening. I'm chief entertainer of the nieces and nephews and second cousins. And supposed to be helping with cooking. See you tomorrow, okay?"

When Erin woke, she thought that the clock on the desk had stopped, but her mobile showed the same time. It had gone midday. She'd slept for fifteen hours!

Even as she showered and dressed, she sensed that the house was deserted. Downstairs, a note from Dad said that they'd gone to Orchid for lunch.

Cautiously, she turned the TV on. A news channel was reporting the "besieging" of Orchid outlets (formerly Whiz-Go) in city centres across the country. "Besieging", though, was the wrong word. Closer shots showed people moving dopily like cattle – a replay, on a national scale, of the scenes common in Everdene a few weeks ago. Erin found some regional news. There was a mention of Hawkes: he'd been quoted as saying he may step aside from politics to spend more time with his family.

She switched off and got ready for band practice.

At Nisha's arrival, Kane became awkward and quiet. Then he sprang into action and was overly eager to help unload the keyboard and its peripherals from the boot of her dad's car. When the car had gone, he stood about in dumb confusion.

"Er, Nisha needs a copy of the music," said Erin. "And maybe talk the arrangements through with her?"

"Good idea," he said.

Josh gave Erin a funny smile.

"Any chance of some more burger vouchers?" he said.

"I haven't got any more."

"Can't you get some from your uncle?"

"We're not after freebies," said Logan. "It's just that you get served quicker with vouchers. We'll pay you."

"I thought we were having a rehearsal?" she said.

"Yeah, but after the rehearsal – "

"Can you believe these nutters?" said Kane. "Queuing for hours last night and didn't even get served. Too many people. So they queue again half the morning. Had about three or four burgers each. I had to go down there and virtually drag them away. Now they're planning their next fix. It's like I told you, Josh. Like Erin said. Her uncle's advert's hypnotic."

"Rubbish," said Josh. "They're really good burgers."

"Did they get squashed into your faces?" said Erin.

"Course not," said Josh. "That's just in the advert."

"Trouble is, you can't get near the place," said Logan. "If we had some more vouchers, Erin, we'd get priority service."

"More like priority gut-rot."

"What would you know?" said Josh. "You're a wimpy veggie."

"I'm veggie as well," said Nisha, "and last year I was second in the school cross-country race. Does that make me a wimp?"

"Second?" grinned Josh. "Bet the winner liked their steak dinners."

Kane and Logan laughed.

"And I used to do floor gymnastics years ago," added Nisha. "I was county junior champion when I was nine."

"Luck," said Josh.

"Don't be a dummy," said Kane. "Luck! What about that new striker Man U have just signed? He's a veggie."

"Then there's Sergei Korsakov," said Erin. "He won an athletics gold medal in the last Olympics. He's a *vegan*."

"Never heard of him," said Josh. "You're making it up now. Only veggies I've ever known are girls or wimps."

Kane laughed and said, "Too much meat's bad for you, anyway."

"Balls," said Josh. He gave Erin a challenging look. "It's good for you. And I think everyone should eat what they want to."

125

"So do I," said Erin.

"No you don't. You'd ban meat, if you could."

"It's not like that."

"What's it like, then?"

"Everyone makes their own choices. I choose not to eat meat. My choice."

"You think it's cruel?" said Josh.

"Yes," joined Nisha. "It's cruel."

Erin felt shaky and a bit nauseous. She'd found herself in that place again – the place where she couldn't cope with conflict, even if it was only verbal. Despite the uneasiness, she was determined this time to stand up for her principles.

"I don't think it's necessary for survival," she said. "As long as you get all the right nutrition from other sources, being vegetarian or vegan's fine. And, yeah, I think factory farms and slaughterhouses can be bad places. Cruelty goes on. Torture, probably. People who like hurting and killing animals get attracted to the industry; they go where they can do it all the time – legally."

"We didn't ask for a lecture," said Josh. "What you on about? Torture? Are you saying all slaughterhouses are torture chambers?"

Erin shook her head and forced herself to go on.

"No. Although, from an animal's perspective ... They feel pain. They've got emotions and intuitions, like us. They sense they're in a bad place, long before they die. But from the average human's perspective – "

"Perspective?" said Josh. "You sound like a politician. They use long words like that, and talk bollocks to avoid answering the question."

"Shut up a second," said Kane.

"She stated it like a fact," said Josh. "Slaughterhouses are torture chambers, and everyone what works in 'em is just evil."

His eyes were glittering, as if he had secret knowledge that he couldn't wait to trap Erin with the moment she slipped up. He kept glancing at Logan, too, but Logan wouldn't meet his gaze.

"The average person," said Erin, "just thinks of them as places where animals get processed into the meat that ends up on their plates."

"Tell her, Logan," said Josh with a chuckle.

"It don't matter," mumbled Logan. "She's not saying what you're trying to make out she's saying – "

"Logan's dad only works in a slaughterhouse, don't he!" crowed Josh. "So according to you – " he jabbed a finger at her " – that makes him a torturer."

"It's okay, Erin," said Logan uncomfortably. "I know you're not – "

"She's rubbished you and rubbished your family," said Josh, enjoying himself hugely. "Called you a liar, and called your dad an evil torturer."

"You really are thick sometimes," said Kane. "All she meant was that *some* people working in the industry are cruel. *Some.* Or a few. Not all."

Josh looked from Kane to Erin to Logan to Nisha.

"Yeah, just some people," said Logan.

"So how are we supposed to get our meat?" said Josh. "If there weren't no farms or slaughterhouses. Like how *she* wants it to be."

"Kill your own," said Erin. And now she was calmer.

"Eh?" said Josh.

"Go out and hunt, and kill your own meat. That's how things were originally. Hunters and gatherers."

"You're contradicting yourself now," said Josh. "You're a veggie; you're supposed to be against killing."

"I'm not *supposed* to be anything. I am what I am."

"Yeah, way to go, girl," said Nisha.

Josh rubbed a hand over his chin and looked at Erin sceptically.

"You don't mind it when people kill animals?" he said.

"I don't *like* it," she said, "and I wish they wouldn't, but it's their choice."

18

Donna Wowcat With A Death Wish

"Protection of rare animals," said Josh. "I get *that*. There's these snow leopards what I seen on a documentary.

They're really cool. I wouldn't wanna see them wiped out. But meat, it's, like, it just comes from cows and pigs and stuff. Normal people just eat 'em. They don't get all wussy about it."

Erin laughed and said, "What's 'normal'? You're right that most people don't think too much about where meat comes from. But that's what I mean about hunters killing their own. At least they're being honest."

"Honest?"

"Well, if you kill your own, you're taking responsibility for it. Not everyone who buys a frozen chicken or packet of sausages from a supermarket would be capable of killing the animal."

"And that makes them liars?"

"Well ..."

"Yes, it makes them liars," said Nisha.

"*I'*d kill my own meat," said Josh.

"Okay," said Erin. "So that's my point. *I* couldn't hurt or kill an animal, so I don't feel comfortable or right about eating them."

"I'd probably kill my own as well," said Kane. "If that was the only way. But I wouldn't be cruel. I'd do it quick. Humane."

"Right," she said.

"Poor Logan," said Josh. "He couldn't kill a flea. You put a bacon sarnie in front of him, though, or a burger, and he'd wolf it down like ... like a wolf what's not ate for a long time. Right, Logan?"

"I might go veggie myself soon," said Logan. "Been thinking about it."

Josh looked him up and down.

"Yeah," he said. "That'll happen."

"I might. One day."

"Yeah, right. Then you'll be a wimp like the rest of 'em. We need meat for strength and energy. Just look at wild animals. Lions and stuff. They're only as fit and powerful as they are 'cause they eat tons of raw meat."

"Okay," said Erin. "What about gorillas? They're really powerful and strong. What do you think they eat?"

"Dunno," he said. "Goats and stuff, don't they?"

"*Goats*!" said Kane. "Priceless! Can you just picture it? A gorilla sitting there tucking in to a goat."

"So what do they eat?" said Josh, smirking.

"Mainly just leaves and fruit," said Erin.

Kane said, "You're such a dummy, Josh. You've got a giant slug for a brain, and that's a compliment. At least Erin's got some decent arguments and evidence to back her opinions up."

"Hate to break it up," said Nisha. "But I heard from Erin that this band can rock. And I can't wait to find out if it's true."

"Yeah, let's make a start," laughed Kane.

He powered up the equipment and they all spent a moment threading their leads into safer configurations on the floor.

It was a scrappy start. Erin occasionally relaxed enough to find the grungy voice she'd been rehearsing, but mostly it eluded her. The debate had drained her emotionally, but she was pleased with herself for making a stand.

There was an awkward silence after the first few numbers. While waiting for Kane to decide which number they'd do next, Josh struck off a few solo riffs on his bass and Logan messed about with some hi-hat.

Then Kane played the opening bars of 'Darker'. Erin was glad he'd chosen a moody ballad. She hadn't used her full vocal range yet, but something was building inside her. With the next song – the industrial 'Spitting Nails' – she was finding her stride, injecting Logan's lyrics with some guts and energy. Kane must have sensed her growing surefootedness, because straight out of

'Spitting Nails', he led the band seamlessly into the cranked-up new version of 'Rich Bitch'. Erin lost herself to it; felt as if the lyrics were being sung through her rather than by her. She was no longer in Kane's garage on a Saturday afternoon, but inhabiting the smoky, diamond-studded world of Logan's 'Rich Bitch':

"I don't care, baby, I don't care ~ I just wanna feel right ~ Push me in the car, you can push me in the car ~ But you better make sure it's Porsche-ah ..."

She didn't know how they would have sounded to an impartial listener, but to her, everything came together with this song. Logan's drumming was inspired. Nisha's keyboard work was spot on. Kane's lead guitar and Josh's bass had never communicated so well (at least not during her few months with the band). For herself, she felt as if her singing had reached a new plateau.

At the end, Logan said, "I think we've got ourselves a band."

"Yeah!" said Kane. He propped his guitar against the amp and went to the fridge to break out cold cans. "Great keyboards, Nisha. And what did everyone reckon to Erin? Pretty good, or what?"

"Pretty good?" said Logan. "She was incredible. She sounds like Donna Wowcat with a death wish."

Everybody fell about laughing. Erin would rather have been compared to her inspiration, Lily Raven (Donna Wowcat was just a pop singer), but she supposed the "with a death wish" bit was kind of cool. She was slightly out of breath and her head and neck felt hot. Her hair was hanging wildly in her face. She dragged it aside, gathered it all together and began to tie it back.

Then paused ...

Josh was staring at her. It may have been out of respect for her voice. But there was something more potent in his look, too. It was similar to how he'd looked while performing his *kata* in the gym. She'd done her research and knew now that such martial arts routines were called *katas*.

In the next second, Josh became flustered, which was totally unlike him. He turned away and pretended to check something on his phone.

Erin sat with Nisha on the two-seater sofa.

Nisha turned and said, "You were really, *really* good."

"Hey, you too. Your keyboard skills absolutely leave mine for dead."

Erin looked for Josh and saw that he was putting his guitar in its case.

Logan perched on an arm of the sofa next to Erin.

"Just so you girls know," said Kane, pacing about. "We're not too fussed about the talent contest. If we do okay on the night, fine. What *we're* interested in is the Battle of the Youth Bands. It's at the youth club, the Friday after the school contest."

"Cool," said Nisha. "I'll put it in my diary. Thanks for bringing me on board, you guys. I've wanted to be part of something like this for a long time."

"Well, you're where you belong now," said Kane. "I ... We're, like, really glad you're here. I mean ... you know."

Nisha lowered her eyes.

"Right," Logan called to Josh. "We going for a burger, mate, or what?"

"Dead right," said Josh, though he seemed distracted.

* * *

Erin was smiling as she cycled back across the western elbow of the woods. The air was warm and the birds were singing. Everything was bursting with life. The rich smells put her in mind of green spores and new growth and superabundance. She'd always imagined that the Earth must be female. The thought struck her now as she paused by the little stream.

She leaned her bike against a birch tree and sat down. It was so peaceful and welcoming here.

It helped her to forget all her worries.

Erin rolled up her jeans, took her boots and socks off and sank her feet into the stream. A small gasp escaped her. The water was cold but soothing. She pressed the soles of her feet against the stony bottom. Flexed her toes. Untied her hair and shook it out and threw her head back. Spread her hands on the ground and curled her fingers into the soil. Smiled and laughed.

She closed her eyes. On the backs of her eyelids she saw orange and red fluctuations from the play of sunlight through the wood's canopy.

The glassy trickle of the stream, birdsong, the drill and buzz of insects, the sun in her face, water and stone against her feet, her fingers in the soil ...

She was anchored. Anchored to the Earth.

As she cycled on, she thought about her new friendship with Nisha, about how everybody liked her voice, about Josh's strange behaviour, and about the band, the band, the band. It wasn't until she got home to an empty house again that her buoyant mood began to dip. Whether her parents had been back, she didn't know, but there weren't any more notes. She made herself some avocado on toast with crushed garlic, black pepper and turmeric, followed by fruit salad. While she was washing up, Mum rang to say that a table had been "specially reserved" at the new Orchid restaurant on High Street, for seven thirty that evening. She spoke as if the booking were a coup.

When Erin said she'd already eaten, her mum said, "Do you realise how many people queuing outside at this minute would happily take your place?"

Erin was tempted to say, "So invite somebody in off the street," but didn't.

"You don't have to eat anything," said Mum, "but it's important that you make the effort to come. We had lunch with Dom, in a special little alcove in the kitchen – actually in the Orchid kitchen! He's really changed. Success goes to some people's heads, but not Dom ... Now, listen: even though you've been rude to him lately, he's going to give you a job. You're not legally old enough to do more than so many hours a week, but he knows ways round these silly regulations and you'll be able to do as many hours as he wants you to." She giggled. "I wasn't supposed to tell you yet, but ..."

Erin quaked as her mother continued to sing Uncle Dom's praises and bang on about how lucky Erin was to be offered the job.

"Mum," she said when there was a pause. "I'll be helping out on that wildlife project over the summer. I told you – "

"*That* silly thing? Voluntary, isn't it? Or you get paid pennies. For what? Nursing flea-infested squirrels and mice back to life? Uncle Dom's offering you a *real* job. For hard cash."

Erin hesitated, wondering if she'd missed the point.

"Oh, sorry, Mum. If you *need* me to work ... If we need the money?"

"We don't *need* you to work, Erin. It's about giving you more interests in your life, instead of fretting about climate change, or the loss of rainforest sloths, or whatever it is this week. You'll be provided with a lovely clown-outfit; the other girls look *so* cute; and you'll have the chance to meet people. It's a fantastic opportunity. I'm only thinking of you. See you at seven thirty?"

"Er, is it okay if I don't? I'm feeling pretty tired ..."

Her mother had hung up.

A mixture of anger, guilt and affront gnawed at Erin as seven thirty came and went. Later, exhausted from thinking about the worsening situation with her parents, she went to bed early and fell into a troubled sleep ...

19

The Swoop

"It's light," said Mum, turning from the piano. "The sun'll be up soon. I was hoping your dad'd be home, but it's another double-shift."

She drew on a liquorice-coloured cigarette in a silver holder, then balanced it on top of the piano and began tinkling away at the keys again.

Erin sat up in the armchair. On the walls she saw framed photos of what appeared to be scenes from theatre productions. There was a smell of incense. And where had the piano come from? She didn't know Mum could even play.

As for the smoking ...

"Are you just going to sit there?" said Mum. "Those dogs have been howling for ages. It puts me off, and it'll wake the baby. Honestly, Erin, I don't know why you have to encourage so many."

Baby? Dogs?

Erin heard a howl and stood up automatically.

"Before you go," said Mum. "There's something ... This new factory job of your dad's. I don't know if you've seen the horrid clothes he has to wear? He *says* it's only in town, but he can't be contacted while he's there, and I just have this *feeling*, this feeling that it's a long, long way away. He's *been told* ..."

She stopped and looked fearfully out of the window.

Erin looked as well, but all she saw was Mr and Mrs Chalmers's monkey-puzzle tree across the road. Monkey-puzzle tree?

Awareness was coming by slow degrees.

"He's been told," continued Mum in a low voice, "that *I* might have to work there, too. He even said *you* might have to, and we could be in serious trouble if we don't. Ridiculous, I told him. It has to be a misunderstanding." She laughed. "Go on, then. See to those dogs, and then it's time you went to bed, isn't it? And I need to finish this composition for the show in ten days."

Erin went out to the hall. She swung open the door and walked up the path. The early morning light sparkled with tiny motes. Children played on the pavements. Cars passed. Mrs Higgins was riding a horse, and Geoff Sharpe was chasing her with a bouquet of flowers, his feet several inches above the ground. Mr Buchenwald was bounding along the bonnets and roofs of a line of parked cars, leaping from one to the next. Erin wanted to tell him to be careful, but he looked as if he were enjoying himself, and seemed highly skilled at the game.

A feeling of *déjà vu* kept nagging at her. Thoughts of other people, other places, other selves ... Other selves?

In the eastern sky, the horizon was streaked with oranges and blues, and the sun was just chinking into view. The air smelled fresh and inviting.

Beside her, the lead dog raised its grizzled head, bayed, then took off. The others followed, and so did Erin.

She was almost asleep again, but had a dreamy understanding that everything was as it should be. She sped on, the dogs accompanying her. Fifty or more. They were wolves, she realised. All wolves. Some crashed about her like a friendly tide; the majority surged forward in the shape of a spearhead. She smiled, and laughed a little, and let her fingers trail through the golden-grey coats that were closest.

The lead wolves turned left at the T-junction; the rest followed, and Erin followed, straight down the middle of the dusty pavement, her red hair flying out behind.

Other dreamers moved aside. Dreamers? Oh ...

As she passed side-streets, more wolves raced up to join the pack, and as the pack swelled, so their collective speed increased.

Erin's tenuous grip on consciousness grew looser. A whiteness crept across her vision. The sky, the suburban landscape – everything was whiting out, and the wolves' baying came to her as if from a distance.

But she was rocketing along still, feeling obscurely like an Arctic explorer travelling through a snowbound wilderness on a dogsled.

An involuntary moan escaped her.

She might have drifted fully into dreams then – except that the wolves nuzzled her and licked her hands. Her attention quickened. She registered that the journey had ended. Or, that *her* journey had ended. The wolf pack continued along the sleepy road, leaving her.

Erin had stopped at a gravel driveway that curved its way up to a large house with a grey stone frontage. Every curtain was open; there were lights on behind the leaded diamond-paned windows; dark figures moved around in the rooms. A sleek Jaguar stood on the drive, and two police cars were parked end-to-end. Leaning against one of these, a uniformed officer talked into a radio. Erin moved closer, but she could only see his lips moving.

Suddenly, Vern Hawkes was bundled from the house by two more officers. His hair was messy. He wore maroon trousers and a yellowish cardigan that was buttoned up wrong. Erin couldn't hear what anybody said, but Hawkes's expressions and gestures were a clear, if feeble, protest of innocence.

The officers came forward. They either didn't or couldn't see her, and in her efforts to get out of the way, she stumbled against the Jaguar. There was a brief resistance, then she felt herself passing right through the bodywork of the car. For a second, she was viewing the world from behind the windscreen – saw Hawkes being handed efficiently into a police car; saw figures still moving in the rooms of his house – then she sank into the driver's seat. She had a sensation of leather and foam and springs, then of darkness and carpet and dirty metal as she went through the floor. She blacked out as she sank into the gravel drive.

Mum and Dad had left before she was up on Sunday morning. Another curt note said that they'd gone to Orchid. She mooched about the house most of the day, wanting to be alone. She kept thinking about the vivid dream. It was similar to the other recent dream, the one about the clearing in the woods. Both had come tantalisingly close to waking dreams, but fallen short.

Late in the afternoon, her parents brought Uncle Dom back. Erin was up in her room again, rehearsing lyrics, when she heard their noisy arrival.

"Erin?" Mum called up. "Uncle Dom's here. Come and say hello."

Erin thought about pretending she wasn't in, but her window was open to the street and she knew they'd probably heard her singing. She went down reluctantly and paused at the living-room doorway.

In Dad's armchair, Uncle Dom wore the dark-green suit he'd been using for TV interviews. His face no longer had the healthy glow of recent weeks; it was puffy and pale, making his eyes look like currants pressed into a lump of dough. Mum and Dad were on the sofa. Dad wore a tee-shirt and jeans, which was unusual, but not exactly alarming – unlike the baseball cap bearing the Orchid logo. Dad had a pathological hatred of hats. He ridiculed them on other people and would never be seen in one himself. Mum's hair had been dyed black by the looks of it, and the style was ... well, hedgehog at best, toilet-brush at worst. She was wearing a black skirt and a bright orange blouse.

"Hallo, Erin," said her uncle.

"Hello."

"Not interested in this job at Orchid, then?"

"Sorry ... no," she said.

"Is that all you've got to say for yourself?" said Dad. "Even if you don't want it, how about some gratitude?"

Erin frowned and looked at Uncle Dom again.

"Thanks," she said.

Her uncle laughed thickly.

"Sticking to your one-word answers?" he said. "Typical teenager. Or is it just when you're speaking to me?"

She was tempted to say "yes".

"Sit down," said Mum. "Instead of hovering rudely."

Erin went to the other armchair, which meant crossing the room and putting the three of them between her and the door ... Not good.

"So," said Uncle Dom. "Have you seen the new Orchid advert?"

"Er, yes."

"But not all of it, I understand?"

Dad slapped his thighs and chuckled, as if this were all a big joke.

"I'm sorry, but I didn't like it," said Erin. "I couldn't believe two good actors would agree to do something so naff, how ever much they're being paid. But it doesn't matter, does it? The acting's not what it's about. The advert could just as easily show forty-five seconds of paint drying. The only thing that – "

"Erin!" said Mum.

"No, it's fine," said Uncle Dom, raising a plump hand. "Never discourage honesty in a child."

"I'm not a child."

He gave her a look that suggested she was mistaken.

"But if you've not watched it to the end," he said. "You'll have missed the main message."

Erin made a scoffing noise.

"That's quite enough of that, young lady," said Dad.

"She should see it properly," said Uncle Dom. "Come on, Wendy. Get the telly on and surf the commercial channels. It'll be on somewhere."

Erin stood up.

"Sit down," said Dad, in his new menacing tone.

She could have marched off. What could they possibly do? Tie her up? But she'd had an idea. She sat and feigned interest in the television.

Mum's channel surfing produced glimpses of various programmes and adverts. She would have kept flicking, but Uncle Dom raised a hand. On the screen, the end-credits of some old film were scrolling up.

"You wouldn't believe how much money Whiz-Go agreed to throw at this promotion," he said. "I've hardly seen a commercial break this weekend that didn't include the Orchid advert."

The truth of his statement was soon borne out. After an advert for insurance, the famous screen couple were making eyes at one another across the plastic moulded table. Erin watched as the waiters brought out the In Your Face Burgers and set about their sorry business.

But as soon as the animated brand appeared, she coolly looked straight at Uncle Dom. It took him a second to realise what she was doing, then he stared right back. And while Mum and Dad sat transfixed, and the animation went through its cycle, Erin's gaze was locked with her uncle's.

Then his eyes glittered oddly, in a look identical to the one that had chilled her so much at the hospital, and when he'd stood in her bedroom doorway.

It was as if he were sizing up a puny opponent.

20

Endangered

The muscles in her arms and legs went taught. She kept blinking and almost had to turn away, but forced herself not to. Uncle Dom's gaze was icy. For a moment, she wasn't even sure that this man was her uncle any more.

"I just fancy a burger," said Dad.

"It must be nearly tea-time," said Mum.

The advert had ended and they were both smiling inanely. Uncle Dom smiled, too. He relaxed and treated Erin to a theatrical wink. She felt her body slump into the sofa, as if released from invisible forces.

Uncle Dom took out his mobile.

"Hi, Bilal. It's Dom. Priority order for home delivery. Four portions of fries, four In Your Face Burgers, and four Mr Scrummys."

Erin was trembling in every limb, but she kept her face defiant. Although she wanted to escape, she sensed that any immediate danger had passed, and wondered if, by sticking around, she'd discover more about what it all meant.

As her uncle rang off, Mum and Dad's faces were eloquent with excitement and anticipation.

Erin said, "I don't want any, thank you."

"Who said any of it was for you?" said Uncle Dom.

"Oh ... I ... You ordered four of everything."

"I did, didn't I?" he said, with a cryptic look.

Dad slapped his thighs and chuckled loudly. Mum had missed the joke, but joined in, faking the laughter. Erin considered their spiteful faces, and wondered who these three strangers were.

"Yum-yum, this is really special. How's yours, Toby? Wendy?"

Uncle Dom was demolishing a Mr Scrummy, and had been enjoying the extended news coverage about the success of the Orchid national roll-out.

"... that was how things looked outside the Kensington restaurant," said the man on the screen. "Other news now. In a dawn swoop by police and customs ..."

While Mum and Dad noisily crammed their mouths and showered Uncle Dom with compliments, Erin picked up on snatches of the news report.

"... illegal trade in animal furs and skins ... Has apparently suffered a breakdown ... Asked for fifty-four other offences to be taken into ..."

Despite her uncle's earlier comments, two burgers and some fries had been placed at Erin's end of the coffee table. She'd eaten a few fries, but they'd been stodgy and were sitting in her stomach like lead.

"Come on, Erin," said Dad. "You're missing out. These burgers are amazing!"

"Young people today," said Uncle Dom in a mock-weary tone. "Waste, waste, waste. I don't know. Well, if she's not going to eat it ..." He leaned across the coffee table, whisked her plate away and began tucking in.

"... Vernon Hawkes," the newsreader said, "MP for Everdene West, had extended his dealings to include rare and endangered ..."

Erin still felt distressed by the psychological battle of wills with her uncle, but the news about Hawkes was burning through her like an epiphany.

At the mention of the name, Uncle Dom glanced at the TV. Erin watched him closely for a reaction, but he couldn't have been less bothered.

"Silly bugger, getting caught," he laughed. "I suppose this means that our golf meet's off for this evening."

There was a witch-like cackle from the sofa. It was Mum. Erin's parents were tossing fries for one another, and catching them in their mouths, like performing seals. On the TV, there'd been a cut to a man with medals on his uniform. Cameras and boom microphones were being thrust towards him.

"... communicating our findings to Interpol," he was saying. "And since Mr Vernon Hawkes now fully admits that he – "

"What about the giant pandas, Chief Constable?" came a reporter's disembodied voice. "What about the snow leopards?"

"As already stated, Mr Hawkes's online conventional fur business was a front for a highly illegal and lucrative trade in the pelts of endangered species. His off-shore accounts and computer records show ..."

Uncle Dom sighed loudly and sat forward. He wiped a smear of grease from his mouth with his knuckles. Then he leaned back again and loosened his tie. He looked paler than ever. Beads of sweat stood out on his brow.

"Oh, dear!" he said.

"What is it, Dom?" said Dad.

Uncle Dom sucked in some air and sighed it out.

"Might have eaten a bit too quickly," he grunted.

Too quickly and too much, thought Erin.

The newsreader came back on the screen.

"Chief Constable Evans wouldn't be drawn on actual price-tags, but this channel can reveal that polar-bear skins have been known to fetch upwards of ten thousand pounds. Allegedly, Mr Hawkes has also co-ordinated deals between acquirers and buyers of the skins of even rarer, protected species, such as snow leopards and giant pandas. Politics now. In the House of ..."

"Glass of water, I think," said Uncle Dom.

Mum jumped up and left the room to fetch it.

Uncle Dom cast his tie aside and undid a shirt button.

"And a spot of brandy," he said.

Dad poured him a large brandy. Uncle Dom had a sip, then passed it back.

"Ice," he grumbled. "Can't drink it without ice."

As Dad left the room, Mum came in with the water.

"Changed my mind," said Uncle Dom. "Sorry, Wendy. Make me a coffee, can you? Hmm, and ask Toby if he'd mind crushing the ice."

Mum scuttled out of the room.

144

Erin couldn't believe her uncle's audacity or how her parents were fawning over him. He didn't look well, but what she'd just witnessed was pure manipulation to get rid of Mum and Dad. Wasn't it? She stood up.

"You'll fail, Erin," said Uncle Dom. "Don't even try. You'll fail."

She shuddered. These were exactly the words spoken in the canal nightmare, by the baby with his face. As she stared at him, he lolled back in the armchair. His body went still and his face took on a greenish tinge.

Erin thought he was dead. Then his eyes opened very wide. They were solid orbs of white. Erin took a step towards the door. Her heart was beating fast. She took another step, and her uncle's head ratcheted round, the white orbs tracking her. On the blank screen of each eye appeared an orchid and a flaming sun.

The images grew brighter and larger; they floated into the air and converged to form a single image, which hung less than twelve inches from Erin's face.

The sun spat out its fiery prominences, the black petals began their anticlockwise rotation. She was too stunned to move or look away.

Then Dad came in with the brandy and crushed ice, and the holographic image disappeared. Uncle Dom sat up and accepted his drink with a smile as if nothing had happened. Dad was baffled. He'd seen something, but wasn't sure what. He looked at his brother, and at Erin, and at the space in the air.

"Uh ... playing a computer game or something?"

Uncle Dom laughed.

"I'm feeling much better," he said.

Erin's mobile rang. It was Kane. She answered, but intended to go upstairs before saying much. Then Mum arrived with the coffee and both Erin's parents milled about like confused sheep, blocking her exit.

"Seen the news?" said Kane.

"Yes," she said.

Uncle Dom stood up and said, "I should go. Notes to prepare for tomorrow. Big meeting with Clark Jefferson in London."

"You knew about the fur trade," said Kane.

"What?" she said. "I ... It was a coincidence."

"*The* Clark Jefferson of Whiz-Go America?" said Dad. "Really, Dom? He's coming to London to meet you?"

"It's all happening, Toby. At breakneck speed. Next week, Orchid is being rolled out across the rest of Europe and piloted in California. Within the month, we expect to take the rest of the States, then go global."

"Fantastic!" squealed Mum, jigging on the spot.

"You *knew*," said Kane, "and you've got to tell us how. Can you come round? Now? For a meeting? Josh is bringing some drinks; Logan's bringing munchies. My parents are out."

Uncle Dom was leading Mum and Dad into the hall.

"... calls to people in Sao Paolo, Rio, and Brasilia. Meat. Meat. Meat. Too slow in Europe and the States; too many restrictions. We need a meat supply that's capable of fast and massive growth ..."

Erin felt sick and dizzy. Chunks of information whirled about and collided in her head. Uncle Dom, the hypnotic power of the Orchid brand, Kree, the Dreamscape – it was all connected; it had to be. How, though? And why?

Warm sunlight was filtering into Crow Woods, dappling the trail as she crossed the wide elbow towards Parkfields. She heard the swish of her tyres and the occasional creak of a tree limb. Insects and birds were everywhere. The little stream gurgled over its stony bed, and looked welcoming as the sun's rays silvered its surface. But she didn't stop. The others would be waiting, and she wasn't sure how much to tell them. It was all still a big puzzle. Josh would pressure her ... and Josh was a puzzle and a problem himself.

She smiled as she saw Rarke perched in a tree, just ahead. Big enough to be a raven. Silver head-feathers. It had to be him. She gripped her brake levers, and winced as the peace was disturbed by the squeal and judder of rubber blocks dragging on metal – far too violent, surely, not to scare him away?

But no. There he was. Still perched on his bough, ten feet up. Looking incredibly proud. Regarding her with curiosity and perhaps a touch of disdain.

For a time, he preened himself in the sunlight. Then he let out a cry and extended his wings. His yellow eyes brightened. He hopped up and down on the branch. He took to the air and circled the tree before flying off.

Erin abandoned her bike in the undergrowth and followed. Up ahead, she saw him in another tree, waiting. He pointed his beak skyward and jiggled his head, sending a ripple along the blue-black feathers of his plump body.

As Erin got close, he flew on.

Deeper and deeper they went. Unless her bearings were way out, he was leading her to the clearing. She hesitated. He'd gone from sight again, but Erin was sensing an atmosphere. It wasn't the same kind of malevolence she'd encountered before.

Something wasn't right, though ...

A loud crack echoed through the woods.

She heard a cheer and some voices near by. There was a tight knot in her chest as she hurried through a brake of bushes, to where the ground sloped upwards. On the slope, by a tangle of exposed tree roots, stood two boys of about seventeen. Only now, as she saw the rifle, did she understand what the cracking sound had been. Lying on the dirt at the boys' feet was Rarke.

His beautiful feathers were already losing their lustre.

147

"Morons!" she cried, running at them.

They were startled by her sudden, hostile appearance, but then laughed as they realised that she was "just a girl", and younger than themselves.

Erin faltered and stopped. One boy was short and wore glasses. The one with the gun was tall, blond, and had a cigarette dangling from his mouth.

In a suspended moment, this second boy's life was laid open to Erin in a short burst of fragmented scenes. His taxidermist father standing over him encouragingly, as the boy, blue eyes needle-sharp, worked on the body of a stoat pinned to a board. An ex-soldier brother whose only way of coping with what he'd done in a mountain village on the other side of the world, was mainlining heroin twice a day. The alcoholic, pill-popping mother who rarely left her bedroom. Leo – the boy's name was Leo – liked taxidermy, roller-coasters, computer games, slasher horror movies, porn, Orchid burgers, banana milkshakes, picking at a scab inside his ear ...

The projector spools in her head stopped turning.

Sunlight fell through the trees. Leaves twitched. The ground was fibrous and springy beneath her feet. The smell of the woods was all about her.

Leo had looked uncomfortable when she'd been reading him. Now he raised his rifle, pointed it at her and made a shot-gun noise with his mouth.

He stooped to pick up the dead raven, and then the boys casually turned and walked away.

"See its silver head," said Leo. "Unusual, that is."

"It's a big 'un," said the other.

Erin stood there with tears on her cheeks.

Okay, so Leo's an arsehole, she thought. *But I knew that already. Why can't the Source give me some* real *answers?*

21

Prelude To A Waking Nightmare

They were in a huge room with a pine floor. Through a series of bi-fold doors spanning an entire wall, there was a view across Thistledown Valley.

Three leather sofas formed a curve around the television. In front of the television, but with his back to it, Kane sat in a low-slung gaming chair. From that position he could swivel to face either Erin, Josh or Logan. Those three were enjoying the luxury of a whole sofa each. Nisha hadn't been able to come.

"So how did you know?" said Kane.

"I told you," said Erin. "I ... *didn't* know."

At least she hadn't known about the fur trade.

"Rubbish," said Josh. He'd been lying on his sofa; now he sat up. "She probably belongs to some radical animal rights group. The sort of people what spray-paint 'vivisectionist' in big red capitals on scientists' cars."

The boys laughed. Erin looked at the floor; said nothing. She kept thinking about Rarke, crumpled and lifeless in the dirt.

"Who cares, anyway?" said Josh. "Hawkes is getting done, that's the main thing. Me: I ain't bothered about them giant pandas – they're wussy and stupid. They only shag about once every five years. Deserve to go extinct. But snow leopards are cool. And that tosser was making a fortune out of 'em. I wouldn't mind ten minutes in a boxing-ring with him. Know what I'm saying?"

Kane smiled at Erin.

"You're not going to tell us, are you?" he said.

"There's ... nothing to tell."

"Rubbish," said Josh.

"I wanted to raise awareness with the demo, and – "

"Yeah, rubbish," said Kane. "Don't get us wrong though. We're glad. People like that *should* be locked up. It's okay if you don't want to tell us how you knew, but *you knew*. Just – hey, thanks for letting us in on the act."

"It was brilliant," said Josh. "What're we doing next?"

In the converted attic, there was a desk, a computer, and stacks of books. The workstation belonged to Kane's dad, but the space was so big that there was still room to walk around. One of the pitched sides had a window, open to the night air, and at this window stood an eight-inch reflector telescope.

"I'm still learning how to use it," said Kane, resting a hand gently on the white casing. "With our old telescope, everything was manual. When you tried to look at faraway objects like Saturn, it was moving so fast and being magnified so much, it was hard to keep it in the screen. The slightest nudge, and you'd be aiming at a patch of sky millions of miles off-course."

Josh and Logan had left earlier, after arrangements for tomorrow's rehearsal had been sorted out. Kane had then made himself and Erin cups of tea and tinned spaghetti on toast.

At one end of the attic, there was a big felt notice-board. Pinned to it were star-charts, a map of the moon, a map of Mars, and a plan of the solar system showing all the planets and their orbits. One poster made Erin smile: she had a copy of it on her bedroom wall.

"What?" said Kane.

"Earthrise," she said.

"Yeah. Classic photo. Imagine walking on the moon, then bringing a picture like that back with you."

"It was taken before the landings," she said.

"What? No, it wasn't. You sure?"

"Yes. Apollo 8 in 1968. They only orbited the moon. I mean, there are later similar photos that were taken during other missions, but your poster and mine, they're from the original 1968 'Earthrise' photo."

Kane flexed his neck and swallowed.

"Right. Know your stuff, don't you? Imagine how people must have felt the first time they saw how amazing our planet looks from a distance."

"Yeah, amazing," she said. "And fragile and beautiful and so blue."

"Yeah. That, too."

He peered out of the window again.

The sky wasn't completely dark, but it was clear, and more stars were appearing by the minute. Because the house was on the edge of town, overlooking Thistledown Valley, light pollution was low.

"... the GOTO system's all computerised. Works a bit like a satnav. You can find and track objects easily."

She longed to see something. Anything. She watched him pressing keys on a handheld control-box. Little motors whirred and the telescope began to move in its mountings. Erin's skin prickled because the movement reminded her of how Uncle Dom's head had cranked mechanically on his neck, the blind white orbs of his eyes tracking her across the living-room.

"You okay?" said Kane.

"Yes!" she said, forcing a smile.

When the telescope had stopped, Kane put his eye to it, then stood back and said, "Check that out."

She looked into the eyepiece. What she saw was a fuzzy oval with a bright centre, and fainter spiral arms that reached out in slow arcs.

"Andromeda," said Kane. "A spiral galaxy, like ours. See, a galaxy is made up of billions of stars, and there's billions of galaxies in the universe. Andromeda's the nearest, and it's two and a half million light years away. A light year is how far light travels in a year. So it's a measure of distance, not time, like some people think ..."

She already knew much of what Kane was talking about, but she listened patiently, not wanting to spoil the moment. He was all fired up, more enthusiastic than she'd seen him before, now that he was immersed in his subject. She tried to imagine having a conversation like this with Josh. Yeah, right!

"What's up?" said Kane.

"Nothing. I was just thinking about how Josh ..." She broke off, realising that so far she hadn't spoken about any of the boys behind their backs.

"Yeah, there's no stopping him," said Kane, grinning. "Works to his own set of rules and laughs at everybody else's. He's got his good points, though."

Erin frowned as she remembered some of the intense and puzzling looks Josh had given her earlier – occasional, brief looks that had punctuated his more general cynical banter, of course. And every time she'd turned to him – feeling his eyes on her – he'd looked quickly away.

"Is he getting to you a bit?" said Kane.

She didn't want to talk about Josh. Not to Kane. Not to anyone.

"Is astronomy part of your dad's job?" she asked.

"Not really. He's a physicist, but he's working on the really small stuff. Particles. Quantum mechanics."

Erin stood back from the telescope.

"The resolution's not great tonight," said Kane. "It looks clear out there, but you can get other problems, like with temperature, or with atmospherics."

He pressed keys on the GOTO control-box again as he talked. The motors whirred and the telescope started to orientate itself to a different position.

Kane laughed and said, "My dad talks about some really weird and cool stuff. You know, atoms are mostly just empty space? If you imagine a grain of sand in mid air, in the middle of a cathedral, and then even tinier particles buzzing around the grain of sand, but so far away from it that their orbit puts them at the walls and roof and floor of the cathedral – I mean, that's the scale of an atom! Crazy, or what? So even though our bodies feel pretty solid, or a lump of iron or whatever seems solid, it's really made mainly of nothing. And then *some* particles – like they see in the work going on at CERN – some particles behave as if they exist in two places at once, or they can disappear and reappear somewhere else. Some theorists believe that, like, there could be other dimensions occupying the empty spaces of the quantum world. Really loopy, don't you think?"

She wanted him to say more, but he shrugged and seemed embarrassed. He smoothed a hand lightly over his cornrows and waved a hand at the telescope.

"Have a look now," he said, without checking first.

This time, she saw a large pale disc with a pattern of swirls and striations, which appeared to be in gradual flux. She looked up, to where the telescope was aimed, and there was a bright star among fainter stars.

"A planet?" she guessed.

"Venus. We've been studying it lately. I thought you'd like to see it because, well, I know you're interested in climate change, and Venus is a radical example of what the greenhouse effect can do."

"Really?"

"It looks peaceful through the 'scope. All you can see is how it's smothered by thick clouds. But they're not made of rain. They're made of sulphuric acid. It's the hottest, most violent place in the solar system – I mean, except for the sun, obviously. The surface of Venus is covered in volcanoes. It's hotter than hell down there. Something like about four hundred degrees C."

"Isn't it hotter because it's closer to the sun?"

"Well, yeah, partly, but really it's more to do with what happened to the atmosphere. Venus is choked with greenhouse gases. Otherwise, it'd be a lot cooler. It's about balance as well, though. If Earth didn't have any greenhouse gases, it'd be way too cold to live on."

"Now we're upsetting the balance," she said. "Do you worry about it?"

"Yeah, 'course," he said. "Not much *we* can do, though. I suppose I worry about it the same as I worry about knowing I'll die one day. It's gonna happen, and there ain't nothing I can do to change it. Let's hope Earth doesn't get as bad as Venus while we're still alive." He laughed. "I'm joking. Even if we carry on polluting the atmosphere, it'd probably take hundreds of years."

She thought his knowledge was impressive, but he didn't have a clear picture of climate change on Earth. He'd talked about a balance in greenhouse gases, but did he appreciate how fragile that balance was?

"Don't worry," he said, misinterpreting her silence. "It won't get anywhere near as hot as Venus in our lifetimes."

"Wouldn't have to," she said. "If average global temperatures rose even five degrees, it'd be too much. There'd be droughts, famines, crop failures – on a massive scale. Monster storms and floods. Killer heat-waves. More disease – "

"Steady on, Erin. You been reading 'Revelation'?"

She laughed, looked at the 'Earthrise' poster again and said, "I just want us to stop trashing the planet."

22

Chthonia

Erin was trudging through narrow streets where factory walls towered. Grimy windows were lit sporadically by flashes and sparks. The visible band of furrowed sky was crimson and ulcerated, like a diseased membrane.

The silence and emptiness were unbearable.

It was ferociously hot. Sweat streamed down her face and body. The whole place stank so badly that she kept gagging. The ground was pot-holed and covered with all kinds of filth: food slops, offal, excrement.

Cockroaches ran up walls. A huge bristly rat scurried between her feet and into an open drain. Flies and mosquitoes swarmed in the foul air.

The street ended in a T-junction, where customers from a busy burger place wandered past with their takeaways. Some looked at her suspiciously. Erin saw why: she was wearing jeans and a tee-shirt and they were all in ragged grey garments held up with string.

A loud rumble came from behind and she flattened herself against the nearest wall just in time. A team of oxen thundered by, pulling a wooden cart that carried more of the grey-garbed people. In a cloud of dust, the cart was quickly gone, but she'd seen a scaly green arm as the driver cracked a whip.

She considered the T-junction again and understood that in some way or time, the street ahead of her was Cank Street. A right turn should lead to what she knew as High Street; a left should lead to the town hall square.

Just then, an odd creature appeared. About four feet tall, it had multiple arms and legs and wore a bowler hat and black waistcoat. The rest of its maggot-like body curved down and under, its belly almost touching the ground. Grinning at Erin, it hooked some of its hands into the pockets of the waistcoat.

Erin tried to ignore the creature. She turned left and walked quickly, hoping it would lose interest, but it followed, propelling itself along on its stumpy little legs. Its face was puce, and it had slit eyes and a cruel mouth.

She began running – reached the end of the street and came out in a square with official-looking buildings at its perimeter. One was similar in design to Everdene's town hall. Ragged people roamed everywhere. The lowering sky was becoming redder, angrier, like flayed flesh covered with cysts and boils.

At the fountain, iron griffins spouted what looked like blood. The clock above the town hall was pulsing with an orange light, and a great spider spanned the face, its grotesque black legs rotating anticlockwise around the numerals, showing All Time, and No Time.

Two more of the upright maggoty creatures flanked the open doorway of the town hall, and people clutching documents filtered in and out.

On the side of the square adjacent to the town hall, there was a road whose position matched Luxor Street. It was pot-holed and piled with rubbish, and rumbling along it was another ox-drawn cart full of people.

This time, Erin saw that the whip-cracking driver was similar to a humanoid lizard she'd once seen underwater ... When and where had that been?

The crowds began to disperse, and she understood that they were workers, that it was a change of shift. She watched them shuffling in their grey rags and broken shoes, hands going to mouths, eating mechanically, like cows chewing the cud. And as they trudged and masticated, the Cubist clamshells of polystyrene takeaway boxes accumulated in the unspeakable filth underfoot.

A scream was building inside Erin.

She attempted to run again but her legs wouldn't obey. An awkward plod around the square was all she could manage, as if her route were determined by an unseen hand. By her side, the creature gave nothing away, answering her fears with a tip of its bowler hat and an enigmatic grin.

Round and round she laboured – through the hot, humid, crimson night, until the square was empty and she was desperately tired. At a chime, she looked up and saw that the spider was now stationary on the glowing orange clock-face.

The maggoty creature threw its hat into the air, came right up and tried to hug Erin. She retched at its foul breath, and felt its busy little hands at her waist.

"No!" she screamed, shoving it away.

There was a thunderclap. Then the ulcerated sky burst open and hot blood came pissing down over everything.

The creature skittered towards her again.

"Kree," she cried out. "Kree ..."

Behind the creature, she glimpsed a movement. It was just a swirling and thickening of the air at first; then there was a gentle rushing sound and a mass of particles and colours and shadows converged into a figure.

In the next instant, the maggoty creature was headless.

Its head simply jumped off its shoulders. It hit the ground with a dull, wet noise and rolled a little way. The body writhed and thrashed, then lay still. The many arms and legs twitched a moment longer.

Kree squatted and used the dead creature's waistcoat to clean the blade of his sword. He stood, re-sheathed it and looked calmly at Erin before saying:

"You need to wake up."

As awareness sharpened her mind, a mournful alarm echoed around the deserted square. The tang of the bloody rain was strong in her nose and throat.

Then the ground throbbed, as with the approach of a great number of heavy feet.

"We can't stay here," said Kree.

Within moments, a snarling horde of lizard-like beasts was converging on the square from every direction. Fierce-eyed and scaly, they carried swords and wore black military garb and chain-mail.

"I'm awake," she said. "So why ... ?"

The scene dissolved.

She was still in the town hall square, or a very similar square, but the troops had vanished. The sky was pale, dawn close, and the scintillating air told her that she was in the Dreamscape. Clean flagstones paved the ground. Modern cars passed on the road. The iron griffins at the fountain had changed into winged stone lions spouting water, not blood. The town hall clock was an ordinary clock, with Roman numerals, and the right amount of hands indicating quarter to five.

"Good," said Kree, at her side.

"It wasn't real," she said. "A nightmare ..."

Other dreamers were going about their business: children performed impossible feats on skateboards; an elderly couple in wedding clothes came down the steps of the town hall; a brass band in purple-and-gold uniforms oompah'd its way along past the post-office.

Kree still had something of his boyish looks, but there was a weariness about him, too; he seemed even sadder and wiser.

"It *was* real," he said. "A shift in focus, and we'd be back in Chthonia, the Nightmare Realm. Erin, I don't know what sort of trouble you're in, but ..."

His eyes shone dully one moment, bright the next. He seemed to be fighting some inner battle.

Then he came forward and gathered her in his arms.

A pleasant shiver passed through her. She didn't resist. It felt good and right to be so close to him. She wrapped her arms around his tough, lean body, and felt the coarse material of his tunic against her fingers and palms. He smelled of earth and clay and sunshine and riverbanks.

After a moment, he put his hands on her shoulders and held her away from him at arm's-length. Then he lowered his hands to his sides.

Had she misinterpreted?

"Are you all right?" he said.

"Er, yes," she said. "I think so, anyway. I ... liked what just happened. Were you just being friendly? Or ... ?"

Erin could see the struggle going on behind his eyes again. It lasted a couple of seconds, then he appeared to be back in control.

"Yes," he said. "A friendly hug."

She nodded, but allowed herself a secret smile. It was as if, deep within her, something small and precious had stirred; like a flower opening in moonlight.

"How did you find me?" she said.

"You dreamed me here, Erin. Or not *here*. But to Chthonia. You dreamed me into your nightmare."

"Like at the canal? So it's a place? K'tho ... It's real?"

"Yes," he said. "There is the physical world, then there is the Dreamscape and there is Chthonia. Wait here."

In a gentle, scintillating explosion of particles, he was gone. Seconds later, he returned carrying an extra sword, complete with scabbard and belt.

"For you," he said awkwardly.

"Wha – what for?"

"Protection. If you're going to make a habit of waking dreams, and of turning up in Chthonia ... Those two things can be a bad mixture."

Erin stared at the sword-belt he was holding. Her aversion to weapons and violence surfaced, but her blood quickened for other reasons, too. She had a powerful intuition that her destiny and Kree's were intertwined.

"They were skerri troops we saw in Chthonia, right?" she said.

"Yes. Or, more correctly, their phantoms."

"Phantoms? What was that thing you decapitated?"

"A shlurm," he said. "They're in the thrall of the skerri – they're used as spies, slaves, messengers."

"What about the giant spider on the clock?"

"A mystery," said Kree. "It's been there for more than fifty years. We know nothing about its origins or about its relationship with the skerri."

"And the orange glow behind the clock face?"

"A glow behind the Spider Clock? No. There's never been ..."

They both glanced up, but of course the clock in the Dreamscape had a plain white background with black numerals.

"You must have seen it," she said. "It was bright. And pulsing. Like fire."

Kree frowned. "No. I didn't. It must be new."

"New?" A shiver ran up her back. "How new?"

Kree raised one shoulder. "I don't know. Recent."

She took the sword from him. Her hands shook as she fumbled with the thick belt and clinking buckle. Her mind was full of protests, but some vital part of her understood that, like it or not, she was already embroiled in a conflict. If she didn't find courage, the consequences would be cataclysmic.

And the answers – all of the answers – now hovered tantalisingly close.

23

Modes Of Travel

"Something's happening to me," she said. "I'm starting to see ... Understanding. I think my purpose has to do with my world, and my uncle, and Chthonia. And *you*."

A troubled look crossed his face.

"Kree? You said you'd help me."

He smiled thinly. "Yes, Erin. If I can help you, I will."

"First, I'd like you to teach me how to travel. You know; that trick you do. I've done it by accident, and without realising, but I need to be an expert."

He blinked a few times, then nodded.

"An expert. All right. Think of a place, and then focus on it to the exclusion of all else."

Exclusion of all else? That wouldn't be easy. Along with her growing sense of purpose, the thrill of being so close to Kree lingered in her thoughts. And even if *he* chose to deny it, she knew it wasn't just her imagination telling her that something fragile between them had begun but been left unfinished.

"How about the clearing in Crow Woods?" she said.

"Too easy."

"The railway station?"

"All right. Imagine it as vividly as you can."

As she thought about the station, she began to drift. She smiled as the first of her wolves slunk from the shadows at the base of the fountain. Then Kree blocked her path, arms folded, and the wolves slunk back.

"Not like that," he said. "'Expert', travel is immediate. An instantaneous transfer from one point to another."

Again, she pictured the station and began to drift. Again, the wolves came to attend her. Kree shooed them off and they melted into the shadows around the fountain. It was as if they'd slipped through the cracks in the concrete.

"That mode of travel is frivolous. It's for beginners and sightseers."

"I *am* a beginner!" she said with a smile. She was finding it difficult to take his all-business attitude seriously. "And the wolves were helping."

"Whimsies," said Kree. "We call those kinds of helpers 'whimsies'. If you travel that way, you risk slipping into conventional dreams. An expert traveller maintains focus. Lose focus and you attract whimsies."

"What about Chthonia?" she said. "Was that confused by whimsies? Or was I seeing it how it really is? It was raining blood. And the fountain – "

"Not blood," he said. "All water there has a very high content of iron. Rust, iron oxide; that's what gives the water its colour."

Erin touched a hand to her wet hair, relieved.

"Although," he said, "it's blood that covers the ground. Blood and offal, among other things. They slaughter their cattle in public and don't bother to clean up. The skerri are disgusting and primitive. They don't even use toilets. Can you believe that? If they need to go, they stop anywhere in the street, pull down their trousers and squat. Vile creatures!"

She laughed, but Kree was grimacing, lost in his hatred of the skerri. He seemed to be under immense strain. Erin had thought earlier that it was to do with the emotional "misunderstanding" between them. Now she realised that she'd been naïve. Had something terrible happened? Something he was keeping inside himself or protecting her from? She was about to ask when he raised his chin and said, "Do you want to try again? The travelling."

Erin hesitated, then nodded and closed her eyes.

Don't visualise the route, she told herself. Visualise *being there*. She thought about the main entrance: the ornate stone frontage and the modern concourse. A couple of times, she began to sail through the air, but stopped herself and remembered Kree's words: "An instantaneous transfer from one point to another."

She concentrated harder.

Thought only about arriving … arriving …

"Good. Open your eyes."

The station's Victorian façade was lit by the first rays of the sun as it peeped above the row of shops opposite.

In the bright early morning, dreamers came and went with their baggage. Taxi driver's touted for business.

"Now back to the square," said Kree.

This time, she didn't need to be told that they'd arrived. Although there was no accompanying sense of movement, she was aware of a tiny, subtle shift in orientation, and knew she'd succeeded.

"Good. And back to the station ..."

Several more times, and she felt her confidence building, but on the final return to the square, something went slightly wrong. She arrived alone. There wasn't a dreamer in sight. The fountain was inactive; the winged lions were a tarnished bronze rather than pale stone. A strong wind blew a sheet of newspaper about, and the sun shone dully through thin clouds.

Preceded by a momentary swirling vortex of particles and shadows and diffused light, Kree materialised.

"You've slipped into the physical world by mistake, Erin" he said.

"I think I've done that before," she said.

She brought him up to date about the demo, and about Hawkes's arrest.

"And I sank straight through a car," she said. "I didn't understand before, but I must have been in the physical world. It's the only way I could have witnessed the swoop on his house."

She knelt down and pushed at the ground. After a slight resistance, she felt a cool grittiness as her hand went through the paving slab.

"A dream body has little substance here," said Kree. "In any case, you shouldn't be able to do this yet. It takes much practice."

"But why don't we – ?"

"Sink into the Earth? It all happens on a subconscious level. We're used to being on the ground, so that's where we stay. A waking dreamer can defy the laws of motion and gravity here as easily as in the Dreamscape. The difference is that the physical world lacks solidity for us."

He reached for Erin's hand. At his touch, a thrill expanded in her chest.

She stood up, marvelling at how precisely their hands fitted together. They were standing very close. She looked into his eyes and her thoughts reeled.

Kree disengaged his hand, confusion on his face.

Was his inner turmoil about us, after all, then? she thought. She tried to read him using the Source, but his mind and heart were impenetrable. Still, she felt him bristling at her attempts. He passed a quivering hand over his mouth. An agonised look entered his eyes.

"Kree ... ?"

In the next instant, and without a word, he'd gone.

All she could think to do, logically, was return to the Dreamscape. She created a mental picture of the square with its minor differences. There was a subtle shift, then she opened her eyes to sparkling air and a blue sky. The sun shone warm on her skin. Water splashed musically at the fountain. With the arrival of day, some of the dreamers were departing. The brass-band members had packed up their instruments. A bent old man was locking the town hall doors.

Kree was standing a little way off, his head in his hands. His body shook and he was making a deep groaning sound. Was he crying?

She approached him. No, she realised. Not crying.

When he unsheathed his sword, she was quite close. His gaze was incandescent as he threw the sword and sent it spinning end over end.

It embedded itself in the door of the town hall. From near by, the old man who'd just locked up paused to glare disapprovingly.

"Kree?" said Erin.

He looked startled to see her. His anger wavered. Then he shouldered past her, mounted the steps and pulled his sword from the solid oak. He re-sheathed it and sat on the top step, head in hands again.

After a minute, she went to him.

She didn't know what to say, and was feeling wretched herself, so she just stood there, waiting. The huge doors were set in an elaborate stone arch – a more stately-looking entrance than the one in the physical world. She couldn't resist touching the splintered gash left by the sword. The damage felt real enough.

Erin remembered the maggoty creature's head being chopped off, and became aware again of the sword hanging from her waist.

"Forgive me," said Kree. "Five of my comrades were lost yesterday. The skerri found our safe haven. We're nomadic again, living on our wits. Forgive me."

Five lost? There'd only been seventeen left.

She touched his arm.

He glanced up at her, smiled sadly and got to his feet.

"I'm sorry about your comrades," she choked.

He stood more upright and raised his chin.

"Would you like to continue?" he said. "You're doing brilliantly. As you just discovered, it works exactly the same if you need to locate a person rather than simply go somewhere. You're a swift learner. That can only mean that your purpose has great magnitude. Try again. You wait here, then come and find me."

"Okay. So what if ... ?"

He'd already gone. So she visualised him: his cropped hair and lean face, his big eyes the amber colour of autumn leaves ...

Erin experienced a barely perceptible shift, then she was with him. Over his shoulder, she saw high-rise buildings and blazing neon. Restaurants and bars. Laughing, chattering people on terraces. Yellow taxi-cabs cruising about. She could smell coffee and cigar smoke. The air thrummed with the beat of music; she felt it jangling pleasantly in her bones.

"New York?" she said.

"Lower Manhattan," he confirmed. "Or its Dreamscape equivalent. It's just before midnight, allowing for the five-hour time difference."

A gang of whooping young boys cycled down the middle of the road, zigzagging between the cruising taxis. A big-bellied man in a string vest was shuffling along the pavement talking to himself. Several feet above the ground, a woman with wild grey hair was cart-wheeling.

"Dreamers," Erin murmured.

"It'll get busier later," said Kree, "as more of the population go to bed."

Erin straightened abruptly, her head bursting with energy.

"You see the man on the rooftop over there?" she said breathlessly. "In the physical world, he's in an operating theatre. Undergoing brain surgery."

"The Source," said Kree. "You're accessing – "

"We have to go back. Now Follow me."

She pictured the town hall square and arrived instantaneously. Kree was with her a moment later. Erin looked up at the fat square tower above the town hall. Although they were in the Dreamscape, she glimpsed the Spider Clock with its glowing, pulsing face. Then she saw the clock as it was in the physical world. Then she was straddling all three dimensions at the same time. The vision lasted a second or two, then broke up and fell away. The rush in her head slowed to a trickle and stopped. But she was left with the knowledge that she could shift easily between any of the realms.

Erin had gained other knowledge as well – other insights too shocking to contemplate fully. She tried to push them aside, but knew they had to be faced.

"Kree," she said. "My purpose ... There's a job I have to do in Chthonia."

He made a broken gesture around the hilt of his sword.

"In Chthonia?" he said with a faltering smile.

"Yes. It'll be dangerous. Very dangerous."

He shuffled his feet and looked away. Erin frowned. What was wrong? Where was the courage she needed him to show at this moment?

She staggered as the head-rush and the visions returned – the fiery, dwarf sun behind the clock; the vile experiments in the subterranean lab; the cold-as-steel logic of the skerri's lizard brains, and Uncle Dom's mindless facilitation of their plot. And in that instant, the rest of the puzzle became horrifyingly clear.

"The operation in Chthonia," she said. "We should do it soon."

"*We*?" he said. "No. *I* can't come. It's impossible."

24

Sunshine & Riverbanks

"I'm sorry, Erin. If I can help you in any other way ... But not that. It can't be that. Not Chthonia. I'll show you. We'll go back, just for a moment."

He went.

Erin followed, experiencing the now familiar shift.

The deserted square looked apocalyptic in the rust-coloured rain. Everything stank. The great spider was stationary on the pulsing clock-face.

Two shlurms stood at the town hall entrance. On spotting Erin and Kree, the shlurms put their heads together, then one went inside.

A moment later, the alarm Erin had heard earlier started its mournful drone. Kree folded his arms, his expression neutral. A rumbling shook the ground. Erin knew that it was the skerri soldiers. A hideous bellowing was added to the thunder of military boots. Then they appeared at every entrance to the square – a sea of scaly green hides, fierce eyes, gleaming swords.

"We should go," said Kree.

She closed her eyes.

"They were coming for me, not you," he said, back in the safety of the Dreamscape. "They'd love to wipe out the few of us who remain. In Chthonia, they can sense us from far away, and they also have their spies, the shlurms. If any of us spent more than a short time there, we'd be obliterated. But the greater danger is that by finding *me* in Chthonia, they'd find *you*."

"I understand," she said. "You told me before, but I forgot." It wasn't lack of courage at all, she realised.

"What is that you need to do?" said Kree.

"Destroy the generator. It's in the room at the back of the clock – the Clock Room. You saw the glow behind the face this time? That's the generator."

"What is it generating?" he said.

"It's the power source behind the Orchid brand."

"Your uncle's company? He has links with Chthonia?"

"Yes. Every use of the brand in the physical world depends on that generator. It has to be destroyed."

Tiredness was swamping her.

169

In the scintillating daylight of the Dreamscape, the town hall looked so innocent. It had been locked now by the old man, but ...

"I've got a plan," she said. "I'll shift into the physical world, where I can pass through the closed doors or the walls. I'll go up to the Clock Room, shift to Chthonia, destroy the generator; then shift to the Dreamscape."

"Clever," said Kree. "But it wouldn't work."

"Why?"

"I'll tell you what I know about the town hall in Chthonia. It's protected by forces that can't be bypassed. It isn't possible to enter it or exit it from another realm. You can only do that via the main entrance in Chthonia. Whatever happens, don't get trapped inside while you're in Chthonia. The skerri ..." He lowered his eyes.

"Maybe I'll need some help," she said. "Is it possible to train other people to wake up in the Dreamscape?"

"Who?"

"People from my world. Friends. Kane and Logan. And Nisha."

"There are ways," he said. "I can show you. And it's better that you don't attempt the operation alone. Kane, Logan and Nisha? Not Josh?"

"Er, Josh can be a bit chaotic," she said.

Kree's eyes went foggy. Erin could tell that he was using his limited access to the Source.

"You'll need Josh," he said. "If it was me, and I could take only one person, I'd choose him. He's a skilled swordsman and has an unusual kind of bravery. Couldn't you put aside any differences you have and ... Ah. I see."

"What?" she said, flushing. "See what? You mean ... No way. I don't even like him. I ... There's just no way!"

With the suggestion of a sag around his shoulders, Kree stared off into space. He recovered quickly.

"Your only hope is to bluff your way in," he said. "I have contacts. I'll organise some of the clothes worn by the Chthonia masses. And extra swords. We'll cache everything in the Dreamscape. You should be able to get into the town hall, do the job and get out before the troop alarm goes off."

"What about the shlurms?"

"A nuisance, but basically cowards. They wouldn't even rally to help one another. If necessary, you can kill them with impunity. Slice them up ... Sorry. I sometimes forget I'm not talking to a comrade, although you *are* a comrade of sorts, Erin. I know you don't like the idea of killing even elemental creatures. It may not come to that. Anyway, it would draw attention to you."

Her head was whirling with fatigue.

"So we walk in and pretend we've got business?"

"Yes, I'll organise fake documents for you," he said. "Everybody has to register at the town hall before assignment to a factory, even though the work is compulsory. For a long time, the skerri only used the unfortunate inhabitants of Chthonia for slave labour. Away from the towns, it's just shanty dwellings, where the masses try to scrape an existence. But recently, there's been an influx of dreamers from the physical realm, drafted to work alongside the others ..."

His face started to blur.

Erin saw the fuzzy edges of her computer desk. She rolled her head on the pillow. Early daylight shone between the curtains. Then strong hands squeezed her shoulders, and Kree's face snapped back into focus.

He lowered his arms to his sides, but his grip had left a lingering impression.

"Your uncle," he said. "Is his brand and the generator so much of a threat to your world? What else do you know from the Source?"

"Everything, I think. And it all links back to the skerri. They used scientists from my world, during nightmares, to help them design and build the generator. They're getting more powerful. They want to rule the surface."

Kree laughed. "The skerri would be no match for the weapons of men."

"No," she said. "And they won't show themselves yet. Not until they've brought about the collapse of human civilisation by engineering the climate. By making it much, much hotter. Underground, they mostly live near the magma seams of volcanoes, right? So their solution is to create a hell on Earth. To turn the surface of the planet into a duplicate of Chthonia."

"Accelerate climate change?" he said. "How can they do that?"

"It's already happening. Humans have been warming the planet up by burning fossil fuels. Industry, power stations, transport. But that's only part of the story. Methane is the rest. It's an even more potent greenhouse gas than carbon dioxide. About *twenty times* more potent. It comes up through the ground from landfill sites, and from more natural sources like the Arctic tundra. But the biggest source of methane is animal livestock, especially cattle. Cows produce vast amounts, and because of its higher potency, what's going into the atmosphere is a threat that's already equal to the pollution caused by all the cars in the world. *Already equal.* The skerri aren't stupid; they know that the easiest way to create a runaway greenhouse effect is by massive growth of the cattle population. It's the sickest joke of all. Planet Earth could heat up – not, in the end, from burning fossil fuels, but from cows' farts!"

She fought off wave after wave of tiredness as they talked. Knowing how much Kree and his people had suffered at the hands of the skerri, there was something she could hardly bring herself to ask him. But it had to be done.

172

"The skerri have a laboratory, way beneath the Earth in the physical realm," she said.

"We know of this lab," he said with a frown. "But not what they – "

"Is a skerra's phantom the same as a dream body?"

"Yes, it's only a term to differentiate."

"Okay," she said. "Kree, they've been conducting experiments on their own kind. Attempting to lengthen the death process. Under freak conditions, a skerra subject was suspended on the point of death. And what happened next was beyond the wildest hopes of the experimenters. The skerra's phantom occupied and reanimated a dying human."

"Your uncle?" he said.

"When he nearly died in hospital. Uncle Dom isn't a man any more. He's a puppet, a zombie. But killing him wouldn't solve the problem. The phantom could simply occupy another dying human."

"Yes," he said. "And as long as the subject is suspended on the point of death in the lab ..." His frown deepened. "It's the same for my people. If either my dream body or physical body were mortally wounded, both bodies would die. In that respect, we're the same as the skerri. But *nothing* like them otherwise."

"You use toilets, for one thing," said Erin.

"Sorry?"

"You use toilets," she said, keeping her face deadpan. "You don't just drop your trousers and have a crap anywhere."

Kree laughed long and hard.

"Yes," he choked. "*We* use toilets! Or, now that we're nomadic again, I'm sorry to say we have to dig a hole."

As his laughter subsided, realisation settled in his beautiful eyes.

"I'll talk to my comrades," he said. "I know where the lab is. If the skerra's physical counterpart dies, so will its phantom."

"I'm ... sorry, Kree."

He shook his head. "What's to stop them repeating the experiment?"

"It's taken them decades to pull this thing off. They only succeeded under freak conditions, and only the skerri scientists at the lab have any hope of ..."

Erin felt sick with responsibility and guilt. She'd gained all this knowledge in a flash and a burst. It had been abstract, existing somewhere remote. Now that she was putting it into words, it felt too real. And what she was asking Kree to do felt almost like betrayal. She could be sending him to his death.

But Kree was standing to attention, looking like a soldier again. He knitted his fingers together and cracked his knuckles.

"We can't risk anything less than the destruction of the lab," he said. "And as well as the subject, we'll have to kill any skerri scientists we find there. At the end of the week – this coming Friday by your calendar – it's a new moon and the powers of darkness will be at their lowest ebb. Anyway, it will take my comrades and I almost that long to make the journey under the Earth."

"I ... wish there was another way," she said.

"There isn't," he said. "We'll storm the lab on Friday night. You should carry out your operation in Chthonia then, too."

The same night as the talent contest, Erin registered. Not that that was important. But, of course, she was just looking for distractions. Now she focussed on the weight of the sword she was wearing. She ran her fingers over the knurled pattern on the hilt, and with an effort she centred herself.

They sat on the wooden seats around the fountain. The water made a clean, surging sound. Spray rose on the air and occasionally wafted in their faces.

"Kree? Could I ... My friends ... Could *we* get hurt?"

"If you did, you'd still wake up unharmed. And in time, your dream body would reconstitute. Quite a gift."

She tried not to think about what might happen if *he* got hurt.

A coldness crept into her bones.

Kree couldn't sit still for long. He went to the fountain and stood with his back to her, grasping the safety-rail. She got up and followed him over, and he turned just as she reached him. They looked at one another in silence as the fine spray from the fountain descended around them like a mist.

"I don't know if we'll meet again after tonight, Erin," he said. "I may not have time for sleep or waking dreams in the coming days. The journey to the lab will be gruelling. Afterwards, I don't know if you'll be able to ... Your purpose is what draws you."

"*Not meet?* We can't not meet again. That'd be ..."

She was already wrapping her arms around him, her hands pressed against the rough material of his tunic. And there was his smell: clay and riverbanks and sun-scorched earth. He didn't try to hug her back. His body was rigid and unyielding. But then his resistance crumbled and he drew her close.

"In a different time and place ..." he said, his lips level with her ear, "... a different reality. You're so perfect, Erin. So beautiful. But we can't ever ..."

She hugged him tight, trying not to hear words like "but" and "can't". Any sense of time or place melted away. It was just the two of them, his earthy smell, and the glassy plash of the fountain.

She felt anchored to him.

"A moment longer," he said into her hair. "Another moment longer ..."

Then he pushed her gently away from him.

"Kree," she said, reaching for him.

He stepped back. His face was mask-like.

"Forgive me, Erin. I shouldn't have done that."

"You didn't. *I* did. I ... wanted to. Kree, I thought ..."

His eyes grew pale, almost white, and his pupils shrank to black dots. A hardness settled on his face but was betrayed by a tear falling to his cheek. He wiped it away with a trembling fist.

"What – what just happened between us?" said Erin.

The amber returned to his eyes, but he looked sad.

"I've lost so much, Erin. And there's still so much more to lose ..." He waved a hand through the air. "A hundred years from now, a hundred orbits of the sun, and the deepest cares of everybody alive today will be as nothing. It's all so temporary."

"What are you talking about?"

"Time. Loss. You have to live each moment fully, Erin. Be truly alive. Don't hoard and save things too much. Don't forget yourself in some half-awake trudge through the hours, mesmerised by the artificial things. We don't really know anything. Mystics. Scientists. Philosophers. Nobody does. We only know that we are here. In the world. With our fears and joys. For a time."

He laughed bitterly.

"What are we in the end, but a fleeting arrangement of atoms, soon to dissipate?"

Erin stared at him.

"No," she said. "We're more than that. Much more. I'm sorry you're so sad."

She nearly went to him, but sensed that he'd reject her.

"We *could* meet again when it's all over, couldn't we?" she said.

The cynical line of his mouth slowly curved into a smile.

"If it's possible. But as I said, it's your *purpose* that draws you. Once the generator is destroyed, you may lose the gift."

She didn't believe him. There were so many things she wanted to try. So many things she wanted to do. As for the idea of not seeing him again ...

25

Angles Of Perception

"... so never underestimate the brain's capacity to trick and deceive in its efforts to make sense of the world," said Mr Tomlinson, the physics tutor.

He pressed a key on his laptop. On the projection screen, a room's interior appeared. It had a plain red ceiling, plain red floor, and white walls with a black striped pattern. At one end, stood a woman so tall that her head and shoulders were squashed against the ceiling. At the other end, stood a man less than half the woman's height. Across the empty space, they waved to each other.

"So what's happening here?" said Mr Tomlinson.

"Well, like, it's obvious," said Parmajit. "It's the world's smallest man and the world's tallest woman, innit?"

"No. Anybody else?"

Erin's head ached and her eyes felt gritty. She couldn't accept the idea that she might not see him again. *There'd be a way.* After the joint operation, she'd find a way to be with him. She knew she would. Images from Chthonia kept polluting her thoughts. She was tired and jittery. Any sudden noises or movements made her flinch. But something odd was happening on the projector screen ...

The tall woman and the short man were crossing the room, and as they did so, the woman grew shorter and the man grew taller. When they met in the middle, they were the same height. They shook hands, then continued – each to the other's original position. Now, the man's head and shoulders were squashed against the ceiling and the woman looked very short.

"Special effects," said Oscar.

"No," said Mr Tomlinson. "It's an optical illusion."

The two people crossed the room again, becoming the same height as they passed each other, then respectively taller and shorter.

Despite how Erin felt, her interest was sparked by the illusion. The camera zoomed out now, showing that the front wall of the experimental room was missing. At the point where the woman stood with her head squashed under the ceiling, it was about five feet high; where the man stood, it was much higher. From his perspective, the floor sloped up and the ceiling sloped down. The actual shape of the room was a flat-ended wedge, a trapezoid.

"It's called an Ames Room. But why are our perceptions deceived in this way? I wanted to take you to see one of these for real, but the funding wasn't available. In the film, the front wall isn't needed because the camera lens limits what can be seen. At the Ames Room I wanted us to visit, there *is* a front wall, with a window. If you enter the room, you're fooled by nothing, and you have the physical evidence of walking up or down the gradient of the floor. But through the viewing window, you'd see an ordinary room, with parallel lines. The spooky thing is that even when you *know* it's a trick, you still see an ordinary room, and still observe the people growing or shrinking."

"Conditioning," said Erin.

He seemed surprised and pleased by the response. Erin didn't often make contributions in his lessons.

"Can you elaborate on that?"

"Er, I don't know. Sorry."

"You're absolutely right, though, Erin. Conditioning. The brain makes sense of things based on conditioning, assumptions, the evidence of past experience. Our belief that rooms are regular in shape, with parallel lines, is so hard-wired that we're more prepared to accept the idea of people shrinking and growing."

"Can I find this on YouTube, sir?" said Oscar.

"Yes, you can. Or examples of it."

"So if ..." said Erin, but the thought slipped away.

Her eyes drifted to the wall clock. Its hands multiplied into eight spider's legs. She shivered. Then there were two hands again, standing at quarter to eleven.

On the projection screen, the Ames Room film continued playing, the man and woman growing and shrinking as they swapped places.

"Yes, Erin?" said Mr Tomlinson.

A lyric fragment from one of Logan's songs came to her: *Poison darts and broken kite-string* ... It was band practice tonight.

"Yes, Erin?"

"Sorry, sir. I was wondering how the room, the Ames Room, how it relates to ... What I mean is, it sort of proves, doesn't it, that we can't rely on our senses? What we see, isn't always what's there."

"Precisely."

"So, I mean, conditioning could even have blinded us to things that we *used* to be able to see, maybe as babies, or ancestrally. Like ... other dimensions ..."

Parmajit and a few others broke into giggles.

"Quiet, please. Go on, Erin."

"Well, what if there were other, separate realities ... and they existed at a different angle to ours. Occupied the same space. I mean ... *overlapping*. There's lots of empty space in atoms. And with all the conditioning of evolution and modern life, what if we were only seeing part of the truth about the world ... and the universe? But if we could make the right shift in our perceptions, if we decided to ignore the – the Ames Room window in our minds – maybe we could see everything as it really is ... Er, dreams can sometimes seem very real ..."

She was sorry she'd said anything. Her cheeks burned and she'd become self-conscious of her very slight lisp.

"Bleddy hell, Lockwood! Are you *on* something today?"

"That's enough now, Parmajit," said Mr Tomlinson. "Thanks, Erin. You were sort of touching on quantum theory there. And it's interesting that you mentioned dreams. It seems that neuroscientists have shown how our perception of the world is always a two-way process. On the one hand, information is received through our senses and interpreted by the brain. On the other, there's evidence that the brain simultaneously *generates* its own stuff. Memories, expectations, assumptions. So what we *see* is a combination of what's there and what the brain manufactures. Reality is the biggest illusion of all. The brain perceives, reprocesses, and then projects a *version* of the world back out there."

"That's way too deep for me, sir," said Oscar. "You're blowing my mind."

"Shut up, Oscar. Now, the *really* spooky thing ... When brain waves are measured with an EEG, it can be shown that during dreamless, regenerative sleep, brain activity has a distinct signature. But when we dream, the activity is similar to when we're wide awake. Some neurologists now believe that dreaming is a form of consciousness, and consciousness is a form of dreaming."

"That's the best we've ever played," Josh kept saying.

Erin had been distracted all evening and could barely remember singing. At some stage, she had to tell them about the operation – *recruit* them – but she hadn't got a clue how to broach the subject.

Kane was so happy with the band's progress, he couldn't stop dishing out compliments to everyone. He kept crossing his legs and squirming about a lot, too – it was obvious that he was holding on to a full bladder. Finally, he rushed to the door at the back of the garage.

"Dying for a slash," he threw over his shoulder.

Everybody laughed.

Josh and Logan were just talking about going for a burger when Kane came back and said, "Don't know if you're interested, Erin – something to do with Orchid on the news again."

He led the way along the hall, where through one open doorway his parents were glimpsed watching a TV. Moments later, Kane and the others were settling themselves in the room overlooking Thistledown Valley.

"Which one's your uncle?" said Josh, referring to the TV newsroom interview. "That baldy pensioner with a face like a slapped arse?"

"No, you dummy," said Kane. "He's the big-shot guy from Whiz-Go America. I didn't say Erin's *uncle* was on. Just said it was about Orchid."

Rupert Frith was saying, "... neither were any members of the Brazilian government available for comment. So let's get this straight, Clark. The US has no problem with the exploitation of the Amazon? You don't care?"

"Now, hold your horses," said Clark Jefferson. "I never said diddly-squat about not caring. But we've got a business to run. Anyways, the Amazon's no stranger to exploitation. It's a big forest. It can stand a little topiary."

"Topiary?" said Rex Peach, the environment minister. "Shall I quote from these emails again? The 18th of June. Four days ago. Dom Lockwood to Larry Bratwurst. 'Hi, Larry. You can relax about the California pilot program and the proposed US-wide roll-out. Together, we're free-wheeling to outrageous success. No corner of the Amazon should be seen as beyond utilisation. Relevant Brazilian politicians and business leaders are now in my pocket ...' Oh, and here's one he sent to *you*, Clark – "

"Those emails are private," said Clark, "and you're taking them completely out of context. You're playing cheap and dirty. The special relationship between our nations used to be better than this. Anyways, I saw you in the House of Commons coverage this morning, Mr Rex 'Learjet' Peach, spouting off about Orchid being good for Britain, good for jobs, good for the economy."

"And I stand by those statements. But I want to see appropriate regulation. I want to see Black Orchid UK using exclusively British-grown beef, and the US – "

"Legally," said Clark, "the US is doing nothing wrong."

Rupert Frith laughed and tossed his leonine head.

"Legally?" he said. "What about ethics? Can't you ramp up production in Texas? Do you really need to sanction the death-knell for the Amazon?"

"Here's the thing, Rupert," said Clark. "We *do* have plans to up homeland production, but the projected *scale* required by Orchid is just ... well, it's *big*. Needs room to flex its limbs. And let's not lose sight of the wider economic benefits. The Brazilian's are happy bunnies, too. Those cattle farmers in the rainforest, they've been restricted for decades. Reduced to sucking a living out of an old sock by collecting namby-pamby herbs and shit for the homeopathic industry. Their livelihoods are now set to be improved many times over. We at Whiz-Go America – soon to be Black Orchid America – we believe that we can offer global solutions with this business enterprise. Is that so wrong? Is it unethical?"

"Yes," said Peach. "It's unethical and – "

"All right," said Frith. "We're short on time, and we still need to fit in a disturbing undercover report that concerns Orchid."

Rex Peach and Clark Jefferson both looked puzzled.

"I'm not easily shocked," said Frith dramatically, "but our undercover footage is too horrific to put on air ..."

26

MRM

"The report shows that the working practices of Orchid UK's meat suppliers border on the sinister. To quote our man, conditions endured by cattle 'make the average factory-farm look like a Butlin's for fun-loving heifers'."

"Despicable," said Nisha.

With glistening eyes and a trembling lip, Frith glanced off-camera, then back again, affecting a brave smile – the news presenter who has to carry on no matter what; but it was so obvious that he was faking. His floppy fringe had fallen over one eye and he left it there in martyred dishevelment.

"I can also report that it seems Orchid simply wants to 'get the cow into the burger by the shortest possible route'. Apart from the usual gutting, and the removal of head, hide, tail and hooves, the whole animal is fed into an MRM machine. So much for the 'prime cuts' we're led to believe – "

"Easy, tiger," said Clark. "If a handful of dodgy outfits in the UK – "

"Not a handful, Clark. Every trail our undercover man followed from Orchid restaurants to their meat suppliers, it was the same picture. Cattle raised in atrocious conditions; then this mysterious fast-tracking from abattoir to MRM facility."

"Well ... I don't know about that," said Clark. "That Dom Lockwood, he's a real English gent and a good egg. I can't see him being in the loop over something like that, assuming there's a shred of truth in it. But let's be clear. It wouldn't happen on mine and Larry's watch across the Atlantic."

"All right, we have to leave it there," said Frith. "To sum up: allegations of malpractice and cruelty hanging over Orchid suppliers ..."

"What's an MRM machine?" said Josh.

"Stands for Mechanically Recovered Meat," said Erin. "It's that horrible greasy pink stuff that comes in tins."

"Easy-Meat," said Josh. "I really like Easy-Meat, me. I usually fry it in butter and dob loads of brown sauce on it. Or mustard."

"Wouldn't be as keen if you knew how it was made."

"Go on, then. Tell us."

"Okay," she said. "After they've butchered the animal into all the various cuts that go to the supermarkets and the catering industries, what's left – the fat, gristle, sinews, even the skeleton – it gets loaded into this metal container. There's a kind of grid or mesh at the front, and the back wall slides in on hydraulics. Squashes the carcass through the grid. The stuff that oozes out is what goes in the tins you buy off the shelves."

An expression of shock passed over Josh's face, then he smirked and said, "Sounds okay to me. I wouldn't mind a visit to the Easy-Meat factory. I'd just stand in front of that grid thing with my mouth open."

Kane and Logan laughed. Erin exchanged grimaces with Nisha.

Then Kane's dad put his head around the door to tell Nisha he had to go out in ten minutes and would be happy to run her home. It was nine thirty. Dusk was gathering in Thistledown Valley. Since Erin's house was in the same direction, she agreed to leave her bike behind and accept a lift herself.

Nothing like giving yourself a deadline, she thought. As soon as Kane's dad was out of earshot, she took a deep breath and dived straight in.

"I was wondering if you lot might be interested in helping out with another sort of demo. Er, more like an *operation*, really ... Like nothing you've ever imagined, probably, but I need your help. You, too, Nisha."

"Yeah?" said Nisha. "Great. I always knew there was something ultra-cool about you on the quiet, Erin. If you need help busting people like Vern Hawkes, count me in. As long as we don't get arrested."

"We won't get arrested. It's impossible for us to be linked in any way. But it's to do with the Orchid company. And my uncle."

"Orchid?" said Josh. "What've *they* done wrong? Oh, wait. I get it. The meat suppliers. The factory farming report we just heard about? So maybe you should go for *them*? Not Orchid. Or else it's like targeting some department store because they import their products from child-labour sweat-shops in China or India or somewhere. That don't mean the shops are blameless or nothing. But you have to go for the jugular."

"Yeah, fair point, Josh. But as bad as the report on factory farming was, it's not what this is about. Or, not directly. And, I promise you, Orchid *is* the jugular. I can't explain everything at once. First thing is, don't touch any more Orchid products. I know it's easier for me and Nisha, being vegetarians – "

"What?" said Josh. "Give up burgers? I knew it! I knew she was planning to turn us all into wussy veggies – "

"I didn't say you have to give up meat. Not even burgers. Just listen a second. All I'm saying is, don't get them from Orchid."

"But they're the best."

"No. That's hypnotism. And that's the other thing: don't watch any more Orchid adverts. They'll only strengthen the hypnosis you're already under."

"I don't believe in hypnosis," said Josh.

"*I* do," said Logan.

"How could I be hypnotised if I don't believe in it?" said Josh. "What are you planning to do? Rescue all the moo-cows and chuck your uncle into an MRM machine to teach him a lesson?"

"Just shut up and listen," said Kane. "You trusted Erin before, and look what happened. Vern Hawkes got nailed."

"Yeah, and I wanna be part of nailing her uncle, but only if he deserves it. Is it just the Orchid thing, or is he a paedo or summat?"

"I need you to trust me," said Erin.

Josh scowled and sniffed; then he nodded.

"I *do* trust you," he said. "You're cool."

From Josh, that was flattering, and she felt herself blush. Nor was she comfortable being the centre of attention, but her confidence was growing.

"Believe me," she said. "Uncle Dom has to be stopped."

"We'll stop him," said Logan. "He'll be sorry he messed with *us*!"

"Sorry he messed with us?" said Kane. "He doesn't even know who the rest of us are. How can he be *sorry* he messed with us?"

"Yeah, well ... I'm just saying, ain't I?"

Nisha had to turn her head to hide her amusement.

"So what's the 'operation'?" said Josh. "Where are you even getting this stuff from? You working for the animal rights equivalent of MI5?"

"I know how weird it seems," said Erin. "But I don't want to say too much yet about ... about my sources."

"*Sources?* You're *fourteen*. What's going on with you?"

"We'll be targeting Orchid directly," she said. "Striking a ... a killer blow to its nerve-centre. We're going to take down the whole company."

On his sofa, Josh flipped from his back to his belly, buried his face in a cushion and screamed with laughter.

Even Kane, Logan and Nisha looked at Erin as if she was off her trolley. Kane summed up the collective feeling: "Take down the whole of Orchid? Just like that? And not be arrested or linked to it in any way?"

"Yeah," she said.

Then Kane's dad put his head around the door again.

"You lot planning a bank robbery?" he said. He was smiling so it seemed unlikely he'd heard very much. "Meet you at the car, girls? One minute."

"Okay, Mr Whitman," said Nisha.

"Thanks, Mr Whitman," said Erin.

She waited until his footsteps had faded along the hall.

"If I told you any of the details now, I doubt if you'd believe a word of it. So instead of telling you, I'm going to show you."

"Show us what?" said Kane. "When?"

"Everything. Tonight."

"Oh," said Nisha, "I have to go straight home. I won't be able to – "

"Me too," said Logan. "It's not far off ten."

"Tonight's over," said Josh.

"No," she said. "Tonight's only just beginning."

27

Initiates & Veterans

The sunflower-yellow ceiling was inches from her face. She'd done it. Taken herself through the deepening layers of physical and mental relaxation, plumbing right to the brink of sleep while remaining conscious. Then willed herself *up* ... and *out*. Not allowing doubt to creep in. Suspending herself in the "leap of faith" moment.

Now her dream body was bobbing up near the ceiling. In the light from the streetlamps, entering the gaps around the curtains, she saw where the edge of the yellow ceiling met the Kandinsky wall. She thought about looking down, and the thought itself caused her to roll over in the air.

About seven feet below was an empty bed with the covers thrown aside. She willed herself down to the floor, to the chair where a pile of clothes were neatly folded. Her movements felt clumsy, but she was gaining control. A minute later, she'd swapped her silky white pyjamas for combats and a tee-shirt.

At the door, she stroked the thermal cloak Kree had given her, but decided to leave it behind. She didn't want to risk losing it or getting it ruined.

Erin reached for the door handle, then paused. Although important work awaited, she couldn't resist checking something ... She shifted to her bedroom in the physical world. A sleeping copy of her lay at an angle in the bed. The left arm, in a dark-green pyjama sleeve, was flung across the pillow. Under the closed eyelids, the eyes made darting, searching movements. It was more shocking than she'd expected, seeing her physical body from an outside viewpoint. She backed away, locking her fingers into her masses of hair.

Instead of the cloak hanging on the door, it was now the embarrassing quilted dressing-gown, a gift from two

189

birthdays ago, which she occasionally wore to avoid hurting Mum's feelings. In her distraction, she stumbled.

An odd cloying resistance passed through her. It put her in mind of roughness and fibres and scratchy old cupboards from childhood. She looked around. Not only was she on the other side of the closed door, but she was buried up to her midriff in the landing floorboards. From her parents' room, she heard Mum's distinctive rhythmic breathing and Dad's ragged snores. The scratchy fibrous sensation continued as she sank the rest of the way into the landing. She popped out through the hall ceiling.

As she glided to the floor, she heard piano music and realised that she must have slipped back into the Dreamscape.

The music stopped.

"Is that you, Erin?" her "mother" called from the living-room.

Maybe Erin should say hello or something? It was night, so she could hardly say good morning. What did they say here?

"Er, yes, it's me," she called. "I was just going out for a bit. Okay?"

"Fine. See you later."

The street was busy with dreamers; the night air had its familiar sparkle.

At the front of the house, her wolves were waiting.

Right, she thought. Nisha first. And Erin knew she should be disciplined enough to make an instantaneous shift – knew Kree would disapprove of anything less – but the look of recognition and affection in the eyes of the lead wolf were too much. Erin tousled the rough, golden-grey fur of his head. He groaned contentedly, nuzzled her then loped off, the others tearing after him.

As the last of them brushed past her legs, her dream body snapped to attention and she shot forward, as if she'd been scooped up by an invisible sleigh. Fifty wolves sailed ahead to the T-junction. They didn't turn left or right. Just kept on going. Across the road. Into the air. Up, up, above the gardens and houses and rooftops, straight into the starlit sky.

Over Crow Woods they all flew, with Erin at the rear. Over the dark landscape beyond, eerie-looking in the light of the waning crescent moon.

Faster and faster. Higher and higher. Vertigo made her nerve-endings fizz and her stomach flip. She smiled and laughed with the exhilaration. They were going so fast that her vision blurred and her thoughts reeled. She worried that she'd lose her grip on consciousness, be sucked under by the powerful lure of sleep and dreams. She had to stay alert. Had to picture Nisha, Nisha ...

Annoyingly, somebody else's face kept intruding.

Then her mind *did* go blank. For how long, she didn't know. When awareness returned – in a head-spinning rush – the wolves had gone, and she was high above the Earth. Hundreds of miles below, the blue planet was gradually turning. Continents and oceans and weather systems were laid out in a vision of such beauty, she almost cried. Then she saw Josh, drifting close by, smiling as he gazed down on the blue Earth. Josh? What was *he* doing here? She willed herself over to him and gripped the snakeskin jacket he wore.

"Wake up," she said.

It seemed a strange thing to say to somebody whose eyes were open. He turned to her and his happiness intensified. His irises were such a deep shade of brown that she couldn't make out where the pupils began. His eyes were stunning. *Wasted on him!*

"Erin!" he said. "You're really something, you know."

She could tell that he was still dreaming.

"Er, Josh. Wake up."

He brushed a strand of hair from Erin's cheek and let his fingertips trail down her neck. She caught her breath as he touched her skin. Something glowed and rippled in her chest. The feeling spread all over her.

Josh buried his fingers in her hair, caressed the nape of her neck and the back of her head. His eyes half closed as he moved his lips towards hers.

"Er, wake up," she said. "We're not ... I don't ..."

Then Josh looked puzzled.

"Are you awake?" she said.

"Wha – ?"

He stared down at the majestic Earth, then back at her. He jerked away from her, like a kite pulled on its string. There was a risk, she knew, that the shock would be too much, that he could wake to the physical world instead of waking to the Dreamscape. So she caught up with him and had no choice but to grasp his hands in hers – the "anchoring" technique Kree had talked about.

"It's real," she said. "I said I had something to show you. Said you might not believe me. And this is it."

Josh cast about apprehensively and struggled against her grip.

"I ... was dreaming," he said. "I wanted to ... We ... Er, then I dreamed about flying and ... What's going on?"

"Don't let go," she said. "As long as you hang on to me and try to relax, you'll be okay. I'll explain everything. Don't worry. We'll find one of the others soon. Nisha first. Keep holding on ..."

The night was a blur of hard work and perseverance. Based on Josh's scepticism about so many things, Erin thought he'd have the most difficulty with the "leap of faith" required for waking dreams, yet he excelled – he even claimed he'd already had similar experiences that he'd never told anyone about.

The next day, they were all texting her or seeking her out at breaks, bombarding her with questions. There was also more bitchiness to deal with from Paige, Madison and Beth, over Nisha joining Kane's band. Considering Nisha had been kicked out of Pink Ocean first, it defied logic, but Paige made sure the story on the gossip circuit had Nisha cast as the traitor.

When Erin got home that evening, her mum was ill. The doctor had prescribed tablets for chronic indigestion and acid, but she still had to give the operatic society a miss. After Erin had made the apology phone call for her, Mum said, "You're a good girl. And I suppose I shouldn't be nagging you to come back to the society, when all you want to do is sing in a pop group."

"Rock, Mum. We're a rock band."

"Rock, then. What's it called, this rock band?"

"It used to be called Big Red Baboon's Bum."

"Delightful!"

"But we've been trying to think of a new name, and we're still not sure, but Nisha had a good idea. We think we might call ourselves The Source."

"The Sauce?" said Dad with a chuckle. "Is that brown sauce or red sauce? Or is it maybe parsley sauce?"

"Ha ha, Dad," she said.

Then he phoned for the usual order and an Orchid takeaway was soon delivered. Despite being ill, Mum helped Dad demolish it. Ten minutes later, she had to take some of her tablets and go upstairs to lie down.

When they met in the Dreamscape that night, Erin emphasised the importance of training, but all too often the others whizzed off on their own adventures and she had to find them. Late into the night, she gave them their first glimpse of Chthonia and revealed the details of the operation. Then she told Josh about his role of teaching everybody some moves with the swords. He was pleased about this, and modest, but had other concerns.

"This Kree character," he said. "How do we know he's genuine? I mean, he's obviously got you worked up."

"It's not like that," she said.

"No? What's it like, then? The rest of us don't know nothing about him and we're supposed to trust him? Why can't you set up a meeting?"

"I told you that's not possible. But we can trust him. I promise. His people are really special. They're a lot like humans and ..."

Josh's expression darkened.

"Yeah. Like I said. He's got *you* worked up."

Erin ignored him. She just hoped Kree was right when he'd said they'd probably be in and out of the town hall without so much as a skirmish.

In the small hours of the morning, she took some time out for herself while the others practised entering the Dreamscape at will.

With only three days to go before the joint operation, she was desperate to see Kree. Maybe he was right about them being too far removed from one another's separate realities, about it not being possible to be together. Maybe he was right about that ... And she didn't want to put anybody's safety at risk, but she'd thought of a way to get a tiny bit of reassurance for herself.

Having made a shift into the physical world, she pictured his face – the perfection of his mahogany skin, his large eyes whose amber tones fluctuated with subtle changes in light. She felt herself sinking into the ground. An immediate transfer had been her plan, but it wasn't happening. She concentrated harder, continued sinking, and was startled by the uncomfortable experience of her dream-self intermingling and passing through cold earth and clay. Deeper, she sank ... but slow ... slow ... slower. Everything slowing down. Coldness, darkness and pressure closing in.

Then she stopped moving, and a wave of fear crashed over her. She was inside the bedrock, encased in stone. She tried to move but was paralysed ...

A small, silent scream was shaped in her throat.

Her mind exploded with ideas and concepts. She saw vivid, cartoon-style representations of atoms, the electrons buzzing around the nuclei. Something came back to her from one of Mr Tomlinson's physics classes.

"All things in nature began their existence in the hearts of stars. From a tree to a stone to the air we breathe – every atom, including all the atoms of our bodies, was forged by stars and supernovae. We're made of star-dust. 'Star stuff', as Carl Sagan used to say."

Then she was aware again of the crushing bedrock. But the fear had left her. She understood that she wasn't really trapped. It was psychological. So she calmed herself and didn't attempt to move. She visualised Kree's face, remembering his looks of tenderness in unguarded moments, his intoxicating earthy smell.

She thought only of arriving ... of being wherever *he* was ... The pressure lifted. She was free. Her sense of orientation shifted, then cool air caressed her skin.

She was standing by the wall of a tunnel lit by soft, bluish light. There was a faintly acrid smell, and a trickle of water somewhere.

Close enough to touch, Kree and eight companions laboured along single-file. Like him, a few were young. Most were white-haired, ancient, and three of these ancients carried torches – long-handled with a wire cage that contained glowing chunks of rock. The word "phosphorous" flitted into Erin's thoughts.

At the front of the line, Kree stopped and raised a hand. Erin froze. The silence was total. Then her ears detected the almost imperceptible crackle of the torches.

"I told you we couldn't meet," said Kree.

He knew she was here! Could he see her?

"I ... I'm sorry," she said.

There were no signs that he'd heard. He wasn't even looking at her. He might as well have been addressing his comrades.

"Don't worry," he said. "Everything is going to plan ..."

He looked tired and his voice had a catch in it. "Going to plan" sounded like a massive overstatement hiding a stark, unbearable truth.

She remembered him saying originally that there were seventeen of his people left, and she knew that five had fallen recently.

There were only nine here now, not twelve ...

"Go, Erin," he said, his voice stronger.

He began walking again, and the others filed after him. Before he passed from view, Erin saw that his eyes were moist and there was a quiver around his lips. He walked on determinedly, but his shoulders were hunched. It looked as if he were leading the last of his people towards annihilation.

Erin's throat felt swollen. Pain filled her chest.

She watched until the last bluish glimmer from the torches had faded into the tunnel. For a while, she leaned against the rock wall in the darkness, then she closed her eyes and formed an image of her bedroom.

28

Across The Lines

Pre-dawn light seeped in at the edges of the curtains, and the magnolia walls were coffee-toned in the gloom. Erin turned away from the sight of her physical body huddled under the bedcovers. She tried not to think about Kree's distress. It was too upsetting. Instead, she thought about some of the moments of laughter they'd shared, and how it had felt to be in his arms.

Then she took a deep breath, stood up straighter and made the shift to the Dreamscape. The corner of a different curtain billowed softly in a breeze at the open window. A different pre-dawn light cast the colourful geometric wall-patterns into dusky visibility. The unmade bed was empty.

The digital clock on the desk showed 4.10.

At four thirty, she had to be at Wembley. In his new role, Josh's activities had led to an arrangement with the Dreamscape people who controlled the stadium, and he'd fixed it to meet there for sword-skill workshops.

Erin sat at the desk and switched on the lamp. She'd been curious about the sleek computer with its lilac veneer and peripherals. As she searched for an on-button, she discovered a slim silver book tucked behind the monitor. It was a diary ... She opened it and saw handwritten text in a flowing script.

Trying to convince herself that she was only having a quick peek, she found the most recent entries. And because she had no conscious knowledge of this "other" life, except for fragments of conventional dreams, it still felt like prying.

" ... thinking about breaking it off with Surinder, he's so anti-social all of a sudden, and self-obsessed ..."

197

"Had that dream again, about the rock band. I'd love to sing, but I believe you have to stick to what you're best at. Carla says my *Aqua Crimson* is good enough for a season at the gallery! And I've got this zappy idea for ..."

"... still can't believe Uncle Dom's gone. It's totally cruel and unfair. He was the best. Keep thinking of all the times he took me to the National Ballet ..."

Unable to bear any more, Erin let the book drop from her fingers. She began to form a mental picture of Wembley Stadium.

Then she heard a woman sobbing downstairs. Her "mother"? Erin told herself that she should just go. It was nothing to do with her, was it? But her curiosity, and mostly her concern took her out to the landing. She peered over the banister and saw her parents in the hall. Mum was crying her eyes out.

Erin went down a few stairs and stopped again. It was impossible to think of these people as anyone other than Mum and Dad.

"... fresh packet of sticking-plasters," Dad was saying in gentle, supportive tones. "And, look! Some nice gloves."

"Don't care," sobbed Mum. "Every nail's broken!"

"There, there. I packed sandwiches, too. Er, we really should go. They won't wait, and if we miss a shift ..."

Both were dressed in the grey ragged clothes that everybody wore in Chthonia. But why? This was the Dreamscape.

"... we'll be in serious trouble," said Dad, as he guided Mum through the doorway with a hand in the small of her back.

The door closed. Erin hurried downstairs. Through the frosted glass, she watched their fuzzy shapes receding, then she went after them. As she reached the low gate at the end of the path, she saw them walk into thin air. One second, they were trudging along the pavement, the next they'd faded out of existence.

Erin visualised the street similar to how it was, but with everything dilapidated and slipshod; with broken houses and broken people.

It worked. None of it looked quite how she'd imagined, but she was definitely in Chthonia.

In the punishing heat, sweat sprang from her every pore. A neighbourhood hell unfolded before her eyes. A rough similarity of layout was recognisable, but nothing else. There were flaming braziers and bonfires, and row upon row of shanty homes, cobbled together with rocks and sticks and corrugated-iron. Clouds of acrid smoke wafted about. Between the shanties, a narrow road swam with mud and rubbish. A large black dog ran past with a squealing rat clenched in its bared fangs.

Approximately where Erin had seen her parents disappear, they'd now reappeared, and were picking their way through the mud towards an ox-cart. It was so crammed with workers that she couldn't see the driver's seat, where she knew a skerra would be sitting with his whip. From the back of the ox-cart, the hands of other ragged workers reached out to help her parents aboard.

"Mum?" said Erin. "Dad?"

"How did *you* get here?" said Dad. "You're not supposed to ... No, don't come any nearer. Go away."

But Erin went to the back of the cart.

"Hide yourself!" said Mum. "We haven't declared you. We lied. You'll get us thrown in the dungeons."

"Dungeons? No. Listen. You don't even have to go to the factory. All you have to do is wake up. You're ... you're having a nightmare."

The cart lurched away.

"Go home," called Dad in a low, urgent voice.

"No, Dad. Listen."

"Go home, if you can get back there, and hide yourself in the shed."

"Sssh!" warned one of the other workers.

The ox-cart gathered speed, its creaky wooden wheels leaving ruts in the mud.

There was nothing Erin could do. In confusion, she raised a hand and her "parents" waved back.

She sensed that it might be a bad idea to linger.

"Girl!" came a voice. "Here. Over here."

A woman with matted hair was calling from outside a shanty. Her pretty face was etched with worry and she was cradling a bundle.

"Here, girl," she said. "Please help."

"Er, hello," said Erin, approaching warily.

"Take him," said the woman, holding out the bundle.

The baby had a grubby face and a hollow look in his eyes. A foul odour rose from the swaddling rags. Erin almost accepted the baby automatically.

"That's it. Good girl. Just take him."

"Sorry, I ... no."

"Please. Oh, please. You ain't got a clue. My hubby, he's working triple shifts. It'll kill him. Me – I gotta do one of them shifts, see? It's our only hope."

Erin shrank away, mumbling apologies.

"Just take the babe, eh?" said the woman, smiling weakly. "Take him for a couple o' weeks, till we get straight. What d'ya say? You're a good person, I can tell y'are. Little Ollie ain't no trouble."

"I'm really sorry. I can't look after him."

"Go on, get away with you, then," the woman said. "Toffee-nosed little slut! We don't want your sort round here. With your fancy clobber and fancy talk."

Erin closed her eyes and pictured Wembley.

She arrived in the middle of a vast amphitheatre. The dusty ground was stained with dried blood. A broken spear lay near by. The crude stone seating that swept up in every direction was deserted. Still in Chthonia ...

A moment of rapid refocusing and she was standing on neatly cropped turf. The stands of the stadium were empty, except for Josh's contact, who sat by himself, eating a hotdog as he watched the beginnings of the sword-play.

In the morning, Dad left early to go away with the accountancy firm for a two-day conference. Mum's stomach was still delicate and she was lying on the sofa sipping peppermint tea when the doorbell rang. Erin had been about to set off for school. It was the last thing she felt like doing, but as she'd told the others, it was important they all behave normally and avoid drawing attention to themselves. The caller was Logan. Standing beside his bike, slightly out of breath, he looked at Erin with a pathetic, lost-dog expression.

"Can I come in?" he said.

"Er, we should be getting to school."

"Please," he said. "I ain't got no-one to talk to. No-one like you."

She opened the door wider. Logan wheeled his bike in and leaned it against the wall, then Erin led him to the kitchen.

"Is your mum okay?" he said, sitting at the table.

"A build-up of acid. Too much rubbishy food. Orchid."

Logan's expression became fraught.

"Something bad's happened, Erin." He swallowed hard. "I crossed a line, and it's made me into a different person. I didn't know about the line. I crossed it without realising, and I don't know if I'll make it back over."

"Line? Are you talking about the operation?"

A violent sob convulsed his body. Erin placed a hand on his arm. Logan seized her fingers and brushed them with his lips.

"Sometimes … I really hate myself," he choked.

"What is it?"

He shook his head and stared at the floor.

"What is it? What's wrong, Logan? What's this line you've crossed?"

He sniffed. Any possibility of completely breaking down seemed to have passed, but his lost-dog expression was back.

"I've just been at the doctor's," he said. "She warned me last year. Told me I was clinically o-beast."

"You mean obese?"

"Yeah. They've got this thing called a BMI chart and she told me last year I was in the clinically o-beast sector. Today she told me I've crossed that line. Now I'm *morbidly o-beast*. That's the line I'm talking about."

"Oh. I … I'm sorry, Logan."

"Still, it's good to have labels, ain't it?" he said with a crooked grin. "You know where you are with labels. I was cutting down … I was! I was cutting down before Orchid opened. Now I'm eating more than ever. Shovelling burgers and chips and crap into my fat idiot face. I can't stop. We have 'em for tea every night. Dad loves 'em. But I go out again later, by myself. And on nights when we have our meetings, or band practice, I go back to Orchid after. Buy another two, sometimes three. Sit outside on the pavement to eat 'em. Next to the litter bin or in the gutter. Just so I feel even worse about myself. Then I have to go round the back to spew up. And I'll start riding home then, pretending that that's it. But it's not it. It never is. I always turn round to go and get more."

"Er, I don't know what to say," she said. "You have to make sure you don't watch the advert any more – "

"You know where you are with labels. Clinically o-beast. That one's not too bad, is it? Sounds sort of scientific. Like there's still a bit of hope if you do what the doctor tells you. But morbidly o-beast. *Morbidly.*

Speaks for itself. You're done for. You're a write-off. Time to think about planning your own funeral."

His face began to pucker again.

"What am I gonna do?" he whispered.

Erin patted him on the arm.

"The doctor," said Logan, "she reckons that some people who are morbidly o-beast, they can just drop dead. I've got to go for this heart-trace thing. She said if I'm not careful … If I don't take drastic action … I could just … you know."

"Oh, Logan."

"I feel like a freak. It didn't help that Paige and Madison and Beth were taking the piss yesterday. Saying I'm the fattest in the school, and that our band shouldn't even bother to play at the contest, because we're crap."

"Their opinions don't mean a thing, Logan," she said. "Celebrity gossip and reality shows are the important things in their lives. They've said stuff to me in the past, and yeah, I've let myself believe it and felt bad. Still do, sometimes. But, Logan, these places that people try to take us to in our heads – they're not real. And you're not a freak. Or, if you are, I am too. Freaks who don't fit in. Good freaks. And the obesity thing … Okay, you need to follow the doctor's advice. But a line on a chart … It's invented. It doesn't change you. You're still you. No different from yesterday. You're still a great drummer and a great person."

"Tell you what, Erin. As true as I'm sitting here, I'll never touch another burger in my life. Never. Never."

29

Carried Away On White Wings

She'd dropped into the school library after history to check a reference. It took ten minutes, and by then most students had left the premises. When she got to the main entrance, an ambulance was parked outside.

A fine summer rain was falling. It was a hot, muggy day, and the classrooms had been stifling all afternoon. A few stragglers loitered about, gawping and gossiping and barely hiding their excitement. The rear doors of the empty ambulance hung open. Mrs Bolum, the deputy head, stood with folded arms and an indomitable face, presumably on guard as the paramedics went about their business in the school.

"Do you know what's going on?" Erin asked a lad with acne and bad teeth.

"Some girl. Went arse over tit down them stairs in C Block."

All the stone stairways in the building were divided into two flights, except for the very long ones at the far end of C Block. Handrails had been fitted years before, and warning signs emblazoned the walls.

Erin was about to walk away, not wanting to be just another "ghoul", when there was a clattering at the entrance. The head tutor a teaching assistant held the main entrance doors wide open while the paramedics brought the trolley through and wheeled it to the back of the ambulance.

The patient was covered up to the neck with a blanket. She lay very still. It was hard to tell what was wrong, but she might have been unconscious, or sedated, or ... It was Nisha! Erin rushed forward.

"Back, girl!" said Mrs Bolum, barring the way.

"What's happened?"

"She fell down the stairs. Everything's under control."

204

"I'm a friend, though. Nisha? *Nisha?*"

"If you're a friend," said Mrs Bolum with a steely look, "the best thing you can do for her now is stay out of the way and let the ambulance crew do its job."

Erin couldn't see what was happening. She heard an efficient voice giving instructions and another person responding. There were scraping and dragging sounds, and the distinctive clunk of the doors.

The ambulance sped away. The blue light and siren weren't being used at first, and she didn't know if that were a positive or negative thing. Then the blue light and siren burst into life.

Erin's heart thumped against her ribs.

She started tapping out a text to Nisha.

"... that psycho mate of Paige Sanderson's," a boy was muttering to his friend. "Beth something-or-other ..."

Erin caught up with them.

"What was that? Did you see Beth push Nisha down the steps?"

The lad with acne gave her a cocky grin. His shorter friend suddenly found his feet very interesting.

"If either of you saw anything, you should go and tell Mrs Bolum."

"We didn't see nothing," said the lad with acne.

"Beth. One of you mentioned Paige and Beth."

"We didn't say nothing about nobody. She fell down the C-Block steps, far as we know." He elbowed his friend. "Come on, T-Bone."

Erin sent texts to Josh, Kane and Logan. She was tempted to ring Nisha's landline number. Then she realised that she'd only add to the family's stress, even if they were home, and that the school would have informed them already.

The hospital was closer to the town centre. If she went there and inquired politely at reception, maybe they'd be able to tell her something?

With the idea of catching a bus from outside the station, she was about to cross the road when a gleaming white Porsche, with darkly tinted windows, pulled into the kerb. The passenger window slid smoothly down and, grinning across at her from the driver's seat, was Uncle Dom.

"Need a lift?"

"No...no. Thanks."

Still at the kerb, Uncle Dom revved the engine and it thrummed into life. He tapped his plump fingers on the steering wheel.

"Where are you going, Erin?"

"Er, nowhere."

She started to walk, but suddenly he was out of the car and on the pavement beside her with a swiftness that belied his far-from-nimble proportions.

"What do you think of the new motor?"

"I ... It's okay."

She tried to move around him, but he wouldn't let her. Tried to back away, but he'd encircled her wrist with his strong grip. His small dark eyes bored into her from their surrounding rolls of fat. He smelled of sweat, and of something harsher and more chemical. Bad aftershave?

"It's all right," he said gently. "I'm your uncle."

Erin looked around urgently. Where was everybody? It was an ordinary Wednesday afternoon, yet it was as quiet as a bank holiday. She thought about kicking him in the ankles or screaming out...

"Let's not have a scene. I'm your uncle. Your uncle. Your uncle ..."

His voice was tender and monotone.

"You've been having a bad time, Erin. All alone. Up against events and forces you barely understand. You're only a schoolgirl. Leave things to others."

She yanked her arm, but his grip was like iron.

"I don't want a lift, and I've got to go."

Uncle Dom smiled and opened the passenger door of the white Porsche.

"This baby goes like an absolute dream," he said. "I know a road in the countryside. A big, big dip. It goes all the way down for about a mile, then up the other side for another mile. A clear, open road, just inviting you to floor the accelerator. I hit the bottom of it this morning at a hundred and twenty-five, and I can tell you, my dear," – he let out a torrent of bubbling laughter – "when you're going down it and coming up the other side, it's exactly like being on a roller-coaster ..."

A lorry rumbled past.

Erin yanked her arm again, but he wouldn't let go.

She kicked him in the shins. He didn't react. She could see pedestrians now, not far away, but none seemed to care about the developing scuffle.

"Come on now, Erin, I'm your uncle!" he trumpeted, his teeth yellow, his breath meaty.

Then Erin was bundled roughly and efficiently into the passenger seat. The smell of new leather pervaded the interior. She began to scream, but something wet and linty was pressed over her nose and mouth. She struggled, but it was as if a switch had been thrown.

Her mind was numbed. Her limbs went floppy.

Disconnected thoughts flowered in her head. The chemical smell she'd detected ... It hadn't been bad aftershave. No. Unravelling. Everything unravelling. Well, of course ... they have to use chloroform when they take you away. Standard procedure. Yes, I understand now, Mr Tomlinson. Never enter an Ames Room without your rose-tinted sunglasses. Ah, what's that you say? To sleep ... perchance ... Soft leather against her cheek. What a car! What a car for a silly little Rich Bitch. *Push me in the car, you can push me in the car ~ But you better make sure it's Porsche-ah ...* Rich smell of new leather. Rich bitch ... poor cow. Used to be a cow, this leather. Cow's face, laughing. *La Vache Qui Rit* ...

Then she was flying high above a barren landscape.

She didn't really care, and there was nothing she could do anyway.

The wind was caressing her face and blowing through her hair.

Talons gripped her tight around the waist ...

If she looked up, she could see the hard eyes and hooked beak of an eagle, a giant white eagle carrying her away. Many miles in the opposite direction, she knew that Nisha was being carried off by another white eagle.

Far, far away from one another. The distance between them increasing with every passing moment. Every wing-beat. White wings. The white wings of death. Where had she heard that expression? Didn't death carry you away on white wings?

Was she dead, then? Were they both dead?

30

The Power Of The Brand

Amid the reek of leather, she felt confused and weak and had a thumping headache. As her vision cleared, a blur of black and orange swam into focus. The Orchid brand. Uncle Dom's device was ten inches from her face.

Her right arm was twisted awkwardly, trapped against the seat. She struck out with her left. There was little strength behind the action, but the device flew from his hand and went skimming into the back.

He gave her a disappointed look.

Through the tinted windows, she glimpsed fields and hedgerows, a grey block of sky. Her thought processes were sluggish. She tried to sit forward.

"It's all going to be okay," he said.

Then he clamped her head in his hands. And his eyes rolled back in their sockets. On each of the bulging white orbs, the orchid-and-sun image appeared.

She screwed her eyes tight shut. No good. While still clamping her head, he was able to transfer his thumbs and index fingers to force her eyelids open.

Erin attempted to strike out again, but her movements were so weak. Her will was being drained by the power of the brand.

"It's been a long struggle," said her uncle. "It's time to rest now."

The twin images converged into a single image. The flaming orange sun spat out its prominences and flares; the petals of the black orchid rotated anticlockwise. Erin was falling. Falling into the fiery depths of the sun. Its gravity was phenomenal. Impossible to resist.

And there was something beautiful about the idea, too. The idea of simply giving herself up to the sun. The sun didn't lie, and it was promising great happiness followed by oblivion, a painless annihilation in its living furnace.

What could be better? It was where everybody and everything had originated from, after all. Star dust. Nothing more, nothing less.

Abruptly, the hologram was extinguished.

She felt almost sorry. But it was okay. Uncle Dom was here, smiling. He'd been right. Everything *was* going to be fine. No more struggling.

"Good," he said. "Let's get you back to town."

He settled himself behind the wheel and secured his seatbelt. As they pulled out of the lay-by, Erin checked her own belt, but it had been done up already.

The windows slid down with a friendly whirring.

"We could put the air-con on," he said, "but it'd be a criminal shame not to enjoy the country air." He breathed in noisily through his nose and exhaled with a happy sigh. "So clean and fresh. And this light summer rain's so nice, isn't it?"

"Yes. So nice."

Fields and meadows flashed by. Tall grasses changed colour as they swayed and undulated: pale green, dark green, grey. Along the waysides, cow parsley stood four feet high, its flowering white tops nodding in the breeze. Curtains of fine rain fell across the road. Erin smiled as every now and then a dash of rain caught her in the face. It reminded her of something. Hadn't she sat near a fountain a long time ago, and experienced a similar sensation? By a fountain with a friend. Spray wafting into her face. She couldn't place the memory now. It was like a deeply buried dream. Nothing important.

"Here we are!" said her uncle. "Hold tight."

Ahead, the road swept down in a monstrous dip that went on and on.

There were no other vehicles in sight, and Uncle Dom accelerated abruptly. Erin felt herself being pushed back into the seat. The Porsche had already been travelling fast, but now it was doing over a hundred miles per hour and still accelerating. Erin's stomach was churning by the time they reached the bottom of the dip, but she smiled and laughed.

"A hundred and forty!" her uncle yelled with delight.

The car was so powerful that it was halfway up the other side before it even began to slow down. It was like flying. Erin felt as if she'd become detached from the world altogether ... She had a memory of a white eagle carrying her away. When had that been? Oh, yes: she fainted or something, didn't she? And then dreamed about an eagle. It had seemed important at the time ...

Uncle Dom laughed loudly. At the same time, he swung his meaty hand up and across. The hand hovered. For a moment, it looked as if it might float down and settle on Erin's leg, but then he coughed and returned it to the wheel.

"Just a funny old uncle and his favourite niece," he said cheerily. "Out for a country drive. What a lovely time we've had."

"Yes," she said. "Lovely."

They cruised by an abandoned industrial zone. Over a wire fence, hunks of rusted metal and machinery parts lay about. Weeds and grass grew in clutches, but mostly the ground between the defunct hardware was barren.

"Bit hot and muggy," said Uncle Dom. "Perhaps I'll close the windows and put the air-con on after all. Or ... No, I'll just take my jacket off."

While keeping the car on course with his substantial gut wedged against the bottom of the wheel, he undid his seatbelt and struggled out of his jacket.

They passed through the outlying villages. Green Dalby, Pressflower, Woodchurch, then came to the edge of Everdene. Now they rounded the southern perimeter of Crow Woods and joined the main drag.

Erin couldn't help admiring the craftsmanship of the Porsche. Every surface she touched felt rich and good. It must have cost tens of thousands.

They passed the polytechnic, the hospital ... Hospital? A thought almost bubbled to the surface. Wasn't somebody ... a friend ... ?

A minute later, they'd turned into Cank Street and pulled over.

"I would have dropped you at the newly acquired High Street branch," he said. "But I thought this'd be more appropriate. You missed out when it first opened. You'll get served nice and quick, too. Plenty of staff."

"Oh...yes," she said. "I missed out when it opened."

"Good girl. Off you go, then. There's the entrance. Interesting word, *entrance*. Don't you think?" He laughed and repeated the word a few times, his voice sounding like a slowed-down recording: "Entrance. *En*-trance. En-*trance*."

Erin undid her seatbelt and found the door-catch.

"Take these," said her uncle.

He pushed a wad of vouchers towards her, and the instant she saw what they were, she grabbed at them.

"Tut tut," he said. "Rude to snatch."

"Sorry," she said, clutching the precious vouchers and swinging her feet to the ground. "Thanks, Uncle Dom."

He patted her on the head like a dog.

"What are uncles for? If not to spoil their favourite nieces? Go on, then."

As she hurried away, the Porsche took off down the road. Erin watched it go for a second, then made for the entrance. She hadn't eaten a burger in years, and she *really* wanted one.

People stood outside, chatting happily over their takeaways. Erin felt a kinship with them – felt as if they could all be close friends just waiting to meet her. It was the smell, too; it gave her a warm fuzzy feeling. Surely, there couldn't be a more welcoming smell in the world? The hot sizzling fat, the savoury burger tang hitting a spot at the back of the nose and throat. Even the damp concrete, the exhaust fumes – it was the smell of the town centre, her rightful home.

Closer, she found two organised queues, one going in, the other coming out, both moving fast. Inside, all tables were occupied, mostly by noisy families and groups of teenagers. Parents and children crammed burgers and fries into their mouths. Very young children and even babies were being encouraged to do the same, their squeals of protest ignored. And in the aisles between the orange plastic tables, the clown-outfitted waiters rushed about with orders.

"Excuse me, *madam*," said a waitress cattily. "Voucher holders over there, if you don't mind. *Please.*"

Paige was almost unrecognisable. Her face was thickly made-up. She wore a bowler hat, baggy trousers with braces, and an Orchid logo tee-shirt.

"I suppose you'll be working here as well soon, Lockwood? With it being your uncle's company? It's okay, but the kids are like a virus. Send me absolutely insane. Anyway, just so long as you realise some of us were here before you. There's a pecking-order. Dom's made me supervisor of the junior staff. At *both* branches. So you might as well get it straight in your stupid little head: your first job will be cleaning the loos. Right?"

"Oh ... I suppose ... If you're the supervisor."

"That's right. Now. Voucher holders are being served at the Voucher Counter, if you please, *madam.*"

At that moment, a child ran between them and tripped over Paige's size 23 clown shoes. The boy got to his feet, snivelling. Paige seized him by the arm, leaned close and gritted, "Watch where you're going, brat!"

Then she turned, cupped her hands under chin and smiled at a family on a nearby table.

"Could I bring something to your attention, sir and madam? You've been chosen by our Happy Family Team, via the CCTV. They thought you looked like such a nice family. So Orchid would like to offer you a special deal on another round of burgers. It's buy one, get *four* free. Oh, what a lovely little girl! Did you colour that in all by yourself, sweetums?"

There were about twenty staff squashed in behind the Voucher Counter, and takeaway bags and money were changing hands at a dazzling rate.

"What can I get you, madam?" said a lanky boy.

"Oh, er, I'm not sure," said Erin.

"Mr Scrummy? Double-Decker Taste-Bud Heaven? In Your Face Burger? Black Orchid Special?"

"They all sound nice. I'll try a Special."

"Good choice! One? Two? Three?" The boy extricated some vouchers from her tight grip. "Go on. Why not have three? Spoil yourself."

"Okay," she laughed. "Three Specials, please."

"Coming riiight-up-aroooney!" the boy sang. "Luke, mate. That's three Specials for the lady."

On the way out with her takeaway, she recognised six more faces from school behind the plastered-on make-up. It looked fun – all the dressing-up, learning a script and meeting people. She'd be earning money, too. She couldn't think now why she'd turned down the offer of a job here. Still, Uncle Dom was a great big pussycat really; he'd surely give her another chance.

The light misty rain had stopped; the sun had broken through. Already a heat-haze was rising from the damp pavement.

Erin found a space among the crowds and slipped the first Special from its Polystyrene clamshell. Palate watering, stomach growling, she stripped away the greaseproof wrapper and raised the juicy-looking burger to her mouth.

This was going to be fantastic ...

31

Iron In The Soul

215

Before the burger completed its journey, it was swiped from her hand. In dumb surprise, she looked at the scattered halves of the sesame-seed bun and its filling on the pavement. Then she registered Josh standing there. She dipped into the takeaway bag again, but he swiped everything from her hands. Before she could rescue the bag, a boot came down to flatten it. Then she was pushed firmly against the narrow section of brick wall between Orchid and the chemist.

"Snap out of it," he said.

"Yeah," said Logan. "What d'you think you're doing?"

In his free hand, Josh held a burger himself. Now he threw it aside. Logan gathered the detritus from the pavement and deposited it, along with his own half-eaten burger, in a litter-bin.

"That's *really* it, now," he said tearfully. "I'm finished. I'm never eating any more burgers. Never, ever again. Seeing you like that, Erin ..."

She frowned. What were they talking about? She fingered the rest of the vouchers in her pocket and tried to scramble back to the entrance.

Josh grabbed her.

"No," he said, his face stern and his eyes burning. "I'm stopping now, and Logan's stopping now. And *you* – you're not even gonna start."

"We need you, Erin," said Logan. "The operation."

"Operation?" she said.

"In the Nightmare Realm ..." began Logan. He glanced from side to side, then lowered his voice. "You know. The operation you've been training us for. The generator ... Josh! We've lost her, Josh."

"No, we've not. Shut up a second. Erin?"

"Let go of me!" she said.

216

"Not till you cool it. There ain't no way we're letting you go back through that door. Give me them vouchers."

"What? No! They're mine! Get off! Please. I'll share. I *will*. I've got about twenty. We could ... No, Josh! They're mine! Don't you ... If you ..."

Josh had ripped up the vouchers and stuffed them in the bin.

"The end. Me and Logan ain't touching another, and *you're* a veggie anyway. Yeah, and even though I don't agree with veggie-ism, I know it means a lot to you. Right. So ..." He sniffed and rubbed a hand over his face.

"Well said, mate," said Logan. "Well said. Come on, Erin. We're supposed to be meeting Kane. You can't let us down now. Nisha's okay, by the way."

"Nisha?" she said, fighting to put her broken memories back together. "Oh, Nisha ... She fell down the ... stairs."

"She's okay," said Josh. "Been texting us. Bruises and that. And shock."

"But she's ... all right?" said Erin. "That's good." Her head was aching and it was like clawing her way through sand to form coherent thoughts. She felt as if *she*'d been the one to fall down a very long flight of steps.

"They wanted to keep her in overnight," said Logan. "She refused. Her dad and brother took her home."

"Doubt if she'll make it to Kane's ..." said Josh.

Erin checked her mobile. There was a text message: *Thanks for your kind words, babe. I'm doing fine. N xx.*

"We'd better get going," said Logan.

Erin glanced at the litter-bin and thought about her shredded vouchers. She considered the happy crowds. Then she took a step again towards the entrance of Orchid. *Entrance* ... And that smell ...

"I'm so hungry. Couldn't we get some takeaways? I've got money – "

"No," said Josh. "Not from Orchid. Snap out of it. Or we'll frog-march you away from here if we have to. Right, Logan?"

"Right. Let's get far away from this planet-trashing, Chthonia-sponsored cesspit."

At the garage, she still laboured under a cloud of mental paralysis as the boys elicited what they could of her story. Then Kane made cheese and tomato on toast for everyone. Erin ate a slice, but it tasted like warm soggy cardboard. She would have preferred to sit at one of those orange tables with a big fat Orchid burger. No. That was crazy thinking. Orchid was the enemy ...

"Is the toast all right, Erin?" said Kane.

"Not bad," Josh cut in, reaching for more. "Me, though, I'd have put Easy-Meat under the cheese before grilling it."

"*You'*d find a way of spoiling any dish," said Nisha from the open double-doors. Behind her, the pampas grasses were swaying in the breeze.

"Look who it's not!" said Kane.

"What's all the slacking about?" she said with a beaming smile. "I thought you'd have been warming up the instruments by now."

As rough as Erin felt, she was so happy to see Nisha. The girl looked fragile but determined in the ruby-red salwar kameez she sometimes wore.

Erin went to her, and they hugged.

"You really come for the rehearsal?" said Logan.

"Yeah, Lo. If you guys are still up for one. I've got about an hour before Dad comes back for me."

When she'd been updated on events, she told her own story of how she'd felt a hard, deliberate push just before falling down the C-Block stairs.

"Wonder if it's all connected," said Kane. "Erin?"

Erin hesitated. A flaming sun surrounded by black petals seared into her thoughts again. With an effort, she pushed it away. By slow degrees, the camaraderie of the group was eroding the hypnotic spell. Thanks to Josh and Logan, she'd been rescued from the brink. She was reaching a fairly safe point now. Powerful cravings kept gnawing at her, but she felt strong enough to fight them off – maybe even strong enough for what lay ahead.

In forty-eight hours, they had to perform in front of Uncle Dom and the other judges. Then, later, in the dead of night, they had a job to do in Chthonia.

"Erin?" repeated Kane. "I said I wonder if everything's connected?"

"I'm not certain. I doubt it, though. I think Uncle Dom's been on to *me* from the start, but what happened to Nisha is to do with the talent contest. I heard some boys talking outside the school. I think it was Beth who did the pushing."

"Paige and her mates all work for him now," said Josh. "He *could* have been behind it. Why not? He could know everything."

"Nah," said Kane. "Beth's always been a psycho. Anyway, I don't think we should practise tonight if Erin and Nisha don't feel up to it."

"Oh," said Erin. "I don't know. A rehearsal might help blow a few cobwebs away for all of us."

"Yeah," said Josh. "That's what we *need*. The music. To play together. Thrash into some numbers. Blow the cobwebs away."

But they chatted on, and the instruments stood idle.

"Me, Erin and Josh have got a pact now," said Logan. "No Orchid burgers. When we saw Erin about to eat one, that was it for me. I was shocked. Knew I had to give up, there and then."

"Not using Orchid goes without saying," said Kane. "And not watching any of the adverts. Erin told you that already."

"Erin's brilliant," said Nisha. "She holds this whole group together. She's stronger than anyone I know."

"Stronger than the brand," said Kane. "That's why the operation'll succeed on Friday."

Erin looked away. Then she said, "It's a mistake to think it'll be easy. It won't. It's going to be – "

"It's gonna be a nightmare," laughed Josh. "Literally."

In the background, the radio was playing the new Lily Raven song, "Iron in the Soul". Erin smiled. She remembered how everything had started – her uncle's supernatural recovery in hospital, the Dreamscape, Kree. It had been around the time of Lily Raven's last hit, "Dark Like Night".

When Erin had first heard "Iron in the Soul" a few days ago, she hadn't been impressed, but now it really spoke to her. It was a departure for Lily Raven. It didn't have any lyrics, just a lilting, dulcet voice, almost indistinguishable from the instruments; and the music was ethereal, not of this world. Erin was sorry when it ended and gave way to the DJ's hammy lines. Then came a gutsy number from Funnelweb, which had Kane reaching for his "air guitar".

While Erin's quiet mood continued, the conversation of the others strayed to their extra-curricular adventures in the Dreamscape.

"That stuff's for tourists," she said. "And it uses conscious energy that we need to conserve for Friday. I'm sorry if it's boring of me, but we have to limit our use of the Dreamscape to training." She felt herself flush. A few weeks ago, she'd had a lot less confidence speaking in social groups. Now she was telling everybody off!

"Friday," said Josh. "Why wait till Friday?"

"We've been over that," she said, more gently. "It's a new moon."

"I thought that was the worst time. In all the horror films, new moons are when all the bad stuff happens."

"You're thinking of a full moon, Josh," said Kane.

"What's the difference?"

"A new moon is when there's no moon. When it's completely in shadow."

"Okay, Mr Astronomer. Thanks for the heads-up. But I still don't see why we can't meet Kree. I prefer to meet someone before I trust 'em."

"If you trust me, you can trust him," said Erin. "Remember: way below the Earth, they're trying to make it to the lab for the new moon. They can't afford to stop and sleep, so Kree can't visit the Dreamscape. As well as that, the ... the *integrity* of the Dreamscape may even have been compromised."

"Yeah, there you go with your long words again," he snorted. "I was really starting to like you an' all."

"Leave it, Josh," said Kane.

"I just like to know what I'm dealing with, and *who* I'm dealing with. If the Dreamscape ain't safe, we could've been spied on while we've been training."

Erin fought back a growing shakiness and nausea. She could see the corrosive effect that Josh's words were having on the others.

"Or we could've been spied on in the physical world," continued Josh. "By Paige and her tame bitches, for example. Who's to say we might not be walking into a trap on Friday? So if we went in tonight ... Element of surprise."

32

Fudoshin

"We have to stick to the plan," said Erin. "There's too much at stake."

"Bollocks," said Josh. "What if the whole thing's a set-up? What if Kree's a double agent? He could be screwing us over! Could be a complete dickhead."

"You should just trust Erin," said Nisha.

"I *do* trust her. I *do*."

"Instead of all this swearing and being suspicious and negative, and behaving like a total numpty from the Claymore Estate."

"I *am* from the Claymore Estate!"

"Sorry," said Nisha. "I didn't know."

"So what's wrong with the Claymore Estate?" said Josh, though he had a playful smile on his lips.

"If you don't know the answer to that," laughed Nisha, "you're such a lost boy."

The trouble was, Erin couldn't deny that it was entirely possible the skerri knew about the joint operation.

"I still think we should go in sooner," said Josh.

"No," she said, sitting up straighter on the garage sofa.

Josh grinned down at her and said, "Just give me one good reason we should trust Kree. That's all I'm asking."

"Okay. Kree and his people – their brains are wired differently from ours. They just don't *do* deception or lies. Or violence. Except in self-defence. They're on the edge of extinction. Kree's lost almost everything. But considering the stresses he must be under, he's got this amazing calmness about him, a serenity ..."

There was a strange gleam in Josh's eyes. Was it jealousy? When he saw that Erin had noticed, he tried to cover it by laughing loudly.

"Sounds like you're describing my sensei," he said. "Is this Kree some ugly old dude, then? About eighty? Looks like Yoda from *Star Wars*?"

"Er, he's our age. But I don't think age works the same for them."

"He's *our* age?" said Josh, the gleam back in his eyes. He nodded slowly and added, "Something going on between you, is there?"

Logan shushed everybody and turned up the radio.

"... another mystery," a woman was saying, "is why Orchid supply chains don't go the way of other fast-food manufacturers: bulking up with sugar, salt and fats."

"Yes, why *is* that?" came a male voice. "Let's ask Larry Bratwurst. Larry, product analysis has borne out earlier claims that Orchid pretty much feeds the whole animal into an MRM machine. It's a mystery, since the company is losing money by *not* cashing in on supplying prime cuts to supermarkets and the catering industry. But why aren't you bulking up your products?"

"You can't have it both ways, Brian," came a throaty American voice. "First you castigate us for MRM machines, then you question why we're not making *more* money by chucking a bunch of garbage into the mix."

"Yes, it's a puzzle. Unless you consider a leaked document called 'The Future'. It propounds that the number of Orchid outlets should be 'multiplied without limit', while at the same time, no significance should be attached to profit. Authored by Mr Lockwood, it appears to be a business plan, but reads like a thriller. 'Highest priority, the massive expansion of the world's cattle population'. And, 'Burger conglomerate to stay in place as a convenient front'. Then a stipulation that the cattle-farming should '*only* be founded on land reclaimed from rainforests'. Tamsin, let's bring you in here ..."

Erin cocked her head. Tamsin Obai was an academic and an independent green lobbyist whose articles and blog Erin had been following for years.

"If this leaked document is real," continued Brian, "what could it mean for the environment?"

"Precisely," said Tamsin. "So to answer that, let's start by looking at current land-use practices. We *could* feed the country, the world, many times over. Instead, we use the vast majority of arable land to grow cereal crops, mainly feed-wheat. Right? Not for bread or breakfast cereals. That only accounts for a tiny fraction. Something like ninety-five per cent of all agricultural crops are grown to feed cattle. It doesn't make environmental or long-term economic sense – "

"But my question ..." said Brian, "The leaked document. If it's real, what could it mean for the environment?"

"Unfortunately, it would be a double-whammy from hell," said Tamsin. "Destroying rainforests is surely bad enough. But to then use that land for concentration cattle-farming is insane. You're *removing* a carbon-sink-cum-oxygen-generator, and *replacing* it with a powerful generator of methane. Ripping out the lungs of the planet and replacing them with a gigantic, flatulent backside."

"Ever the poet, Tamsin," said Larry. "Cattle-ranching has been going on in the rainforests just about forever."

"Not on this proposed scale," said Brian. "Allow me to quote the document again: 'Relevant politicians already on board ... Amazon rainforest to be the pilot for a global model.' And the timeframes, Larry. Within – "

"I'll tell you what's happening here," said Larry.

"No," said Tamsin. "Listen. If you wanted to radically speed up global warming, you'd be hard-pushed for a better way than destroying rainforests and engineering an exponential rise in methane production. But even out of pure greed, nobody would have a good reason for doing that. Something just doesn't add up here."

"I'm sorry," said Brian. "We're out of time – "

"And as you put it a minute ago, Brian," said Larry. "this supposed business-plan of Dom's 'reads like a thriller', and that's exactly what it is. A bunch of fiction. It's a work of propaganda put out by the animal rights and monkey-wrench crowd, the deluded eco-warriors. Deliberate wholesale destruction of rainforests! Brave New World MRM complexes! No! It's all lies. The aim of Orchid is legitimate and sincere. We're just trying to make an honest buck – "

His voice was cut off by electronic pips.

"The seven o'clock news," came a serious female voice. "Police hunting a brutal killer in Helsinki – "

"This leaked document," said Nisha. "If the truth is starting to come out, maybe we won't have to go in?"

"Sorry," said Erin. "It's just a few small voices asking questions. If anybody gets in the way of the plan, they'll be dealt with. That's why I'm doubting if Uncle Dom knows about our operation."

"But look what he just did to you," said Nisha.

"He saw me as a threat from the start. What he did today, he's tried before. I don't think he knows about any of you, or about the timing or details of the operation. But to be on the safe side, I think we have to assume we're being watched."

Kane turned off the radio, stared at a space in the air and said, "Two nights from now. I just hope we're ready."

Logan wrung his hands and shifted position on the arm of the sofa.

"Anyway, we probably need the extra two days," said Nisha. "More training. You know, to *make sure* we're ready ... I'm not sure *I* feel ready yet."

Josh sniffed, then addressed the whole group.

"Okay. I'm picking up on the un-readiness. So ... Friday. We *have* to be ready. Battle-ready. And I think that's my department. Best thing we could do, forget about any more band practices. The band's cooking. We'll be fine. But the real training ... We've still got our Dreamscape training, but let's start using what time we've got left in Kane's garage differently as well. There's a Japanese word my sensei comes out with all the time. *Fudoshin*. It translates as 'unmoving mind' – a quietness of the mind under stress."

He glanced at Erin. She looked away and then back. She'd never heard him speaking so sensibly.

"*Fudoshin* takes years to fully develop, but you can make partial contact with it and benefit from it through training. Right. There's some old bits of wood on that rack over there. We'll use them as dummies and go over some more moves together. Get some focus where it's really needed."

Josh alternated his attention between the two pairs – Erin and Logan; Kane and Nisha – giving advice and short demos where necessary. Kane suggested moving the action out to the front garden, where they'd have more room.

"No," said Josh. "Remember what Erin said. We have to assume we're being watched. And anyway, all our training at Wembley's been open-air. It'll be good to get in some practice in a tighter space."

Then Logan went to the toilet and Josh worked with Erin for a while.

"You've been doing great," he said, taking up a position close behind and reaching around. "I don't know if... I'd try moving the grip of your right hand just another inch or two forward."

"Er, okay."

She could feel his chest against her shoulder blades. His muscular arms were following the angle of her arms and his right hand was on her right hand.

"Just there," he said.

His lips were close to her ear. There was a combination of firmness and gentleness in the way his hand lay on hers. She remembered the moment above the Earth when he'd nearly kissed her.

"Er ... yeah," she said, "that feels like a better grip."

Did he really need to stand so close?

"Now," he said, covering her left hand with his. "Bring this one back a tiny bit. That's it. And get your elbows tighter into your body."

"Okay ... okay. I think I understand."

"Yeah ..." said Josh, trailing his fingers lightly along her forearm before standing aside. "You'll be fine."

She let out a breath. At the other end of the garage, Kane and Nisha had lowered their "swords" and were joking together over something. When Erin turned to Josh again, he was rubbing his chin and frowning.

"What's up?" she smiled. "Lost your *fudoshin*?"

He laughed, then gave her a searching look.

"I was thinking about when you came to find me that night," he said. "I'm still not sure where the dream ended and the waking dream began."

"Oh ..." she said. "Anyway, the first person I was looking for that night was Nisha. Not you. Something must have gone wrong ..."

She couldn't look at him.

"I've had dreams before about floating above the world like that," he said. "And now I've seen all this stuff in my Dreamscape bedroom. Him – the other me – he's really into environmental issues and animal rights." He laughed. "Weird, eh? I was really liking his snakeskin jacket, then I found out it was imitation."

Erin laughed but still couldn't look at him.

227

Logan reappeared.

"Er, right," said Josh. "I'll leave you two to carry on."

"Josh?" said Erin.

"Yeah?"

"Thanks for showing me that better grip position."

"Yeah. No problem."

33

Sacrifice

"Darker" began with some eerie A-minor notes from Nisha's keyboard and a tickling of the hi-hat from Logan. Then Kane struck up the opening guitar riffs and Josh came in with his bass. A little apprehensive, Erin waited for her cue.

From their bench, the judges watched respectfully. Uncle Dom sat in the middle. On the right were the music tutor Mr Ramirez and the head tutor from another school, Mrs Winterson. On the left were the aging local rocker, Nick Lovell, and an elderly but sought-after voice coach, Jennifer Burbage.

The blue and red lighting Kane had chosen washed the stage at exactly the right moment. Erin searched the crowd in a last hope of seeing her parents, even though they'd apologised earlier and wished her luck. Mum's stomach had been playing up again, and Dad, only just back from the conference, was "tired".

Erin sang. She explored her range – to the extent that the grungy ballad offered such exploration. Her voice took possession of the hall. She felt its power. Felt its effortless egress from her throat.

"Poison darts and broken kite-string ..."

The crowd was silent. All eyes on the band. On her.

Virtually every person in the hall was captivated. She felt centred in the moment. Knew that she was hitting every note perfectly. Knew she was singing with a confidence she hadn't experienced before.

"Darker" ended with a reversal of its intro: a last exchange of riffs between Kane's lead and Josh's bass, a tickling of hi-hat from Logan, the haunting A-minor notes from Nisha's keyboard.

The elderly voice-coach was staring at Erin. She had a twinkle in her old eyes as she stood and began to clap energetically. Apart from Uncle Dom – who brought his hands together in a feeble, token applause – the other judges joined the standing ovation.

The audience went crazy.

Erin and the rest of the band walked to the edge of the stage, linked hands and took a bow. It seemed a long time before the applause began to fade.

"That was The Source, everybody," said Mrs Bolum, the deputy head, into her radio-mike. "Let's hear it for The Source."

Erin left the stage and the others followed her into the wings. In the access corridor, they met Pink Ocean, who were next up to perform. The three girls wore pink mini-dresses and their faces were covered with sequins.

"That was rubbish, Lockwood," said Paige, eyes bright with malice. "We saw it on the changing-room monitor. Who ever said you could sing?"

Beside her, Madison and Beth were grinning cruelly.

At first, she re-experienced the hurt of a hundred previous humiliations from Paige, or people like Paige. Then a light went on in her mind. She realised that she could *refuse* to be affected. It was like what she'd been trying to talk to Logan about: the metaphor of the different realms. Paige was pushing buttons that were meant to send Erin to a realm of hurt. But she wasn't going to go there this time; she was going to stay in the feel-good realm she'd entered on stage.

"No, Paige. It was brilliant. *We* were brilliant. Good luck with yours. I hope you get a good response."

With that, she led her smiling friends to the dressing-room. They'd opted for a simple costume of black jeans and tee-shirts, so they didn't have much changing to do.

As they gathered their things, they saw three sparkly-faced girls on the monitor, absolutely murdering a Donna Wowcat song.

The next call was the holding-bay, where the stage-crew had transferred the instruments. When everything had been loaded into the waiting cars of Kane and Logan's dads, the band joined the audience for the rest of the show.

An hour later, the judges went into recess. Then their bench was moved onto the stage, and Emma Jacobs, a local councillor, sat by a table containing the trophies. As foreman of the judges, Uncle Dom spoke.

"We've seen some impressive talent here this evening. So let's have another round of applause for all those who've taken part."

He went on to praise the stage-crew, the technicians and the organisers, then raised his voice dramatically to say, "Here are the results. In third place ... it's the street-dance company Transcendence."

Amid the applause, the fifteen members of the dance troupe filed up to receive their trophy. They definitely deserved a place, Erin thought.

"Second ..." said Uncle Dom, milking the suspense. "It's the extraordinary voice of Ali Khaled."

Eleven-year-old Ali ran up to the stage, punching the air. Erin had heard him sing, and thought his trophy was well-deserved.

"Believe me," said her uncle when the fuss had died down, "selecting a winner was very tough for myself and the other eminent panel-members. But our decision was unanimous. And I'm sure you'll all agree with me, with *us* ... first place belongs to ... Yes, it's ... Pink Ocean!"

The other judges sat po-faced at the announcement.

A stunned silence fell over the crowd.

Then Paige, Madison and Beth squealed as they skipped up to the stage. Their families and friends clapped and cheered, but it was a pathetic sound in the otherwise quiet hall containing several hundred people.

Furious, Uncle Dom clapped louder. The other judges sat mute and still. He gave them a glare, and like trained chimps they now put their hands together. He swept his glare around the gathering and raised a wave of muted applause, along with some cautious booing.

"Pink Ocean!" he cried. "Let's hear it for Pink Ocean. Winners of the Schools of Everdene Talent Contest."

Disgusted, people left in droves.

A puzzled journalist, still with a job to do, was trying to get three gleeful but obscurely embarrassed girls to pose for a photograph. The local councillor stood beside them, clenching her teeth and smiling out at the rapidly emptying hall.

"Let's go," said Erin, touching Kane's arm.

"Yeah," he said. "We can't assume that we were better than Transcendence or Ali, but the audience's reaction speaks volumes."

As they walked to the car-park, Erin felt as flat as her friends looked, and had to keep reminding herself that more important things were at stake.

"Offer you a lift?" said her uncle from his gleaming white Porsche.

She regretted not having left already. It was warm, almost ten o'clock now and not fully dark. The delay on the car-park had been the fault of Kane and Logan's dads expressing their horror at Pink Ocean's victory.

The two men now eyed Uncle Dom warily.

"I'm getting dropped off by Kane's dad," said Erin. "But ... thanks."

"Yeah, she's with us," said Mr Whitman.

Uncle Dom smiled at her.

"Nonsense," he said. "I insist. I'm dropping in to see Toby anyway. I'm *going* to your house, Erin. Can't get a better lift than that, can you?"

"The thing is, Mr Lockwood," said Kane. "On the way, we were going to discuss our rehearsal schedule for the Battle of the Youth Bands competition next week. So we wanted Erin to come with *us*."

"Yeah," said Josh.

Uncle Dom drummed his fingers on the steering wheel and Erin thought she could see suspicion building in his face. Or was it her imagination? It was vital that he still believed she was under the influence of the brand. She couldn't risk him guessing the truth. Couldn't take any risks at all.

"We can discuss rehearsals over the weekend," she told Josh and Kane.

They stared at her.

She smiled and added, "Besides, and no offence to you, Mr Whitman, but out of your car and my uncle's, which would *you* choose to have a lift in?"

Mr Whitman laughed thinly and said, "No competition there. You go with whoever you want to, Erin."

"Yeah ..." said Josh, his eyes brimming with urgency. "Whatever seems the right thing. It's up to you."

Kane and Logan shuffled their feet on the gravel; both looked panicky. Nisha stepped up and kissed Erin, then hugged her and whispered, "Be very, very careful."

Erin opened the door of the Porsche and got in.

"See you later, everyone," she said.

Her seat-belt wasn't even secured when the car took off, spraying gravel from the back wheels.

"Who *were* those horrible people?" said Uncle Dom.

"Friends," she said, her voice shaking. "The rest of the band. And Kane and Logan's dads."

He grunted, swung the car out to the road and zoomed straight through a traffic-light that had just turned red.

"*See you later*?" he said.

"Sorry?"

"You said you'd see them *later*. It's gone ten o'clock. Where and how are you planning to meet later?"

"Uh ... No. We're not. It's ... just an expression. You know. See you later. It just means soon. Like tomorrow, or whatever."

"Is that right?" he said.

"Yes. Er, you're going the wrong way ..."

Uncle Dom gave her a sidelong grin and her heart sank. He was on to them. He had to be. He was going to take her somewhere secluded again and ...

"The Source," he said.

"Sorry?"

"Your band. It's called The Source. A bit odd?"

"Yes. Er ... It's Kane's band really. Not mine. I only joined recently. So it was already called The Source. For years, I think."

She shivered. Had it been a cryptic comment? Did he know everything and was now simply toying with her?

"I ... Why are we in the town centre?" she said. "I thought we were going home? Thought you were coming to see Dad?"

He pulled into High Street. Music was spilling from bars and restaurants. Young people in trendy gear tripped along the pavements in the summer night air, laughing and talking. Taxis cruised about.

Uncle Dom parked the gleaming white Porsche on double-yellow lines directly outside Orchid. Then Erin understood.

Of course he didn't need to subject her to the brand again. He only needed to check the success of her exposure two days ago.

"Fancy a burger?" he said.

"Oh ... yes ... of course."

If I refuse, she thought, he'll hypnotise me again.

234

"I ... I've used all the vouchers," she said feebly.

He locked the car behind him, and led her inside with a tight grip on her wrist. The orange moulded tables were packed.

"Bilal!" he called to a teenager behind the counter. "Two Mr Scrummys in the back, please."

He opened a door onto the busy kitchen, dragging her behind him. Moments later, they were sitting opposite each other at a table in a curtained alcove. Uncle Dom loosened his tie and jiggled his fat head.

"Not nervous, are you?" he said. "I thought it'd be nice. Just a funny old uncle and his favourite niece having supper together."

"Yes ... it *is* nice. I think I'm just a bit frazzled. It's been a big night."

"You could eat a Mr Scrummy, though?"

"Er ... yes. Yes! I could murder one."

He laughed appreciatively, then Bilal arrived with the burgers. Erin's pulse raced. She felt nauseous from the smells of hot fat and sizzling meat.

"Good job, Bilal. By the way, do you want some extra shifts? Paid at double time. Had clearance from the local authorities today – starting next week, we stay open until 5 a.m. on Fridays and Saturdays. Catch all the clubbers straggling home, eh?"

"Thank you, sir. I'd love to do it."

"That's the spirit. This is Erin. She'll be working here after some training at Cank Street. Paige made a special request to show her the ropes."

"I'll look forward to working with you, Erin. Thanks again, sir."

"Can't fault that boy," said Uncle Dom, watching him weave between the busy army of short-order cooks.

"He seems nice," said Erin.

"Yes. So. Aren't you going to thank me for the job?"

"Thanks, Uncle Dom."

"Good. Right. Let's eat these while they're hot."

Half an hour later, the ordeal was over and she was dropped off at the front of her house.

"I won't come in, after all," he said. "Your training starts tomorrow morning. Report to Paige at Cank Street. Eight o'clock. Got it?"

Erin nodded, relieved that he'd seemed convinced by her act. But she was desperate to get away. She felt sure the burger she'd forced down was also desperate to find a way out – probably from both ends of her digestive system.

The whole episode felt like a betrayal of her principles. But sometimes you just had to make sacrifices for the greater good. She faked another smile.

"Goodbye, Uncle Dom."

"Goodbye? You mean goodnight, don't you?"

"Yes. Of course. Goodnight."

34

Into The Jaws Of Hell

Tense and alert, they sat waiting on the iron bench. Rust-red water spouted from the mouths of the griffins at the fountain. The sky was a ploughed field of scarlet. It was 4.06 a.m., and mosquitoes were everywhere in the hot, still air.

"Where is he?" said Logan, wringing his hands.

"Over a minute late," said Kane. "Even a minute's a long time in our tight schedule. Maybe one of us – "

"No," said Erin. "He'll be here."

On the pot-holed road bordering the side of the square adjacent to the town hall, an ox-cart passed with its slave-labour cargo. From the opposite direction came another cart. As the two drew level, the skerri drivers hailed each other.

"Erin," said Nisha. "I understand how, with the square being busy between the shifts, it'll be harder for the skerri troops to reach us. But won't people get hurt?"

Erin didn't answer.

"Won't the skerri just carve their way through?"

"Of course they will," said Kane.

Crowded on other benches around the fountain, oblivious of the scurrying rats and cockroaches, the ragged workers were eating takeaways. Hundreds more stood in groups or shuffled about as they ate.

"All these people," said Nisha. "They don't even know they're in danger."

"It's better not to think about it," said Erin. "Kree and his comrades are probably getting ready to raid the subterranean lab any time now. We have to stick to the plan. And remember, any of these people who get hurt ... They'll heal. Just like we'll heal if we get hurt."

"You sure about that?" said Nisha. "Because, you know, I feel pretty mortal sitting here. I feel like flesh and blood that could *stay* hurt."

"I just want it to be over," said Logan, "and for none of us to get hurt."

Then, from the belly of the blood-red sky, Josh came sailing down on his preferred mode of transport – a surfboard. Seconds later, he stood before them, legs spread, hands on hips, a manic gleam in his eyes.

"Sit down!" said Erin. "Why are you dressed like that?"

He wore jeans and a dirty white tee-shirt with a skull-and-dagger motif.

"It's all good," he said with a cocky grin, squeezing between Erin and Kane on the iron bench and stashing the surfboard underneath.

"You've got to hide that sword," said Logan.

"Yeah? At least I won't be scared to use mine."

"Shut up, Josh!" said Erin. "Please. You're acting way too crazy."

"In less than twenty minutes," said Kane, "this square is gonna be a lot emptier and a lot scarier. What you've got to do, Josh – no surfboard, no frills – make an instant transfer to your Dreamscape bedroom and change your clothes."

"No," said Erin. "We can't afford to lose even another second."

Her hands had begun to shake now, but she got up. The others got up, too, except for Logan, who was staring into space.

"Logan," said Kane.

"Now?" said Logan. "Like, now? We're going in *now*?"

He stood, smiling nervously, a distracted look in his eyes. He took a deep quavering breath and gave a nod.

"Remember," said Erin as they walked in a tight group with Josh in the middle, "inside, we become subject to the usual laws of gravity and physics."

238

"And we'll be 'locked in'," said Josh.

By the same power that barred access to the town hall from other realms, while within the walls of the building there was no exit from Chthonia.

If they were caught, or trapped inside ... Erin refused to think about it, or about what she trod on as she covered the short distance to the wide steps.

The bowler-hatted shlurms, posted either side of the doorway, closed ranks.

Erin went towards them, pausing one step below. This still meant that she stood a foot taller than the shlurm officials, who hooked some of their many hands into their waistcoat pockets and regarded her with disdain. She knew that, although unlikely to communicate with her, they'd understand anything she said.

"We were told to apply here for work permits," she said, presenting the false documents. "The vacancies at the Westbridge factory?"

One shlurm scanned the papers, slit eyes sceptical. The other bobbed its maggoty head about, trying to get a look at Josh. Then the shlurms leaned close to each other and spoke in their thin whiny voices.

Kane stepped up beside Erin.

"Can we just talk to whoever's on the desk?" said Erin.

The shlurms opened their cruel mouths a chink, revealing sharp teeth. One began to frisk her, the other began to frisk Kane. The hilt of Erin's sword was quickly found. She tried to push the shlurm away and its teeth punctured her hand. Kane sent the other flailing against the edge of the stone doorway.

Erin and Kane retreated to the pavement. At the top of the three steps, the shlurms had put their heads together again, in urgent angry conference.

Above the town hall building, the face of the Spider Clock pulsated and glowed, and the spider's legs rotated anticlockwise.

Blood oozed from Erin's hand. The pain was making her nauseous. She caught an extra-strong whiff of the putrefaction covering the ground, and nearly vomited.

"We *need* to get in that entrance," she said.

"Yeah," said Kane. "So how ... ?"

Josh broke out from among them. Erin heard the scrape of steel as he unsheathed his sword. In seconds, he'd felled both shlurms and kicked their twitching corpses down the steps. Logan gasped and backed away.

"They ... weren't even armed," he said.

"They work for the skerri," said Josh. "That's enough. And we ain't got time to wussy-foot around no more. The situation's in flux. We've got to go in fast and hard. Do the job and get out of here before the troops show up."

Kane, Logan and Nisha looked at Erin.

After a split second, she nodded. "He's right."

More shlurms came to the doorway, but when they saw what had happened to their colleagues, they backed inside again, whining feebly.

Josh pursued them, sword held high.

Erin was first to join him in reception. It had a wooden floor and a big desk with brass fittings. A shlurm behind the desk backed up to the wall. In every corner of the room, more shlurms cowered. But guarding a wide staircase, two skerri in dark-blue security uniforms reached for their swords. In the light from the wall lamps, their bloodshot eyes glittered.

A fan turned slowly on the ceiling.

Josh ran straight at the skerri, his warrior cry echoing dully around the warm dusty space. Strong, but slow-witted and lumbering creatures, they were taken by surprise just long enough for Josh to thrust his blade into one of their stomachs. The creature buckled to its knees, bellowing. Josh withdrew his sword and swung it upwards to block an attack from the other skerra. Their blades clashed. With a powerful kick, the skerra sent Josh reeling to the ground.

Erin hurried to help. The skerra swept its sword sideways, and the blade would have hacked into her thigh, but for being blocked by her scabbard. The force of the blow juddered through her and rattled her bones. Simultaneously, Josh sprang back into action and Kane came forward. While the skerra was distracted, Erin swung her sword at its neck. Blood sprayed out.

For a single heart-beat, she was paralysed. This was her, *her* – dealing out death and mayhem. She'd wondered how she'd feel when the moment came. Now the full horror of it spread through her brain like poison. She felt dirty and savage. Then her heart beat again and her thoughts were crystal clear. Polarised. This wasn't about *her* crappy sensitivities. Too much was at stake. She had to act, make every sword stroke count, worry about her feelings later.

The skerra staggered. Blood oozed from its gaping neck in a flood. Erin could see death in its eyes even before Kane delivered a thrust deep up inside its ribcage. There was a resounding thud as its body hit the floor.

Nisha was standing over the first skerra, the one with the stomach wound. It lay slumped against the wall, howling, trying to stop the abundant blood-flow with its scaly hands. With bowed head, Nisha drew her blade across its throat.

Logan had watched the entire scene, mute and frozen, sword unsheathed but held as if it were infected with a deadly disease.

In the square, the mournful sound of the troop alarm had started up.

Erin's face was bathed in sweat and the bite-mark on her hand was stinging badly. The alarm was too soon. Way too soon. They'd hardly begun. From the foot of the stairs, Josh was gesturing urgently. She nodded, then they both went tearing up the curved staircase with Nisha, Kane and Logan close behind.

On the first landing, Josh stopped.

Erin bumped into him, then heard what *he* was hearing. From higher up, but descending fast, came the pounding of boots. More security. There was a door on the landing, which Josh opened.

"Empty office," he said. "Even if they check it, we can defend better from a doorway than we can if we're below 'em on a wide staircase. Yeah? Erin?"

The skerra were so close that the landing floor vibrated and shadows were advancing down the curved wall.

"Okay," she said.

35

The Clock Room

Once inside the small gloomy office, with the door closed, they took up stances and waited, swords raised, as the muffled rumble of descending boots grew louder. Then they heard a noise behind them.

A shlurm had been hiding under the antique desk at the window. Now it stood up, and was cupping two of its hands to its mouth and screeching.

"It's giving us away," said Nisha.

Logan was the nearest. He raised his sword and rushed forward, but then hesitated. The shlurm carried on screeching.

"Kill it!" said Kane.

Logan made threatening lunges across the desk.

"We'll let you live if you shut up," he said.

The shlurm screeched more piercingly than ever. Logan hoisted his sword over his head, but still he hesitated.

"Do it now!" said Josh. "Now!"

Finally, Logan brought his sword down. The shlurm's head was neatly cleaved from the top-dead-centre of the skull to the chinless mouth. Still attached at the neck, the head bowed forward and yawned apart. The two halves of the bowler hat dropped onto the green leather inlay of the desk.

Everybody froze as the tramping boots sounded very loud outside. The floor vibrated and the door shook in its frame. But the skerri seemed to be passing by. Erin and the others kept planting and replanting their feet, kept changing their grips on the hilts of their swords. Mercifully, the thunder of boots faded down the stairs and everybody let out a held breath.

"I've never killed anything before," whispered Logan.

The shlurm's head lay open on the desk. There was no blood. The small brain had been perfectly dissected, and looked like two halves of a broccoli.

"You had to do it, Lo," said Nisha. "Had to. Don't feel bad about it."

"We ain't got time for trauma counselling," said Josh.

Logan had backed away from the desk, but was still mesmerised by the grim evidence of his deed. Kane grabbed his shoulder. Tried to get him to move. But Logan stood there, as obdurate as a water buffalo.

Outside the window, dawn was close. Under the lightening crimson sky, the square looked hellish. The skerri troops were advancing like a tide, their blades flashing and glinting. People were being slaughtered if they were in the way. Above the alarm, faint cries of terror could be heard.

"They're ... they're coming," said Kane.

"I had to do it though, didn't I?" said Logan.

Kane slapped him across the face.

"We've got to move. Now!"

Logan looked bewildered, but more alert. He followed Kane and the rest back out to the landing. They raced up the staircase.

Already, they could hear the security guards returning from below. On the second landing, Erin found the short corridor she was searching for.

At its blind end, two skerri waited in defensive positions by a closed door. Behind that door lay the service stairs that led to the Clock Room.

More afraid now of failing than of being injured or killed, Erin rushed after Josh into the corridor. The skerri came at them. Swords clashed in the confined space. The air was thick with grunts and shouts and spitting and swearing. Flesh wounds went unnoticed.

Erin swung her sword low, and a skerra's leg was amputated at the knee. It dropped its own sword involuntarily. Bellowing with pain, it fell on top of Erin and she was slammed against the floor. Then the skerra's powerful hands found her throat. Its bloodshot crocodile eyes were inches from hers. Drool hung from its snarling mouth. Its breath was like an open sewer.

Erin's windpipe was being crushed.

She was blacking out.

For a moment, she found herself running along a cool sandy beach with her wolves. The tide hissed gently and the air smelled sweet. The stars had never looked so good. Then she was back in the hot, stinking corridor – because she was "locked in". There could be no escape, not even into unconsciousness or dreams. Loss of consciousness could only signify her death in Chthonia.

The skerra squeezed harder, its grip relentless. Erin couldn't breathe. For a second, she knew nothing. Then she returned from how ever close she'd been to the brink. She saw the skerra lying dead and Nisha retrieving her sword from its carcass. The other skerra was dead, too, and Josh and Kane were kicking down the door that led to the service stairs. Josh kept looking back, though, shouting to ask if Erin was all right.

"She's okay!" cried Logan.

Erin let him help her up. It wasn't easy because the floor was so slippery with skerri blood. Logan's lips were trembling.

"Thanks, Lo," she said hoarsely. Her throat felt broken inside. "We've got to keep going now, no matter what."

"I know," he said, despite his obvious fear.

Some way behind, the main stairwell was thumping and crashing so loudly that it could only mean the security guards had been joined by the troops.

Then the first shadows fell across the landing and Erin knew that they were all scant moments from being slaughtered.

"Go!" she cried.

Josh and Kane shot up the service stairs, followed by Nisha, Logan and lastly Erin. It was a steep shaft closed in on all sides, hot and dark. Erin clambered on, higher and higher, sweat stinging her eyes. Just as she heard the skerri at the bottom, she became aware of a dusky orange light above.

In glimpses between the scrambling bodies of her friends, she saw the underside of a trapdoor, its edges defined by the light leaking through. Then it was thrown open by Josh or Kane, and the stair-shaft was flooded with a tangerine glow. Squinting, she followed the others up to the Clock Room.

One by one, they arrived in the dazzling space above.

Erin shielded her eyes. She couldn't see very much, except that they'd come out by a bare brick-wall and that the floor was made of steel. The light source, which had to be the generator, was in the middle. They hadn't been attacked yet, so she reasoned that there couldn't be any skerri up here.

"Quick!" said Nisha. "Close the trapdoor and find something heavy."

"There's nothing," said Josh, who'd already been haring around, checking every corner. "Apart from a massive stack of old-fashioned school-desks."

"I'll give you a hand," said Logan.

"Nah. Won't be no good. They're them stupid flimsy little things with inkwells and a flap what you lift up. We could pile some on the trapdoor but they won't make much difference."

Erin gazed down into the long stair-shaft. The lumbering skerri still had a way to go, but they'd only be another minute or so.

She was panicking now, battling to think straight.

Then the answer came to her, shocking and stark.

For a moment, her focus had slipped. Here they were, in the Clock Room, trying to think of strategies to hold off the skerri. But saving themselves wasn't the point. It was of little consequence what happened to them. The operation was to destroy the generator. In the process, they could be maimed, killed, obliterated. And over time, their dream bodies would recover. Wouldn't they?

She turned and walked away from her friends, leaving them to their grisly fates, and headed for the source of the light.

"What are you doing?" called Kane.

Erin kept her eyes down, and kept them open just enough to see her way across the chequer-plate floor. The light was blinding, the heat intense.

"They're coming!" said Logan. "Close the trapdoor."

"No!" said Nisha. "The desks. I know they're not heavy enough to – but what if we chuck them down on top of the skerri?"

"Yeah!" said Josh. "That'll slow 'em down. Brilliant, Nisha. We'll make a chain from that corner and ..."

Erin had reached a waist-high safety rail. In the brightness, she couldn't see what lay on the other side, so she pulled a handful of her ragged clothes over her face. The fabric was scorching, but through the thick fibres, she now had her first glimpse of the generator. Six feet in diameter, it looked like a captive dwarf-sun, crackling and roaring, spitting out its prominences. At its base, it was cradled in the black petals of a giant orchid, which rotated anticlockwise. It occurred to her that the Orchid brand was represented by a view that looked down on the generator from above, rather than by the side-on view *she* had now.

The whole thing hovered several feet above the floor with no visible means of support. Erin knew that it wasn't a real sun or a real orchid. It was a piece of technology, incredibly sophisticated, but fragile and breakable. Two paces would take her within striking distance, and the sword would have to be enough.

"It's working," shouted Kane. "The desks. Logan, keep 'em coming. Faster! Faster!"

A glimpse was all she'd allowed herself, and even in that glimpse she'd felt a wave of the generator's hypnotic power hitting her. She had to steady herself and take a deep breath before swinging her legs over the iron rail.

Erin walked forward, and it was like entering a furnace. Smoke rose from her clothes. A sob rattled out of her broken throat as her hair ignited.

She hefted her sword with what strength she had left, and struck out.

Her ears were pierced by a sound that was a combination of shattering glass, tearing metal and the tortured cries of a multitude of creatures. She fully expected to be hit by an explosion, but the reverse happened. The fiery sun turned in on itself – it imploded. All its heat and light and mass were sucked into a black dot in mid air. Then the black dot disappeared, or became too small to see. The orchid petals curled up and floated to the floor like burnt paper. Nothing else remained. Just a few flimsy ashes on the steel plate, whose surface had been tinted blue from the heat.

Then Josh rammed into her, knocked her down.

He beat her flaming clothes with his hands. He tore off his tee-shirt and wrapped it around her head. She could smell the singed remnants of her hair. Josh lifted her and heaved her back over the barrier, then he rolled her over and over on the floor to put out the flames.

Finally, she lay still, half stupid with exhaustion.

"You're okay, Erin," he said, squatting over her. "You did it, but – "

"Josh!" shouted Nisha. "We need more help!"

248

Erin got weakly to her feet. Her eyes had gone funny from the generator's glare. The others were shadowy figures frantically dragging or throwing the school-desks to each other and feeding them into the stair-shaft.

She turned away. Beyond the circle of the safety barrier, most of the end wall was taken up by the huge clock. It didn't have a mechanism. The face was of opaque glass divided into panes by the metal frame and numerals. Reddish light from the sky was filtering in, and the fuzzy shape of the black spider could be seen, stationary, behind the glass.

She checked her watch: 4.46.

"The desks are all gone!" shouted Logan.

Erin realised that Josh was still at her side. She thought he'd gone. His expression told her that he knew it was hopeless.

"We're trapped, ain't we?" he said.

She licked ineffectually at her dry lips with her swollen tongue. Josh's tee-shirt lay in a smoking heap near their feet. Erin looked up and gazed at him.

"Pretty much," she said.

36

Loss

"Better get back and help the others," said Josh. "Sorry if I screwed things up for us. You know, earlier. The surfboard. The clothes. Being late."

"No," she said. "Without you, we'd never have made it to the generator. Anyway, I think Kree miscalculated. He thought we'd get back out before the troops arrived, but I doubt if we would have."

"We fight to the bitter end, then. And when we're dead here, we wake up in our rooms. Turn our computers on and meet in the ZedWhy chat-room."

"Er ... yeah," she said.

"*If* your Kree's right, that is."

She broke eye-contact. Kree *had* to be right ...

"You've been fantastic, Josh," she said.

"Yeah, you too. Don't take this the wrong way, but for a girl and a vegetarian, you ain't half got some bollocks."

Erin was surprised that she had the energy to laugh.

"Er, guys," said Nisha, joining them. Her eyes were full of dread and her voice shook. "Kane and Lo ..."

The boys were thrusting their swords down into the stair-shaft. The points of skerri swords were catching Kane and Logan in the legs and guts. In the heat of battle, they showed no signs of noticing. A dead skerra was pushed up and over the edge of the trapdoor and the heads and shoulders of two live skerri appeared. Kane and Logan slashed and jabbed. One of the attackers slumped over the edge of the hole. But then the wounded skerra was heaved aside from below, and another came up to take its place.

"We'd better help," said Josh, even though it was obvious that no amount of help could stop the inevitable.

With their overwhelming force and numbers, the skerri would break through at any second. And once the bottleneck of the trapdoor had been breached ...

Nisha closed her eyes and frowned hard as she tried and failed to exit Chthonia. She opened her eyes again.

"Is there really no other way out?" she said.

"No," said Josh.

"But we're only locked in to the Nightmare Realm while we're inside the building. So, if we can get *outside* the building ..."

"Obviously," said Josh. "And the way out's blocked."

"If we could get through a window."

"There ain't no windows."

"Yes, there are," said Nisha, pointing at the twelve-foot-diameter clock.

Through the opaque glass, between the fuzzy shapes of the spider's legs, the sky was now a pinkish-brown. Erin exchanged glances with Josh, then her ears were assaulted by an increased ferocity of the battle at the trapdoor.

"*Can we have some help here?*" cried Kane.

"Erin?" said Nisha. "Can't we break through the clock and...and get past the spider somehow ... ?"

Josh was already on his way. Nisha rushed after him.

Erin was too exhausted to think clearly. She was suspended between the two unfolding scenes.

At the trapdoor, steel clashed against steel as boys and skerri grunted their mutual hatred and fury. At the clock, Nisha had already smashed one of the bigger windows, and now had to dodge a monstrous leg curling inward.

Josh thrust his sword through a lower-centre window. But the pane, which broke easily, hadn't been his target. His sword had found the body of the great spider. There was a hissing shriek, then four black legs crashed through at different places around the clock-face.

Nisha took a swipe at one leg; another hit Josh in the head and he collapsed to the floor and lay still.

The fog in Erin's brain lifted as the outside air entered. The hot staleness of the Clock Room was sharpened by the smell of wet rust.

"Josh ..." she said.

Kane and Logan had reached the end of their endurance. Both were seriously wounded and bleeding. In a final effort, they tried to shut the trapdoor and stand on it, but their combined weight presented no obstacle. They were tipped off as easily as if they'd been a couple of bags of wood shavings.

They didn't stay to fight. They hurried towards the clock, pausing only to grab Erin by the arms and drag her with them. She stumbled as they rounded the curve of the generator barrier. Kane and Logan were moving quickly and mechanically, like robots, their blood-flecked faces rigid.

In a backward glance, Erin saw the skerri pouring out of the floor. Their grins were savage, their eyes eloquent with promises of torture and slow death.

"We can still make it ..." said Nisha.

But even as she spoke, the great spider was squeezing itself in through the broken clock-face. Josh had been stunned. Now he was recovering, staggering to his feet, his muscular body slick with sweat and blood. Kane and Logan raised their swords. Erin went for hers, but discovered that it had been lost.

The spider was through.

Shrieking horribly, it straddled the steel floor, its plump body suspended between the upside-down V-shapes of its spine-covered legs. The head was horny and misshapen. Its eight eyes glistened amid the matted fur, and from the place where a mouth might have been, a pale green froth oozed.

Erin knew, without looking behind, that even the skerri had paused in this creature's foul presence.

Thrusting its huge head forward, the spider let out a deafening hiss. The vapours it breathed were acidic and probably toxic. Erin's eyes and nose stung. She swayed and felt faint. Nisha, who was closest, sank to her knees.

Then Josh's sword sliced into the creature's fat body. Only a superficial cut was left on the tough hide, but all the spider's eyes were now trained on him. He ran off to one side, then made taunting noises and waved his sword about.

"Go!" he shouted to the rest of them. "Go!"

The spider scuttled after him at alarming speed. He sprinted to the far corner and turned to defend himself.

"Josh!" cried Erin.

Then she couldn't see him or the spider. The skerri had swiftly blocked off that part of the room. And in a pincer formation now, they came – unhurried, silent, sure of their revenge.

"Josh ..."

"We can't help him," said Kane. "We have to go! Don't you see?"

"He's sacrificed himself," said Logan. "We gotta try to escape. Else what he's done for us, it'll be wasted."

He has *an unusual kind of bravery*, Erin remembered.

The skerri steadily closed in, primed to charge if any moves were made towards the broken windows of the clock-face. Yet the spectacle of this hideous, drooling, lizard army paled beside what they were to witness next.

Behind the advancing skerri, the spider scuttled up the wall, and up the pitched face of the ceiling – with Josh somehow attached under its belly.

It took him into the apex of the pyramid-shaped roof, where its form was lost in the shadows. There was a sound, which wasn't exactly a scream. It was more like Josh's warrior-cry. But then it was muffled and cut off, and followed by a series of rattles, clicks and whistles.

There was a moment of absolute stillness and silence.

Then the skerri surged forward.

Kane, Logan and Nisha hurled themselves at the clock. Erin stayed where she was, staring up into the shadows of the roof. Kane darted back, grabbed two handfuls of her sooty clothes and impelled her to move.

Cuts and slashes were ignored as they all scrabbled their way through.

A shard of glass dug into Erin's side as she squeezed between the metal bars of the frame. She pushed harder, twisted herself, and was out.

Scaly hands grasped at her ankles, but she was already falling. Below, she saw the square seething with more troops, and saw the bodies of the innocent.

She eased her fall into a softer, controlled descent, and amid the pain and fear and horrors whirling round her head, she carved out a single pellucid moment in which to focus her thoughts...and made the shift to the Dreamscape before her feet had touched the ground.

37

The Portals Of Death

The sky was blue and the sun's rays were glancing over the buildings of Luxor Street. In the sparkling air, water cascaded and gurgled at the fountain. An old man was just locking the doors of the town hall, and the members of a brass band, all in purple uniforms, were packing away their instruments.

"We ... *left him*," sobbed Logan.

They stood on the flagstones under the clock: Roman numerals; hands showing a couple of minutes to five.

"No we didn't," said Kane. "It was what he wanted."

"That was the bravest thing," choked Erin.

The boys were soaked in blood, not all of it theirs. Nisha had a gash above her eye and three fingers missing from her right hand. Something felt dislocated in Erin's throat, her nose was bleeding, and the remnants of her clothes and hair still smouldered.

"My focus is going!" said Logan.

So was Erin's. Her friends' forms were dissolving, becoming ethereal. Images of her room kept intruding.

"The operation's over," she said. "I told you we might lose the gift."

"What about Josh?" said Kane. "He's awake in his room now, right?"

"Of course he is," she said, but sounded unconvincing even to herself.

"How can he be?" said Logan. "His dream body's still trapped in Chthonia, so how ... ? Kane? You're fading."

"He'll be logging in to ZedWhy now," said Erin.

"Waiting for us," said Nisha.

"We can't be losing the gift," said Logan. "What if ... What happens if Josh ... ?"

Logan's form dissolved. So did Kane's.

Tears streamed from Erin's eyes.

"He'll be safe. He has to be safe."

Nisha hugged her.

"Don't worry, babe. Josh is safe. Kree was right about almost everything else. So he'll be right about this."

Erin nodded. "That was the bravest thing ..."

Then Nisha faded away and Erin was alone. She didn't try to stay any longer. Just closed her eyes, relaxed, let go, and immediately felt her duvet around her neck. Daylight streamed in at the edges of the curtains. The stars on her ceiling had never looked so lifeless, the magnolia walls never so dull.

A violent shiver wracked her body as she got out of bed. She unhooked the quilted dressing-gown from the back of the door and slipped it on.

Then she sat at her computer. Within a minute, she was chatting with Nisha, Kane and Logan in ZedWhy.

There'd been no word from Josh.

Erin rang him on his mobile without result.

While staying logged in, they all lay on their beds and tried to project their dream bodies, intending to shift to Josh's room in the physical world.

No-one succeeded.

It was true: they'd lost the gift of waking dreams.

Erin rang Josh's house and asked a sleepy, angry, older brother to "Please, please, just go to Josh's room and check on him."

Four days later, under the bright sunshine of a hot afternoon, she turned away from the mounds of clay at the graveside, and mechanically followed the retreating crowd. It had been a long service, and the sweltering chapel had been overflowing with people, many of them curious strangers.

The leaden feeling in her guts, of recent days, was getting worse. Her sleeping patterns were erratic and dreamless.

At the cemetery gate, her spirits lifted a little as she saw Nisha, Logan, Kane and Mr Whitman waiting by a car. She turned to her parents. Dad's head was bowed. As he sobbed, he partly shielded his face with a hand.

"Erin should come along to the do," said Mum. "It's only respectful."

"No, Wendy," said Dad, sniffling. "Let her go to her friends. It's enough that she came to the service."

"Well...all right," said Mum.

Erin gave them each a hug, and stopped herself from walking too quickly towards Mr Whitman's car.

"Any change?" she asked Kane.

He shook his head and opened the rear door for her.

As she slid onto the seat and Nisha and Logan got in either side of her, Mr Whitman said gently, "Sorry to hear about your uncle."

"Thanks, Mr Whitman."

"I don't suppose it's much consolation," he said, "but after surviving that big heart-attack, you could say that he lived the rest of his life to the full. The times I saw him on TV, he seemed a happy and enterprising sort of guy. Passionate."

"Yeah," said Erin. "He was kind of *driven*."

Mr Whitman dropped them at the main entrance, and they were at Josh's bedside in two minutes. He was hooked up to an IV, and his heart-rate and blood pressure were being displayed on a screen. Another piece of equipment monitored his brain-wave activity.

After Erin's phone call, Josh's brother had found him on his bedroom floor, sweating and convulsing. He'd been unconscious ever since.

"You lot again?" said a smiling young man as he checked the electrode pads attached to Josh's forehead. "Summer hols already?"

In fact, it was the last week of school before the holiday, but the head tutor had decided – considering their friend's hospitalisation, Nisha's "fall", and Erin's family bereavement – that they should all be excused.

"You just missed his folks, his brother and his cousins," said the young man. "Hope I get as many visitors if I'm ever in this state."

"State?" said Erin. "Is ... is he getting worse?"

"No," he said. "Sorry. Turn of phrase."

He glanced at the door.

"Anyway, I'm not his doctor; I'm not supposed to ... You seem like good kids. Don't quote me, but I think he's on the mend now. That first seventy-two hours ... Wow! Fits; raging fever. Dreaming constantly ..."

He gestured vaguely at the EEG tracer.

"Never seen anything like it. But last night and today, no dreams. I've seen plenty of comas, and this isn't a coma. He's in deep, deep dreamless sleep now, and he's gradually, very gradually surfacing."

On Thursday morning, Josh woke. By Friday afternoon, every test had been carried out, and cautiously the hospital let him go home. A clutch of viral illnesses had been hinted at, but nobody could put a label on his condition. Josh agreed to get plenty of rest, then stunned everybody by turning up at the youth club that evening with his bass guitar. It was the Battle of the Youth Bands. They'd assumed they'd be performing without him.

And even though they won the night, they knew that Josh wasn't his old self.

"When we left you," ventured Kane later, back at the garage. "In the town hall in Chthonia. What happened?"

"Nobody left me," said Josh, in a slower, deeper voice than usual. "We all did what we had to do."

"Yeah," said Logan. "You were totally ace, Josh."

"Yeah," said Kane. "Incredible. But what happened ... ? I mean, you know ..."

Erin sat closer to Josh on the sofa, and took his hand.

"I ... don't remember much about it," said Josh.

"You must do," said Kane. "That thing ran you up into the roof, so you were still inside the town hall. Locked in. You must have been conscious, or drifting in and out of consciousness the whole time that thing was ... Sorry."

Josh seemed to have only just realised that Erin was holding his hand. He looked into her face. There was a softness and warmth in his eyes, and a rock-steadiness that caused her pulse to quicken.

"I just wondered, that's all," said Kane.

"He doesn't want to talk about it," said Erin. "He doesn't have to talk about it yet, or ever, if he doesn't feel like it."

Josh interlocked his fingers with hers.

"Ain't nothing to talk about, Kane," he said. "The operation succeeded."

"Yeah," said Kane. "You've only got to watch the news. Orchid's finished. Erin's uncle's dead – so Kree delivered as well. It's all over."

"No," said Josh. "Not over. We've only dealt with the supernatural threat to the planet; now we have to deal with the continuing human threat. Pollution. Dodgy farming practices. Poor use of land. Destruction of biodiversity. Climate change. We have to campaign and keep on campaigning like never before ..."

Erin squeezed his hand.

38

Regeneration

Scorching weather continued for the rest of July and on into August. Three mornings a week, Erin worked as a volunteer on the wildlife conservation project. Josh sometimes showed up as well, claiming he'd always had a soft spot for badgers and owls.

Other times, they all went to the swimming baths, or hiked in the shaded sanctuary of Crow Woods. The trails had been baked rock-hard and the air was soporific. Insects buzzed in the undergrowth. They explored the cool, hidden dells in the north, and the tinder-dry perimeter in the east, where the sun had created a false autumn by burning the leaves to crisps.

"What do you make of those two?" Kane said to Nisha one afternoon over iced coffees in Ultra. "I mean, do you think they're dating?"

"I don't know," laughed Nisha. "They seem close. Keep your voice down."

"I think it's really good," said Logan.

Nisha, Kane and Logan were crowding around a computer terminal. From where Erin sat with Josh at a table in the window, she could hear them.

In recent weeks, she'd spent a lot of time with Josh. He often called her and arranged to meet. Between talking about music or films – or the environment! – he seemed content to sit quietly with her. Sometimes they'd hold hands. But that was it. And she sensed that he still needed space and time.

"Gotta go," she heard Logan say to the others. "Promised I'd help Mam. She's been trying out these different dishes and we're doing Thai tonight."

"Nice," said Kane. "We have Thai sometimes."

"I'm still off the red meat. Just eating chicken and fish. Ain't lost much weight yet, but the doctor says my cholesterol's coming down already."

"Fantastic," said Nisha.

"After everything what's happened," he said. "I'm starting to feel better about lots of stuff. Not as fazed by the looks some people give me. Or by the name-calling. It's like what Erin says, 'you can choose *not* to go to the realm of hurt'. You can choose to ... Hey, that's it! I'm gonna write us a new song about it. Sort of, *No way, baby, there ain't no way ~ Not letting you push my buttons that way* ... With a bluesy beat maybe, and heavy bass. *I ain't going to the realm of hurt no more ~ No way, baby ~ no way, no, no –* "

"*Ain't gonna play that vi-de-Oh ~* " sang Nisha, "*In my head no more ~ My head no more ...*" She laughed and threw her arms in the air.

"Like it!" said Logan. "Maybe we should co-write it."

"We should. I'll text you later if I come up with more ideas. Compare notes."

"Cool as. But first I'm riding straight down that High Street, past all the fast-food places, and straight home to help cook that Thai meal."

"Way to go, Lo," said Nisha.

"See you later," said Kane.

Logan was making for the door, waving happily.

"Catch you later," called Erin.

"Later, Lo," called Josh.

As Logan left, Josh took Erin's hand under the table.

And there was that feeling she kept getting every time he touched her or smiled at her. It was as if, deep within her, a precious, delicate flower was opening; similar to how she'd felt about somebody else once – somewhere and some-when, in a different reality.

"Nearly four," Kane said to Nisha, "I'd better go soon as well. Got that private tutor. I know it's years away, but I'm definitely doing a physics degree. It'll be a lot of studying ... And I'll still be a member of the band and everything, and be involved in the new eco campaigns Erin and Josh have been talking about. But you and me, Nish ... Us ..." He lowered his voice. "Sometimes, I'm not sure what I want. But I want us to stay friends."

"Why wouldn't we?"

"I know, Nish. But I didn't know if ... I mean, I *really* like you."

"It's okay," said Nisha. "I understand."

"You do?"

"Yes. Don't worry. I think I saw it before you did. Saw that we were maybe only meant to be friends."

"You did?"

Nisha laughed and pecked him on the cheek. "So ... Friends."

Erin was with Josh in the shaded veranda of the disused cricket pavilion. They stood looking out over the park. A group of children and some parents were throwing Frisbees on the expanse of pale, parched grass.

"Hey," said Josh softly.

"Hey," she said.

And now they were facing one another, standing close.

"What do you think about what the others were saying?" he said with a playful grin. "A few days ago in Ultra."

"Er, what were they saying?"

"They wondered if we were dating," he said.

That new look was back in his dark eyes – a warm sparkle to temper the old brashness. She let her gaze wander to his lips, then glanced away.

"So are we?" said Josh.

"I ... don't know," she said. "What do you think?"

"I think there's one way to find out."

He reached a hand around her waist and drew her gently towards him. The other hand he buried in her hair. Then he brought his lips firmly to hers.

Erin kissed him back, and felt as if something had broken loose in her chest and in her head. She lost all sense of where the boundaries of her body ended and his began. Then Josh paused, but still held her, and neither of them could contain their happiness. They simply gazed and gazed, and smiled and laughed, their faces a couple of inches from one another's.

"I think it's definitely yes," he said.

She nodded but didn't speak. Words were redundant.

They kissed again, and she gave herself up to the intoxication of it all.

At home later – her thoughts still whirling, her body still singing – she found her parents in a happy, secretive mood. They were sitting very close together.

"What's going on?" she said.

They beamed at each other, and then beamed at her.

"Erin," said Mum. "We've got two pieces of wonderful news!"

"Really? Two? Oh ... well, good."

"First," she said. "You're going to have a little brother or sister in about seven months' time. We found out an hour ago."

"No? Wow! That's fantastic."

Before the matter had been fully discussed, Dad smirked and said, "The other news is partly medical as well. I had some tests recently, and it turns out I'm not allergic to *all* animals. Only cats. Come and see ..."

She followed him to the back door.

"The personnel manager from work," he said. "She's emigrating to Australia, and I didn't know if ... And he was going to the rescue centre anyway, so we could still take him there and you could pick another."

Erin approached the large yellow-grey dog that was eyeing her cautiously from the lawn. The dog licked her hand when she offered it to him. She stroked his head and he whined affectionately and nuzzled her.

"Apparently the softest mutt in the world," said Dad. "A lot of Alsatian in him, and some husky. Looks like a wolf, if you ask me. Name's Jack."

She knelt down on the grass and threw her arms around Jack's neck.

EPILOGUE

The Blue Yonder

One morning in early September, Erin woke from a vivid dream. She sat up abruptly in bed, and there was a flicker of geometric patterns on the wall. Just a flicker, or a trick of the light ... The dream hadn't been a waking dream, but it had been so, so vivid... She'd sat on a moss-covered rock beside the pond and Kree had sat next to her. Behind him stood six of his comrades.

"I never had the chance to ask," she said. "Why did you even agree to help us humans? You could have just stayed out of it, and kept yourselves safe."

Kree smiled and blinked his amber eyes.

"How could we stand by, once we knew what was happening? After all, we have a shared ancestry with humans."

"Right. And I was wondering, Kree ..."

But the dream had broken up there.

"Go well, Erin," he'd said before she woke. "Go well."

Later that day, she went walking in the woods with Jack. The weather had turned cooler and she was wearing her yak-wool jumper with the butterfly design.

On the eastern horizon, across a wheat field, dark clouds were towering.

An hour into the walk, Jack found the clearing. Erin stopped by the twisted alders at its entrance. Although there was no sense of any atmosphere, she didn't care to go further inside. It reminded her too much of a friend she could no longer visit in the Dreamscape. She called

Jack, and he came away from where he'd been sniffing around the ruin of the old hollow oak.

As Erin was about to head home, she got a text from Josh: *Me and Lo in woods. Walking. On way to town to meet Kane and Nisha. Where are you? X.*

In woods! she texted back. *Meet you at town side of Elbow in five. X.*

She found the main trail again. And as Jack snuffled and howled happily, and kept running ahead or off into the undergrowth to one side or the other, the woods grew darker and eerier. The air felt charged, expectant. Erin remembered the ink-blue cloudbanks she'd seen building in the east. Thunder rumbled behind now, and she was impressed that Jack didn't seem the least bit spooked.

"Come on, boy," she said. "We might beat the rain, if we hurry."

The storm-clouds were coming steadily west, scrolling over the woods to blot out the daylight. There was a baritone growl of thunder and moments later a flash of lightning. Unafraid, Jack trotted along at her side.

When the rain came, it was sudden and heavy.

But there wasn't far to go now.

She left the trail and jogged under the canopy, looking out for the hazardous tree roots threading the ground like rope. Another clap of thunder was followed instantly by a burst of lightning that rendered the woods spectral.

At the edge of the elbow, Josh and Logan were already waiting.

"Here, boy," said Logan.

Jack leapt up playfully and Logan wrestled him to the ground. Erin laughed and Josh laughed, then they moved into each other's arms and kissed.

"Hey," he said.

"Hey."

"Like the jumper. South American?"

"Nepalese," she said. "I've hardly worn it in about a year. I liked it so much I didn't want to wear it out or lose it. But now it's really too small. Look how far the sleeves come up my wrists."

"Yeah," said Josh. "Nice wrists, nice hands, nice everything." He kissed each of her wrists in turn, then kissed her on the lips again.

"So this is probably the last time I'll wear it," she said.

"Right. Better to wear things while they still fit you."

"I know. And live life without holding back too much."

"Well ... yeah," said Josh.

When the play-fight with Logan was over, Jack kept running a little way out from the cover of the trees and back again, trying to lead everybody across the common and towards town.

"Stay, Jack," said Erin.

He sat beside her, wagging his tail.

They all sheltered beneath the spreading boughs of a horse-chestnut. For a while, it absorbed the downpour, then the rain leaked on their heads. Torrents of water gurgled in a drain or ditch somewhere. The common stretched two hundred metres ahead, and the turf was already awash. On the far side, the houses and road were distorting and blurring. Cars had to use their lights.

"We could be stuck here for ages," said Logan.

Jack began to pad out into the rain again.

"Stay, boy," said Erin.

"What was that about not holding back too much?" said Josh.

Erin smiled. The air had a sharp, clean smell. She breathed it deeply and felt a surge of happiness welling up inside her.

"Let's go for it," she said.

With Jack at her heels, she ran straight into the open. Liquid mud squelched and sucked at her feet, and splashed up the legs of her combats. Laughing, the boys followed. Jack bounded around everybody in circles. The rain came down, the lightning flashed, and everything was lost in a deep blue haze. It was like being on the bed of an ocean. Like sailing above the clouds.

Erin paused, remembering a vision of the Earth from space. Then she ran again, laughing, into the blue.

Author's Note: If you have enjoyed this novel, please consider leaving a brief review or comment on Amazon.